SELFSAME

LOWER EARTH RISING: BOOK 1

EDEN WOLFE

ESN INK

FROM THE AUTHOR

This story is the first novel in the Lower Earth Rising Series, which I wrote as a response to what appeared to be a real risk of nuclear war.

Writing is how I dealt with that fear, and also has been an incredible way to connect with people around the world. And that's why I created the Selfsame Readers Club.

I share exclusive material with Club members, like short stories and unpublished material, as well as first-notice of any free book promos.

When you join, you get "Deviants", a novella about Rose's struggles in Cork Town, as my gift to you.

Our world is a wild place; Lower Earth is my escape from the madness. Come join me on a voyage into *what if…*

~Eden Wolfe

www.edenwolfe.com

LOWER EARTH DIRECTION, YEAR 402

FOURTEENTH GENERATION
SINCE THE DUST
UNDER THE REIGN OF QUEEN MAEVA II

GEB COUNTY DIRECTION

Commandante - Irene (Irilena), warrior priestess of Gana
Great Geneticist - Lucius of the first line
Primary Overseer - Roman of the first line
Senior Overseer - Uma of the nineteenth line
Experimental Sequencing - Adam of the first line
Male Bioinformatics Unit - Isaac of the first line

GANA PROTECTORATE

Chief Priestess - Habana, warrior priestess
Keeper of the Chief - Batrasa, warrior priestess

OUTER COUNTIES MANAGEMENT

Prefect on Three-Year Cycle

DARK COUNTIES PROTECTORATE

Prefect on One-Year Cycle

CENTRAL MASS PROTECTORATE

Under Command of the Queen's Guard

STRANGELANDS SECT

Head Sister - Sahna, former warrior priestess of Gana

Rainf
Strangelands
West fields
Leeside Mountains
Lakes Region
Minor Rainforest

FORGOTTEN islands
WEST GANA
EAST GANA
rainforest
Central Mass
East Fields
Geb

SELFSAME

1

____

Aria dropped her spear on the grass and stepped into the water's edge. The pond water lapped at the base of her leather boots. She let the muscles down her back relax and her shoulders lower. Even though the leather cloak sat heavily on her, she never dared to leave it behind. She watched a water spider skid across the pond surface. The combat pitch behind her was still empty.

The next attacker would come soon.

Aria took in the wet air, letting the smell of moss and algae fill her nostrils. But only for a moment. She relished the seconds between fights.

She rested her hand on the lava rock pendant and uttered a blessing to the settlers, to those who had come first, those who had fought and won and rebuilt life on Lower Earth when the world was dying. She prayed for strength beyond her current state, despite all she had already invested in her training. She had to be more, had to be better. She had to be ready for the day when the men of Upper Earth arrived on their shores. She prayed it to the Queens of Before.

Her prayer didn't last long. A scent wove its way to her.

Woman approaching. 170 degrees. Southwest. Heavy steps. Rushing. Breaking branches and slashing brush. Clumsy. Run scenarios: easy to subdue.

Aria sighed. The farce of "physical challenges" was tiresome. Batrasa's creativity was waning with age and the prisoner women were motivated out of a selfish desire for favor more than providing a real fight. Ariane needed threats that were closer to the eventual reality of Upper Earth's men. The disappeared women on the Forgotten Islands were hardly sufficient.

A hundred feet away now. Assess capabilities: limited. She is at full run. Insufficient lung capacity.

She rolled her eyes. The woman was panting from the effort, already mostly spent in the excitement of the attack. Aria let her reach within two arms lengths.

Aria spun, stomach grazing the ground, spider stance, and safely out of the trajectory of a rusty knife the woman swung in Aria's general direction.

"What the - " the woman paused for a half-second, and Aria was upon her.

The woman didn't stand a chance. She was on the ground, on her back, arms spread and wind knocked out of her. Aria didn't let her move.

"Get off me!"

Aria pressed her knee further into the woman's throat. She assessed her attacker from her vantage point on the woman's chest. The woman was more feminine than others, long dark hair while most on the island had it cropped short. She had high cheekbones and dark eyes that matched her dark skin. Broad hips and long legs that kicked left and right in an effort to free herself. Clearly a former priestess from Gana. Her face pulled into a frustrated grimace.

"I said, get off me!" The woman tried to lift her arms, but

Aria had her pinned on each side. The knife fell from the woman's left hand.

Her heartbeat accelerates. She is defeated. Maintain pressure on left side of neck, induce unconsciousness on any struggle. Signs of another weapon in her right pocket.

"I am not getting off you until you surrender."

"I am going to rip your head off, the instant you let me free."

"You won't."

"I will."

"No, you won't."

"And why wouldn't I?"

Aria bent her head down to speak in the woman's ear. "Because you know I'd have a dagger in your heart before you could even raise a fist."

The woman exhaled, exasperated. "Fine. Then I give up."

Aria stood, letting the blood flow again into the woman's arms. The woman brushed off the dirt and massaged her forearms.

"This is getting too easy," Aria shouted into the air, knowing Batrasa wasn't far.

"She was doubly armed," Batrasa emerged from the shadows of the brush, "She had both knives and a razor-edged chain."

"Not that it made any difference."

"I see your point." Batrasa rubbed her forehead.

Aria walked to the old woman, a warrior priestess herself, noting how her former jet-black hair had changed within a matter of months. It was almost completely white now. "You have to make this more challenging, Batrasa. Your silly games are hardly enough to prepare me anymore. What's the point of bringing me out to this island if you aren't going to throw your best at me?"

Batrasa inhaled. "My responsibility is the quality of your training. Just because you cheat doesn't mean-"

"Cheat? How am I cheating? She came at me, I neutralized her within seconds, done."

Calm. She is provoking.

Batrasa coughed. Aria had to turn away from the stench of it. Acrid, the smell of decay.

She's degenerating. It won't be long now.

Batrasa composed herself, standing tall again. "And you think your reaction time was good enough? You think you've got this all figured out? No wonder the Queen won't let you in the capital. You're cocky and careless in your response."

Control blood rush. Reduce stimulation, reduce blood pressure. She's seeking a reaction.

Aria returned her heartbeat to normal. "You don't give me enough valid opportunities." Batrasa coughed. Aria recoiled as another waft of Batrasa's breath reached her. "How many times have I complained about the quality of your simulations? It's unacceptable. If you're going to bring me all the way out here, get me on a boat for a day, just to give me the same old exercises-"

Scent of sweat, 120 degrees.

Aria spun around but it was a moment too late. The attacker had a rope around her neck and tightened it.

"Hello, Queen Ariane," hissed a masked woman, thick in the shoulders and with breath that smelled like sulfur.

"I am no Queen." Aria resisted the pull of the rope.

Maintain oxygen, prevent swelling. Run scenarios: She is former Queen's Guard. Only they are designed with such strength. Limited ability to assess consequences; weakness in predicting outcomes.

"Oh, but you will be. If you can get out of this, that is."

Aria managed to speak, "You underestimate me."

Another voice approached behind her, "You underestimate us."

Aria heard a knife unsheathe.

Focus on sound. Determine the number of attackers.

She listened for a period that was no more than a split second.

Four. At least two knives. Rope tightening. Run scenarios: method of escape: whip crack.

Aria crouched as quickly as she could with the rope still around her neck, and then snapped upwards. They had no time to react. The woman's hands loosened on the rope and Aria rammed her head into the second woman's face, breaking her nose. Aria ran before the third and fourth could lift their arms toward her.

She was across the combat pitch within moments. It wasn't only that Aria had the greatest speed on the pitch – she had greater speed than anyone. She'd known it her whole life; it was part of her design. No one in Lower Earth could match her.

"And now," Aria calmed her breath again, "Now I would run. So you can come at me again if you'd like, but I'll cross the island before you can tie your shoelaces." Aria looked at their feet. "They don't give you shoes?"

Batrasa approached Aria from the left, "Too many used the laces to hang themselves."

Aria kept her eyes on the women, each breathing heavily, something between defeat and despair across their faces. Aria closed her eyes and listened to the sound of each of them breathing.

Woman to the right, nearly in tears. Disappointment. What were they promised in exchange for winning the attack? Run scenarios: most likely their freedom. A valuable prize.

Aria walked to the woman to the right, the smallest of the four. Dark hair and green eyes.

Green eyes. She comes from Geb. Her betrayal was great. They are rare here.

All the women of the capital had green eyes, though the outer counties still had some variance. Aria's were chestnut brown, cracked with green around the far edges.

No one had eyes like Aria's eyes.

As she approached, the woman lowered her head.

"You. How is your confinement on this forgotten island?"

The woman's eyes remained on her feet.

"Do they treat you poorly here?"

"No, ma'am."

Her heartbeat accelerates.

"Do you fear me?"

The woman shrugged.

Aria stepped closer to her and lowered her voice. "Look at me."

The woman raised her head, her heartbeat continuing to accelerate. Aria focused her attention into the woman. She listened to the movement of the woman's blood, the air as it entered, as it converted, as it was exhaled.

Accelerated heartbeat is normal in such circumstances. Her breath is shallow. Batrasa planted a seed of fear in her.

"You are right to fear me. But I won't hurt you. I am not the enemy." Aria watched the woman's eyes, which seemed desperate to break her gaze, and yet didn't. "What's your name?"

The woman stared at her.

"I said, what is your name, woman?"

"Ingrid of the ninth line."

"Why are you here, Ingrid?"

Her heartbeat slows, along with her breath. Pride.

She is proud of her crime.

Ingrid's cheeks raised; her eyes narrowed. Aria didn't recognize the expression. She spoke quietly, "You, you want to know what I did? The Future Queen cares what a lowly citizen of Geb may have done to be disappeared?"

She challenges me.

Aria straightened her spine.

"We are all citizens. Equal under the first Directions of the settlers." Aria listened to the blood of the woman; it still rushed but with less intensity. "Come with me." Aria stepped away from the others. Ingrid followed. "Now you are speaking only to me. No one else can hear what you have to say. Be straight and don't play with words. I can tell it is bursting inside you."

Ingrid cocked her head. "Future Queen," her eyes narrowed, "I killed the child that was growing inside me. That is what they say was my crime." Ingrid stopped there, staring deeply, holding Aria's gaze.

She awaits my reaction. I will invite her. I need this more than I need childish battle games.

"You committed a great crime indeed. Do you have no remorse?"

"Remorse? Future Queen, I did what was right. They put an abomination inside me. You don't understand. You don't know what it was. It was no human child. And yet look where I am because of it." Ingrid stood taller and opened her lips a sliver. "I know it doesn't matter that it was an inhuman creature. I was a Willing Woman."

"By all laws, you are a killer."

"I may have been a genetic deviant, I could never be mother to a monster."

"You violated the most sacred trust."

"No one asked me if I wanted an experiment in my body."

"Willing Women are always asked."

"I was in Cork Town! Nobody cares what they do with the women of Cork Town. They took my blood, then they forced life in my womb, and here I am. I know you'll never let me go back."

Heat ran through the woman's veins. Aria could tell there

was more. The thought of it excited her. The group of women and Batrasa awaited their return, but Aria had to know.

"You resent me, Ingrid. I feel it. Why?"

"Why?"

"I want to know why."

Ingrid inhaled deeply, her voice starting low but growing as she grew bolder.

"Where were you when we were starving, *Future Queen?* Playing games, playing with the disappeared people on forgotten islands." Ingrid stepped toward her. "We needed you, Future Queen. We needed a future. They made me believe I was doing my part. They didn't tell me until it was nearly the end that they'd planted this creature in me, some test of the limits of humanity. By killing it I did that *thing* a favor. It was my right and it was the right thing to do. Now I pay the consequences for it. And where were *you?*" Ingrid stopped, and then shouted, "Where were you? Where was every Queen when we were most in need? Where!"

Aria walked away, calm and collected. She'd heard exactly what she wanted to hear, but she also couldn't let the others see Ingrid speak to her that way and get away with it.

Ingrid shouted at Aria's back, "I asked you a question, Future Queen. When we were suffering under the pests, and infant deaths and poisoned water, where were you?"

The other three prisoner women stood dumb.

Aria wandered a few steps away. She took her time, adjusting her long leather coat, buttoning it to the top of her neck.

"You're right, Ingrid." Aria kept her back to the women but cocked her head to one side as she looked out across the pond. "You're never coming back to Lower Earth. Not after what you've done. Not after the disrespect you've shown."

Aria turned around, slower than the earth turned, letting the four women watch her every movement. "Where was I, you ask?" Aria strode tall toward Ingrid, coming chest to chest where she stood more than a head taller than the convicted woman. "I was instilling the history of every Queen who ever came before." Aria caressed her own arms and neck. "They run in my blood; their wisdom etched on my bones. But I had to learn their ways. This is what I had to do in order to become the Queen you all need and deserve. What you call games were my blessed preparations; the generations are now infused in me and all their wisdom with it. How else could I know your movements before you made them? Those preparations will save us when the enemy arrives."

Aria heard doubt in Ingrid's breath.

I must show only as much as is necessary, no more.

"Say what you have to say, woman. You've said so much already."

Ingrid's voice barely spoke, her lips hardly moved. Only Aria could hear her.

"There is no other enemy. We are our own enemy."

Aria took Ingrid's cheeks into her hands and looked deep into her green eyes.

"Wait until you see what the men of Upper Earth have in store for us. You are naïve. And you'll die a captive animal on this forgotten island prison because of it."

Aria walked away from the women but spoke loud enough to Batrasa that they could hear.

"Take them back to the closed area. And get them some shoes. The Queen may have had them disappeared, but they're not animals."

2

———

Batrasa stoked the fire in their safari tent, ensuring the flames licked toward the open side and away from their sleeping space.

Aria dropped into the fabric folded seat. It creaked under her weight. It was barely large enough for her hips.

"You've slackened, Batrasa," Aria loosened the laces of her boots which climbed up nearly to her knee, but she kept an eye on the old warrior woman.

There was no love between them, even after nearly sixteen years, nearly all of her life. So many of Aria's memories were of Batrasa and the Ganese priestesses, but it had always been an arrangement. A Protectorate and her charge. Nothing more.

Batrasa didn't respond.

"Is it age?"

Batrasa pursed her lips and kept poking at the fire.

"Do you resent spending your last days in my company?"

Batrasa laughed quietly, something of a mocking snicker.

Aria listened to what Batrasa didn't say.

Her heartbeat is irregular. Her breath is forced. She wants to say something.

"Speak, teacher."

"You command me?"

"I invite you."

Batrasa stood, but did not turn from the fire.

"Your skills in collective thought are strong, Future Queen."

"But?"

"But you are too confident. There is much you do not know."

Aria started to speak but stopped herself.

Let her say all she has to say. Her blood is flowing hot.

Aria scanned back into herself, the voices of the Queens before her living just under the surface. But she had never mastered how to call on them. The voices would come when unexpected, when they had something to say, and not when Aria sought them.

"You don't see the moving pieces. You are the center of your own world."

Aria sat back in her seat. "You've been saying the same since I was a little girl. I'm failing to see why now it's suddenly a revelation."

Batrasa swung to look Aria in the eye. "Because it was my job to beat it out of you. To make you into what you needed to be." She turned back to the fire. "And I failed."

"You overstate your position, teacher. I am confident but not cocky. I don't take unnecessary risks, and you know that I have good cause for my assertiveness. I have what you don't, we both know that."

"Even now," Batrasa shook her head at the fire, "you still maintain that position. You don't change." Batrasa walked toward her chair on the other side of the safari tent and lowered herself, hands on the armrests taking her weight. "But times are changing, Ariane, and I'm not going to be of use to you for very much longer. You will have to abandon the Aria you've become if you're to be the Ariane this world needs of you."

"You know something about my coronation?" Aria held herself back. For years she'd been waiting for a sign. Perhaps this was it. She was ready. She'd been calling to the Queens of Before about it for years.

Batrasa tilted her head. "What do you know about your mother's coronation?"

Aria had heard the story many times over from the priestesses in varying degrees of detail. "Old Queen Idia died. Queen Maeva stepped in when she was eighteen years of age. Just like I am now." Aria felt her chest puff at the thought. "I am ready for my time, to bring the world into balance. To honor the settlers and keep their wish for life at the fore of Lower Earth's pursuits."

"The Queens in your blood, do they speak of this?"

She knows nothing of the Queens in my blood, as if they spoke in words.

"They give me signs. Comfort and warnings. Screeching in my veins or low rumbling. But they do not read the future, you know that well enough."

Batrasa laughed lowly. "You speak of these voices as though they are a gift."

They sat silent, crackling fire casting shadows against the tented roof.

"They are a curse," Batrasa whispered. "Punish me for saying it if you like, but listen first. You know I didn't want you in my charge. But you don't know why. It's not my role to speak of it, my role is only to prepare and I promise I did it as best I could. I would not put Lower Earth at risk because of my own moral dilemma. But now? Ariane," Batrasa leaned forward, "Ariane, you have to start learning of Lower Earth on your own. Listen carefully to those voices inside you, but do not trust them. They are a byproduct. And one that I do not envy for a second. I saw what they did to Old Queen Idia."

Batrasa stood, unmoving, eyes frozen in an unseen distance.

Perspiration on her forehead. She doubts herself. She has spoken more than she intended. Nostrils heating the air within them; she doesn't calm though she tries.

Batrasa inhaled deeply and looked to Aria.

"Perhaps you shall soon be called to the capital. But the city is nothing like you have imagined. Now sleep. We cast off for Lower Earth before dawn."

ARIA LAY IN BED, HER VARIOUS PARTS OF HER BODY contracting as they did most nights, especially after a day of combat. She scanned from the inside.

Minor tears to muscle tissue in right calf.

She pulled blood from her torso towards the place, rushing hot and fresh. She inhaled and sent the cells which split, recreating and strengthening.

And she was healed.

Elongation of latissimus dorsi. Result of thrust against second attacker. Must lower elbow during turned movement.

She closed her eyes, the heat of oxygen and sensation of waves, the blood rolling over itself to the place. Cells split. Cells recreated. Cells healed.

She opened her eyes. And waited.

The reflection will come.

She called it a reflection, as she had no other name for it. She'd experienced it since the age of three when she first learned to consciously regenerate. A reflection because it was the counterattack of change that came back at her after she healed herself. Like throwing a spear at her image in the mirror, but she became the reflection just as the spear arrived unto herself.

She had no other way of explaining it to herself, nor had she ever explained it to another soul.

The reflection gripped her. She was on the cot when the pain came, lying ten feet from Batrasa who slept deep. A ripping searing pain started in her neck. Then her shoulder. Further down and around, the reflection tore at her, shredding muscle instants before recreating it.

Recreating it stronger than it was before.

It never followed the same path; it was predictable only by its timing.

Aria breathed heavily through her nose as the pain subsided, leaving her skin slick and taut. She closed her eyes but didn't sleep. She hadn't slept, not in the way others slept, not since she'd been born.

The voices of the old Queens rumbled while she throbbed across her ever-strengthening body. She forced herself to rest.

3

____

teps, approaching at 64 miles per hour. Mother is coming.

Aria had been in the process of memorizing the currents of the Gana River. They had been changing in recent months, which she could only attribute to another climatic change.

But her mother's steps, running, were enough to stop her cold. A visit from the Queen could mean many things, but rarely anything good.

She stood and walked to the gate, the entryway of Gana that was the limit of her access to Lower Earth. She knew her mother would hear her moving to meet her. The Queen could hear almost as far as Aria.

Almost.

None of the warrior priestesses would even be aware of the Queen until she was within their territory. The flurry of activity would be manic once word got out, and invariably Batrasa would make comment about the benefits of fore-warning.

But Ariane always heard her before she arrived. And more than a year had passed since the last time.

The flaps of the Queen's dress blew in the wind as Aria watched her advance from afar. The Queen slowed to a walk from a few hundred feet away. Her mother's voice spoke to her even though she was still 3 miles from the gate where Aria stood.

"I see you, child."

"Child? I'm the same age you were when you took the throne."

The Queen cocked her head. "And I was hardly more than a child. You think eighteen years alive qualifies you to be Queen? You haven't changed. Your training here has kept you soft."

She doesn't how I have been preparing myself since the scout was discovered. There is nothing soft in my training.

"Mother," Aria barely spoke, just loud enough so that the queen could hear, the sound traveling on the breeze across the expanse before Gana officially began. "I have dedicated myself to preparation, taken myself to the far corners of the dark counties. The Queens of old are well in me. Healing, collective thought, the ancient accounts. I am preparing. Gana is no fortress."

The Queen's head snapped, upward, chin high and proud. "You think I'm resting on my laurels in Geb? You think because I live in the fortress that somehow my lifestyle is privileged? You have even farther to come than I thought. You have no idea the trials I went through to become Queen. You have been spared all that."

Aria trod carefully. "What I'm trying to say is that you've kept me here. You wanted me shielded, wanted me to focus on my own training and learn the power of collective thought. But now my skills have surpassed Batrasa's program. Remember, you are the one who said I should not be among the people in order to prepare to lead them. I have turned every attention to that cause. I have even practiced in disguise through the Dark Counties to observe their movements. I am now ready."

"You are not allowed in the Dark Counties."

"I am not a common Ganese. I go for my preparation – "

"You are not allowed! Yes, you were isolated, that was an intentional decision. And now you are undermining its very purpose. We cannot risk decisions being based on individualistic loyalty."

"I have no loyalty here. My collective thought is highly attuned."

"I know Archer comes to see you even when I have not commanded it. What is your relationship with him?"

"Archer is a servant of Lower Earth, no more."

"He considers himself more than that to you."

"Then he overstates his position."

"Isn't he the one who named you Aria?"

"It is you who named me Ariane. That is my name."

The Queen cocked her head at Aria.

"The priestesses say you practice dark arts like the Sisters over in the Strangelands."

"That's only because I so far exceed what they can do."

"So you say. But you've become dependent on your Protectorate." The Queen was arm's length from Aria now, her forehead pulling into a line of criticism.

Her eyes are cold and I cannot hear her heartbeat. She is masking it.

"Mother, I spend every moment listening, waiting, preparing. Fighting even, in disguise and without drawing unnecessary attention, dirty brawls, so that I can heal myself from the wounds of the mad, deep wounds that would kill anyone else."

"Upper Earth will not arrive here mad."

"I am trying to - "

"If anything, they will arrive and we won't know it at all." The Queen looked past Ariane.

Run the scenarios: she's avoiding the point. More input required. Test her regard. Question of leadership? Likely not. More likely a scenario yet undisclosed.

Aria straightened her back. "Queen, are you concerned about my abilities?"

"No."

"My acumen?"

"No."

Aria waited. Unwavering but silent.

Something softened in the Queen's face. Her cheeks relaxed, her eyes calmed.

"Ariane. Designed nearly to perfection. My own code, advanced. You, more than anyone, more than I, are connected through collective thought. I can feel it in you, even now. It will make you a fair leader. The people would swiftly come to love you."

The Queen closed her eyes and leaned closer. Aria felt her breath pass between them, landing on her chin. It was hot and sweet, like aged prunes fermenting to wine.

"My Ariane."

She moved closer still, their heads nearly touching.

There is a wave coming across her. She is vulnerable.

"I know you hear the Queens of old, my Ariane. But you do not hear them as I do - "

Their breath moved together in time, nearly imperceptible.

"Ariane, they know our circumstances. They have seen it all before. Ariane, you cannot - "

Aria let her forehead graze her mother's, the white hairs intermingling, sensing the heat of their skin coming together.

And they touched.

The Queen jerked back as though slapped. The vacuum created by her speed sucked Aria in, just slightly, but enough that she appeared to lunge toward the Queen.

The Queen recoiled, a leap backward and her body curved

into a defensive position. Aria could hear the Queen pull the air behind her teeth; she saw the red of the Queen's blood.

She is alarmed. Her blood rolls hot in her veins. It is beating against the inside of her skull. Dread. Terror. What is behind it?

The Queen stood tall, seeming to gain height and Aria felt again like a child looking up to her mother. The Queen moved her mouth, no sound emerging, but Aria heard the air pass through.

"The threat will come," the Queen's eyes narrowed, "If even one comes – scout, traitor, or otherwise – you do as you must, and you do not pause to think. Do not believe your eyes, believe your instinct. You have been taught all you need to know. Never forget what I say to you now."

In the charged silence, Aria watched the Queen, her face dark and unreadable, waiting for a response.

Aria could only nod.

"Beware your loyalties. Never forget, Ariane. They will come, and they will look just like us. Just like you, and just like me. Never forget."

She took in one breath before the Queen was gone, running across the plains as a deer. Moving the way Aria moved, moving like no other on Lower Earth.

Aria considered the Queen's words over and over.

Beware my loyalties. A threat.

She ran the possibilities and scenarios; ratios of likelihood rose and fell. She sought answers from within, the movement faster than human perception but the questions came and went without reply.

Insufficient information. The threat may look like us? Like me? Where is Archer? He must know more. I must find out what he knows.

Aria paused.

Beware my loyalties. Is Archer a threat?

While the Queen had not been to Gana in more than a year, Archer was a regular visitor. But that was to be expected, it was part of his role as the Queen's aide. He had never posed any risk; Aria had known him as long as she'd been alive.

He wouldn't dare step out of line. Not for a second.

After all, Archer was one of those people who had the right to utter a name, and that person would be disappeared before the night turned to morning. He, more than most, knew he wasn't immune to the same punishment.

And regardless, he had only ever been earnestly dedicated to their service, to the Queen and Future Queen Ariane. She saw it in the way his heart calmed on seeing her.

Aria thought of the fire in the Queen's eyes. There was something real inside them. She was not testing Aria. The Queen's heartbeat had beat faster than Aria had ever heard it before.

Betrayal, deceit. The Queen is threatened. But by whom? Upper Earth? Another scout?

No scenario fulfilled the criteria. The pathways in Aria's mind leaped in cycles but came up empty. Activating more than sixty percent of her brain, with a maximum of seventy-seven point two-seven percent, there was simply insufficient input to define the threat.

An animalistic fear, primeval and deep. It shone from the Queen's eyes.

I am to be her hands and feet. Why this fear? It is not only Upper Earth. Her reaction was raw.

The threat will look like me. She fears the threat and she fears me.

While the Queen had many minor enemies across Lower Earth, the Guard was skilled in the art of disappearance. With those dissenters cast into Rainfields or the forgotten islands, all accounts were that the Queen was loved, supported, and respected.

And feared.

Fear is a powerful driver to an enemy.

The remaining men of Lower Earth were in no state to revolt. Even if a few of the strongest amongst them tried to unite, they would be infiltrated at their meeting point. The backroom men had never been able to mobilize into a force. They never would. They had been well controlled, necessarily so given their history. Given the Mist. Aria knew that if a man wanted to commit some treachery, the only real way to do is was through Central Tower. That was where men held their highest seats. And it was the reason for the Green Files with each detailed DNA sequence. The extended file included their affiliations and movements. The Queen reviewed the extended files weekly for any potential traitor within.

They pose no threat. Not now. The only clear and uniform enemy for the nation is Upper Earth.

But what of the women of Lower Earth? Threat takes many shapes. Does she fear for me?

Aria's identity was more or less protected, but that was only until the day she would take over the reign. No one from outside came into Gana without clear authorization, and Aria had not been to the capital since Festival Day in her second year.

Will she advance my coronation in light of the threat? Or postpone?

She had no claim to the throne until it was granted to her - or the Queen died.

Is the threat her own mortality?

The Queen had not yet reached seventy years. She could theoretically have many years reigning ahead of her. The Queen had been eighteen when she'd taken the throne at the death of Queen Idia. Somehow Aria had always believed that when she reached eighteen the Queen would bestow the seat upon her, eager to pass it to her bloodline, the line which had ruled Lower Earth since the first settlers came.

She felt ready. She wanted it so badly. To live out her destiny and guide Lower Earth to a new generation, of more prosperous times. To reinstate the passion for the settlers' ways, the glory of the lava amulet they all wore around their necks.

To pay homage to all that came before as she built a future where viruses and bacteria were eradicated. She'd dedicated years to mastering the structures of some of their most destructive proteins.

The Queen's words rolled through her mind as she assessed the possibilities, running the options available, but the answer glared at her as bright as the sun.

The Queen will not just give the throne over to me.

The meaning of the words rang louder in Aria's head.

The throne is never gifted, the throne is an outcome.

Queens died, like Queen Idia. Queens disappeared, like in the ninth generation. Queens deteriorated, like in the second generation. But no Queen in Lower Earth had ever just handed over the throne.

The firing flew from one pathway to the next in almost reckless succession through her brain as Aria tried to follow it. She closed her eyes and searched her memories. Rushing waves of images took her back through the years; she sought a sign that she may have missed. She quickly dismissed any memories of calm and simplicity, for she had always been extra vigilant in those periods. She so greatly feared her vulnerability in them.

Running through each day in her mind she watched the film of her life in reverse, seeking flashes where something had felt off, moments that hadn't seemed to have meaning. Times when questions had been left unanswered.

She walked back to the river and kneeled at its edge. The currents had nearly come to a complete halt. Aria looked at her reflection, waving slightly in the water's movement. Her brown eyes glistened back at her. The unknowns within the interaction with her mother would not settle as her brain relentlessly sought a solution to the riddle.

Am I the enemy?

Run, run, run.

The voices echoed between her ears.

Aria was not in full consciousness but was already at pace, far from the gate of Gana. Far from her permitted area. It didn't matter that the Queen forbade her to leave Gana, her body did it to her in the middle of the night. She was running without knowing why.

But she knew the destination.

Rainfields.

Her pace quickened. The call would not end until she set stepped on Rainfields' rocky terrain and the voyage would take close to a day on foot. She had to move fast if she were to make it back to Gana before the priestesses realized she was gone.

Rainfields, the birthplace of society as the Final War drew to a close.

Rainfields, where life began again.

Revered Rainfields.

Feared Rainfields.

Rainfields of her waking nightmares.

And still, she ran to them.

Voices, not just in her blood, but in the hills, across the Central Mass. They screeched at her, demanding it, pleading for it.

Begging her to return to Rainfields.

So many nights she cursed her blood for this call.

Why? What is in my blood, this code of the old Queens, that demands communion with such a wretched place?

The Rainfields of the first peoples had been fertile and green, the natural irrigation through its rocky canals making it a haven for those who'd fled to their cliffs. Boat after boat, from nations near and distant, landed at Rainfields, the corner of Lower Earth most accessible to the rest of the world. It had been their savior.

But now it was only a skeleton.

The drought of the second generation after the Mist had all but eradicated any life in Rainfields. The neighboring counties fared better with richer soil and closer watershed. But Rainfields dried up, a carcass of its beautiful memory. The first known victim in the post-war of the ever-changing climate in Lower Earth.

And yet still it called her.

The pull to the cliffs was great. Cliffs jagged and knifelike, arthritic fingers. Sharpened bones that summoned her.

A magnet.

The expanse of Rainfields ran a few hundred miles wide, empty of life but for the gulls that transited past on their cycle back to the Leeside mountains, and the rare soul who'd been disappeared but not jumped off the cliffs.

Aria arrived at their cliff edge and paused. She listened. The wind hummed in the empty creeks of stone below her feet. The song was sad and compelling. She turned away from the cliffs, the wind singing through the jagged fingers. The wind sang lies at her, but she refused to surrender to them.

Without words, it called at her to jump. To fly. To soar.

Aria was well aware of the lies of the Rainfields wind. She'd heard their deceit since she was a child.

She closed her eyes and calmed her blood.

They will never let me be. Why this physical reaction? Why this power to pull me when I am barely conscious? Queens, why this place?

The voices gave no reply. As ever, they did not respond on command.

Aria opened her eyes.

A figure, wind-like, skimmed the distance. Aria only saw it because the moon caught its hair in a gleam. No scent, no heartbeat, no movement of blood perceived.

A mirage.

Aria kept her eyes on the figure, it froze as though in a dream just before awakening.

Mother's words are wreaking havoc in my brain. Must obtain more input. This cannot continue.

She shut her eyes hard and reopened them. The figure was gone.

It is not real. I am still not fully conscious. It is a mirage in my own image.

The figure had moved as only Aria could.

4

———

Queen Maeva felt Ariane's eyes follow her away, but she couldn't stay. She couldn't bear another moment of it. The secrets were starting to weigh heavily. She feared she would give something away.

She ran. Wind-like and unseen by any human eye.

Eighteen years old, Maeva shook her head. *Her expectations are obvious. She knows my story, she thinks it will be her own. Eighteen years old and Queen. If only she knew what it had cost me.*

But she can never know.

Maeva couldn't bear to let her own history influence the generation to come.

But her own trauma wasn't over yet. If anything, the worst of it was yet to come.

If only it were as simple as declaring Aria Queen. She is the obvious choice. She believes the throne is hers for the having. She's been the most adapted out of all of them.

But Maeva knew. It wasn't so simple.

Nothing has gone to plan from the start. The genetic code of Queens is not as simple as that.

Maeva reached a safe distance from Gana, nearly at the

checkpoint that marked a hundred miles from the Gana border. Her feet moved her at the pace of a bird's flight, even at her age. She could see the ocean off to her left and ran to its coast. The water's edge was rocky but tame. Waves crashed in a gentle rhythm. Maeva let it take her inside, the sound dulling her mind's thoughts so that she could hear the sounds which rolled in her blood.

The voices rose up.

Maeva closed her eyes.

The generations of Queens from before spoke in blood sounds, but if she focused, she could call upon them, and words, phrases, or ideas would burst from within, and she knew.

The Queens of Before who were coded into her genetic sequence would tell her what had to be done.

But they were fickle. Untrustworthy. She would sometimes seek them and they'd lie silent.

And then there were the times they exploded, uninvited and all-encompassing, screaming warnings or reproach. Or worse. The Queens of Before had led lives that transformed the face of Lower Earth.

And not one had died naturally.

It was the secret within her blood. It was what she demanded Lucius code out. And it was the reason she found herself in the riddle of her life.

She had to declare the next Queen.

And Maeva didn't know who it was.

For the rest of Lower Earth, it was obvious. Their next Queen was Ariane. Ariane, like Maeva, was descended from the code of the settlers, revered and honored settlers, they who'd been the answer when the world was dying. The line of Queens kept the settlers' blood alive.

The secrets in that blood were well-kept.

The sound of the waves wove with the voices within.

Maeva could make out their warning. She would have to steel herself for the period that would come. It might be years away still, decades perhaps.

Or the day when Maeva would have to declare the next Queen could be just around the corner.

5

Preparing for a new cohort of Willing Women was the most exhausting part of Uma's job. It wasn't the logistics of it that got her down since they were straightforward enough: ensure facility space, print enough brochures, organize the speakers, recruit current Willing Women to buddy up.

She believed in the need for it, but it was the women themselves that irked her.

She stood at the welcome desk for two hours. At least this was a small event, not like the summer campaign that was coming. The women were becoming more and more ignorant about the program. While the Willing Women program had been in full swing for years, many of the hopefuls didn't even have the most basic facts straight.

"Can I keep the baby?"

"What happens if I can't carry it to term?"

"Is there a chance I won't get pregnant?"

Uma smiled and shoved a brochure in each little, fertile face. This wasn't supposed to be her job. She was a scientist. She could have been spending these hours investigating the newest crop killers. Central Tower didn't have near enough resources to be spreading themselves so thin across the laboratories. And yet there she was, convincing girls to use their wombs for what they'd been designed to do.

She was on the verge of losing her patience when a young one approached her. Uma tried to look very busy doing something important.

"Ma'am, excuse me?"

Uma looked up at her, but she wasn't about to encourage her with a word of welcome.

"I just need some advice. See, I'm not sure why I should become a Willing Woman."

"Well, don't then."

"But everyone says I should."

"And why does everyone say that." She tried not to sound as sarcastic as she felt.

"Probably because I'm not good at anything else."

"You're not a Cork Town deviant. I'm sure there's a career path for you."

"I don't think so."

"How about sign painting? There's always a job for a sign painter."

"I spell words all wrong."

It was because of girls like this that the program was so important. They couldn't leave genetics to happenstance. Uma smiled. "Well then, perhaps everyone might be right. Perhaps you should be a Willing Woman."

The girl's eyebrows came down into a frown before lifting as her eyes welled up. Uma took a deep breath and a step towards her.

"Willing Women are important." *You idiot,* she thought. "The country needs women like you, strong women."

"I'm not strong."

"Healthy then."

"I am healthy."

"There it is. Healthy women. We need healthy women. Haven't you heard about the Directive? You'll have to go through all the regular screening first, and I'm not going to lie. It's invasive. But this could be your chance. You could be the one who produces a boy child. Imagine that!" Uma clapped her hands and smiled while looking past the girl's shoulder, waiting for the moment to pass.

"Thank you," the girl whispered and then walked, bleary-eyed, away.

With a sigh of relief and a deep swallow, Uma tried to rid herself of the lump that was growing in her throat. Perhaps she should change her role at these events. She just didn't have the energy for it anymore.

She would soon have to prepare for the summer session, which was always the most difficult campaign event. There would be additional crowds after exam results. Inevitably the young women who'd failed their exams would find their way, usually with someone else dragging her, to the Willing Women event. The girls would have wet eyes and speak in stops and starts.

For Uma, participation in the Willing Women program as an overseer had been both an honor and a responsibility. These were trying times, and while some questions around the program's ethics may have been justified, Uma believed that participation in the program should have been mandatory for all women of childbearing age, except those, like her, who were designed for other callings. How else could they ever expect to grow back into the population from before the Mist?

It's what the settlers had wanted for them.

Uma caressed the lava amulet around her neck.

"The time has come for this session of the Willing Woman campaign to end," Mary's voice rang out over the screens across the city. "For those of you who have offered your services, bravo! You know how this act is essential to keeping life on Lower Earth. The settlers smile upon you today. We salute all women who offer their wombs for Lower Earth's future! Now prepare, everyone, the Settlement Day parade will begin shortly! Settlers, how grateful we are for the days you suffered! We shall all raise our eyes to the sky and we hold the lava rock of Lower Earth in our hands."

Uma gathered up the application forms and brochures to get back to her real work in Central Tower before the parade began.

Comfortably back at her desk, Uma scanned the memo with updates across the Male Program.

The door to her seventeenth-floor office was closed tightly, just in case anyone could hear her thoughts. She didn't need her aversion to the Male Program known. After all, Roman was insistent that they find a breakthrough, and he was her boss.

Boys. A relic of a generation ago. I wonder when we'll finally give up on trying to revive them.

The current age saw young men and men and old men, but no boys. Mary didn't have to announce it across the screens. Everyone could see it with their own eyes. Inside Central Tower, the men who committed their lives to procreation research were split between floors. The Policy said that the distribution of "man-power" ensured equal input from their sex to the different research programs. In practice, however, not all men were created equal. Uma stood and walked to the glassed wall of her office that overlooked the deep plunge from the seventeenth floor down to the ground floor lobby. Bodies moved like ants across the floors, elevators crossed each other, delivering new codes, genetic material, results. The day was in full swing. Just another day trying to preserve their world.

Uma sighed.

She saw Adam emerge from the elevator across from her office.

Adam. He played on so many sides in the Tower, and somehow was allowed to. It didn't matter that it had been almost a decade they worked together; Uma couldn't read Adam any more than a stranger. She watched as he stepped with a tense back, almost awkwardly, into Isaac's office, closing the door and disappearing from sight.

6

———

Adam stepped out of the elevator, conscious that Uma's eyes were on him. But he didn't care, not now. He had the latest survival rate in his hands, and even though they were less than encouraging, Adam saw some good news in it. Everyone knew that the five floors dedicated to the Male Program were active on a 24-hour cycle, and yet no viable boy had been born for a couple of years. All embryos showed signs of degradation in their genetic code. It wasn't even worth proposing them for Willing Women.

Fewer and fewer of us. When are we going to break through?

Adam felt his mortality. He'd witnessed so much in the men around him. Degradation. Heart failure. Sometimes an unknown cause altogether. So far, he had escaped the worst of it, but the thought of what was to come still haunted him. The effects of the Mist were in all of them.

He pushed open the door at the end of the hall.

"I've got the most recent survival rate, Isaac."

"And?"

Adam shrugged. "Better."

"But not good?"

Adam made a huffing sound.

Isaac sighed, "Okay, not good."

"I feel like good is a generation away. 'Better' is at least a step in the right direction."

"You're a statistician, Adam. I'm an optimist."

The door closed behind Sara, though they hadn't heard it open. "Better an optimist than a river swimmer. It was a tough competition."

"And the winner is?"

"No contest, Jan Gillard won."

"That makes three years in a row!"

"She was built for it."

"Good genes, clearly."

The old joke made them smile. Sara, Isaac, and Adam had all been on the team who improved the Directive. The Gillard line was one of their first successes. They had taken it to heart, even though the adaptations for strength had the expected consequences on lifespan.

"Do you think she'll get any slower with time?"

"Ask the statistician."

Adam pursed his lips. "Not likely."

They smiled.

"Well, that is a nice counterbalance to 'Better'. Worthy of grabbing a coffee, I'd say." Isaac lifted himself out of the rolling office chair, awkwardly, nearly falling sideways but he caught the top of his desk.

"Now, now," Adam rushed over.

"I'm fine." Isaac looked up at them. "Perhaps I should spend some time river swimming myself, or I'll find myself in an early grave. This desk work takes a toll."

The other two watched him leave the room, his belly hanging over his slacks, breathing hard.

"Yeah, desk work." Adam shook his head. It was the same pattern he'd seen with so many men of Isaac's generation, a ticking time bomb. "What is our contingency plan if he goes, Sara?"

Sara took in a deep breath, "I'm still thinking about it. I don't trust a single one of the new geneticists. Not one, Adam." Her chin lowered but her eyes remained fixed on the darkening sky. Adam watched her lips tighten as her mind rolled over the idea. Her green eyes shone in the light of the sunset and she looked so young, so despondent. Adam walked to her and gently placed his hand on her shoulder.

"What are you doing?" Sara snapped and stepped away.

"You look upset."

"So you touch me? In the Tower?" She whispered hard, "What's the matter with you?"

Firmly back in reality, Adam walked to the window.

"This place. I can't imagine the future here. It all comes up black when I think about it. I project myself fifty years into the future and I hit a wall. It makes me wonder if there is one at all."

"There never was, don't idealize."

The fortress gleamed in the distance; several lights were on and movement was visible even from the distance of Central Tower. The Settlement Day parade was about to begin.

"Four hundred and two years since official settlement. Four hundred and two years of what?" he said, mostly to himself.

"You know as well as I do."

"We're so close, Sara," his voice lowered instinctively, though he was speaking to the horizon more than he was speaking to her. "Something is just on the edge, I can feel it. But what if we get it wrong?"

"We've weighed that possibility from the start. We'd end up disappeared, wherever that would take us. But Adam - " she joined him at the window, "I'd die for less."

"I'm afraid I might. Like Isaac."

"Isaac needs to drink a little less and move a little more."

Adam wished it were as simple as that.

"Yeah." He half-laughed, "Optimist, huh?"

"More like depressed drunk."

A holler rose from the fortress gate - a special guest arriving. The hollers gained in volume and intensity, squeals and shouts, words like "Long live!" and "Hoorah!" lifted from the main square.

There was only one person greeted with that kind of noise at national festivities. The Future Queen must have just arrived.

Looking down, Sara and Adam caught sight of her inside the metal bars at the fortress ground's entrance. She was adorned in deep blue scales that caught the light of the setting sun. Stunningly beautiful, she glowed. A small radius of people around her left a respectful space, making her entirely visible from the Central Tower block.

"You want to see our future? There she is, in all her glory," Sara spat out, no attempt to hide her disgust.

"Barely more than a child. And we're supposed to put our hopes in her? If she's anything like Queen Maeva, we are in for even darker times."

"She's been practicing combat skills against animals. Killing them. Ripping them to pieces. Queen Maeva commanded that I collect what remained of the carcasses and analyze the Future Queen's efficiency. What for? What good can come of that?"

Adam shook his head. "It's the increase in disappearances that makes me sick."

They watched as the Future Queen turned from three hundred feet away, as if she heard. She looked directly at them. Her face was flawless, skin smoother than milk, a sharp nose, and high angled cheekbones. Her dark green eyes caught the fading sunlight as no others could do. She kept her gaze on them and lowered her chin briefly before walking away.

Sara and Adam froze.

"Did she just nod her head at us?"

"She did. I swear it, she did."

7

———

"Tomorrow's rain will further production in the West Fields. This is welcome news for us all," Mary's voice on the screen rattled on. Lucy was hardly paying attention. Final exams were coming, and this hadn't been a good year. Lucy walked past corner after corner, Mary's eyes and voice following her as she went.

"New advances have been made available for sustainable home heating. If you continue to use stoves and forced air, report to your nearest City Post for more information before the next cold sets in. Fortunately, fuel consumption is at all-time lows. Thank you for heeding advice, citizens! This has allowed the stores to remain sufficient for the colder seasons."

As she walked down the main avenue, Lucy's toe caught on a break between the asphalt squares and she nearly fell. She barely noticed. Algebra had been especially hard, and the thought of the exam for advanced geometry made her head spin. She knew they wouldn't allow aides into the exam room, and she wouldn't dare cheat, but expectations of her were high. The thought of it made her stomach turn. Scratching her shoulder against the sharp bark of an evergreen tree, she wound her way to a bench in the middle of Green Park. She took a bite of her sandwich and made a face at it. Her mother always put too much butter. Her mother was of the mind that butter built muscle, just look at Lucy's strength, did she not run the fastest 5-mile race last year in her age group? But Lucy found butter horrible, the way it squidged in her teeth and made a layer on her tongue.

Even this couldn't distract her from the sense of impending failure. She had been such a promising student, so they all had told her when she was five and six and seven years old. Then something happened. Lucy couldn't place it on a particular moment, but just as she started to grow taller and stronger, it was like she grew dumber too. She wasn't completely useless; she knew she was far from the half-wits and handicaps of Cork Town.

But she had dreams when she was in that space between awake and asleep. Dreams where her mother cast her out. Wild, whirling dreams of wind and thunder and she'd be running. Running to get away, but not sure what from. She would run and run and run and know she was outrunning whatever it was - but then she would arrive, alone, cold, and no idea where she was. The Strangelands maybe? It was only a dream, and in a dream one can cross thousands of miles in a moment. Suddenly it would feel like real life, that sense of pressure on the bottom of your feet where they touch the earth, and Lucy would wake up holding her breath, eyes wide.

Mary's voice perked up again. "We continue to look for Willing Women! The gestation period is now four months. Can you dedicate a minimum of ten months to your nation? If you have reached your age of womanhood and feel called to raise the next generation, report to the Central Meeting House next Wednesday at noon."

Lucy looked up to the screen. Mary was the face of the nation, every day at seven, ten, and sixteen hundred hours she invaded the streets with her set jaw and deep green eyes. There was a quality to her voice that pulled you in, but it was her eyes that made you stop and look, and inevitably hear whatever she was saying. Most women now had green eyes, but hers were somehow that shade deeper.

"Full information will be available, along with Willing Women themselves who can tell you of the experience. The next season is planned for spring this year, with training commencing in two weeks' time."

In two weeks Lucy would either have just sailed by her exams, or she would be sobbing in the gutter. In two weeks her mother would be serving up duck or locking her in her room. In two weeks, she might have no choice but to sign up as a Willing Woman.

8

―――――

The Queen lifted her chest higher, watching the eyes below watching her.

Silently they all waited for her next word. On the edges of the crowd, the Guard stood at attention. They weren't much more than decorative now; decades had gone by since anyone had tried to cause trouble during a Tuesday Briefing. And even then, it had been a backroom man. No one had taken him seriously.

Maeva took in their faces from her balcony, some smiling, some waiting, others distracted. She cleared her throat and every chin lifted her way. They were so trusting, so innocent, so needy.

Mother of the nation, mother of Lower Earth. Maeva felt as much mother to each beating heart before her now as she did to those designed from her own code. That was her duty. She had been born for it, born from the code of every Queen before her. Born from the original settlers' DNA.

Looking across the masses, she saw her own reflection in each of them. Central Tower had done well in integrating the sequence.

We might stand a chance after all.

She zeroed in on a woman near the northwest corner of the square. A couple of hundred feet away, Maeva saw it in her brow. Straight down from the fortress hill, eight stories below her, she saw it in a woman's chin, another's shoulder frame, and yet another's cheekbones.

The code was well incorporated without being obvious. The connection between royalty and people would be undeniable. She would have to congratulate Roman again; the man lived for small courtesies and space to continue his precious Male Program. Roman was like a dog; Maeva would give him a pat on the head and he would be loyal to death. He'd picked up well where Lucius had left off, even if he didn't have the title to go with it. She'd promised the title would remain with Lucius in exchange for his silence. So Roman would have to live with Primary Overseer, and he seemed perfectly content with it.

Though that didn't mean she didn't track his Extended Green File. He had his file, just like the others. No room for complacency. Not in times like these.

She realized that she had stopped paying attention to the crowds below.

She finished with a deep breath.

"And you all know how the Central Tower has been progressing, I don't need to tell you how there are whispers of promise emerging from the sea of their work. Water purification has reached new levels, collection from the Leeside storms is paying off in dividends, and the Water Ministry must be applauded for their efforts!"

A general rush came over the crowd with "Yes!", "Ministry of Water, hurrah!" and clapping until the Queen swiftly hushed them down.

"You also know the due diligence we must sustain in keeping our eyes beyond our shores. Now is not the time, and today is not the day. But one day Upper Earth might be looking to take new steps. We keep a supply of intelligence. Some risk their lives to obtain it." A few hands clapped, but the Queen raised hers to silence them. "We will not celebrate what we fear, but we prepare against our hopes. It is a thankless job, but not unnoticed. I see you, leaders of the munitions and intelligence group. You need not identify yourselves. The settlers know what you face; they too lived through it. You do homage to the settlers. I thank you with their blood."

Maeva lifted her lava amulet into the air, and the tens of thousands gathered below did the same. The blood of the settlers ran through her veins, their voices humming in her head as she brought the amulet back to her chest.

She scanned the crowd, and one by one by she found the members of the munitions and intelligence group among the thousands. She gave each one a nod. All was silent across the square as she took this time to acknowledge each woman and the two men of the group in silent recognition. The air was electric.

She took a deep breath and moved into her standard closing, unrushed and reverent as ever.

"The screens tell you all, they remain your friends. Mary is your friend. I, too, am your friend, your Mother Queen. As ever, you know that I belong to you, even more than you to me. As the settlers were, so must we be accepting, kind, and strong!"

The eruption of cheers across the crowd signaled the end of the Tuesday Briefing. The event was archaic as a practice, but the Queen felt it was her duty to provide routine. She remained on the balcony, watching the women move back into their daily lives - the farmers and manufacturers, the teachers and food servers, and the few men who mingled among them.

Irene forced air out. "When do we start telling them what's

really going on? These Tuesday Briefings are like a school assembly."

The Queen didn't remove her eyes from the people. A group was laughing in the eastern part of the square, and in them she saw her own teeth.

"Some were missing from the crowd, Irene."

"Some? Who?"

"At least four technicians from the fifth floor of the Tower. Run an inspection. I imagine they prioritized their work. It's important that they know these briefings are not optional. Send a strong message."

Irene cocked her head. "It never ceases to amaze me that you can look out over a crowd of, what, ten thousand, and notice that four were missing."

"They are taking liberties. Liberties are not for taking. They are to be earned. Make sure that is clear to them."

Maeva walked out, knowing Irene would follow. "Prepare the court, I'll hear them as scheduled. But first – "

"I know. The reports were delivered today. They are on your bureau."

"Still sealed?"

"As always."

Maeva stopped.

"I can't help fearing that one day some zealous messenger will tamper with them – " her voice trailed off.

That thought sent her heart racing. She slowed its beating, watching from the inside as the blood moved slower out, the calm rolling over her like clouds.

"Maeva, that is prevented at all costs. I only put the most trustworthy guards on it. I use a particular genetic line that focuses on completion of tasks. The content of what they deliver is of no interest to them."

Maeva sighed.

"I'll come to court at the regular time."

Irene bowed her head. "Yes, Queen."

Maeva took in the sight of the Commandante in the afternoon light that shone yellow through the opening in the fortress wall. Irene's uniform was impeccable, the lines of it sharp across her broad and tall figure. A natural Ganese, her dark eyes, dark skin, and thick lips were a contrast to the Queen's olive complexion.

Irene turned and walked tall in the direction of the main fortress building. The Queen went to her bedroom and shut the wooden door behind her, latching the iron lock.

In front of her window, on her small bureau, sat four packages.

She lowered herself into the velvet chair – all velvet was property of the Queen but for the swatches gifted to the museum – and let her back rest against the dark wood.

Each package was slightly different, but all were triple wrapped. That was the protocol.

She started with the thickest. Batrasa was always the most thorough. Batrasa feared for her position, despite her hard veneer. She made up for it by providing even the most mundane of details on Ariane's progress. Maeva scanned the pages.

Excellent collective thought. As expected. Previous close attachment with Archer seems to be cooling. That's promising.

She took her time, reviewing each page, imagining Ariane's daily life. It was all so far removed from her own experience. Secluded, protected. Cared for, even loved. Yet even then, the power of her code was undeniable. The Queen recognized her own arrogance in Ariane's attitude. It was a protective measure. But it presented risk as well.

Her collective thought is far superior to that of the others. It could fare well for periods of intense change. The people will follow her into confinement and quarantine, rationing, reduction of freedoms. Yes, that could serve very well. She always showed the most promise of them all.

Maeva looked out the window. How much had changed since she first came into power, and yet the uncertainty of their land remained. The Mist couldn't be blamed for all of it. They would soon have to redirect some of their research back into climate studies.

But not yet. The work in human genetics was coming along so well.

Maeva opened the bottom drawer of her bureau and dropped the report into it. She would file it later, after court.

She opened the next package, the report significantly shorter. It was produced on the wild grass paper that was typical of the West Strangelands.

Maeva read the first line and pursed her lips.

It was as she expected, though she hoped every time for a better result.

This one will never do. Her qualities are too far perverted from anything a Queen would need to be. The West Strangelands was never a good choice. The Sisters raising her are too severe, their ways too subversive. I should have known. But I trusted Sahna. How could I not? Where would I have been without her? Her training made me who I am.

Maeva remembered Sahna's face, her young face, from the days when Maeva was herself just a child. How she'd loved Sahna's face. Her deep-set eyes alit with rebellion. But the rebel had lived only in her eyes. That's what Maeva loved in her. Sahna could conform and rebel all at once.

And then she'd gone too far.

Maeva shook Sahna from her mind.

No point in dwelling on it. The world is what it is, and there are rules for a reason. She forced me to discipline her.

Her rational mind understood, but the memory of blood — rushing blood, Sahna's blood, blood running over Sahna's body onto Maeva's hands, her arms, her chest -

Stop it, Maeva. Focus.

She closed the Strangelands report and dropped it in the drawer.

Her hands hovered over the last two reports. She wanted good news, which took her to the Geb account. But her heart was gripped by the other one.

Business first, Maeva. Then you can have your moment of weakness.

She set aside the small package and opened the Geb report.

Progress as planned. A hardened character but she is adaptable. Cool strength in the face of an attack. I wish she didn't insist on training against animals, but I suppose it's not unreasonable. Independent and authoritative, as expected. No surprises in this report.

Maeva preferred it that way. She dropped the package in the drawer.

There was only one left. It was thin and unimposing. Nothing like the others.

And yet she still demanded the report be produced. Maeva owed her that much and more.

Get it over with. You know what you'll see there. Just make sure she's doing alright.

She quickly tore open the report from Cork Town. This time it included a photo.

Maeva's heart filled at the sight of her. The fire-red hair, the face of a creature. In the photo, she could make out the form of Lucius behind her. Her lips were slightly agape and her eyes sparkled.

I don't remember the last time I saw her smile.

Maeva's fingers caressed the photo and then she set it to the side. Hers was always the shortest report. This one was no longer than a few paragraphs.

So soft. So kind. How the world would have been different if she hadn't become this twisted version of her. My first-born, my beautiful -

She didn't let herself think about it anymore. She had to stop the thoughts.

Otherwise, the voices came.

And they would pull her, take her back.

Back to Rainfields.

She felt the rumblings inside her, the movement of blood to that deep place which was always a sign of what was to come.

Not now. Not now. I have court. I can't deal with this now!

She stood quickly, throwing everything off the bureau. She had to do something. Anything to distract her thinking. Anything to quiet them. She picked up her chair and threw it across the room. Faster than most could see, it flew like a bomb, crashing into the bedpost. Wood smashed into splinters at the force of it.

But it worked. The voices calmed.

They were getting worse. Something was happening; something in their world wasn't right. The voices knew, they always knew. They ran scenarios against all which came before, but had no words and spoke in tongues. Maeva knew enough to hear their warning, though she wasn't yet ready to make her final selection. The day would come when she would have to cull.

She reset her hair into a tight bun, inhaled, and opened the door.

Before she'd reached the court, she could hear the bustle inside. Irene was waiting for her.

"Maeva, you look – "

"Is the court ready?"

"Several hundred came directly from the briefing."

The Queen rubbed her temples. "I have such little patience. This obligation has grown tiresome."

"It's only once a quarter, my Queen. You know what it does for them."

The Queen closed her eyes and rallied her patience. These court sessions pulled her away from the matters of management, genetics, and menaces to society, and brought her

squarely down to squabbles, petty retaliation, and minor terri-
torial disputes.

Irene pushed open the heavy carved wooden doors and the
din in the room settled as the ceremonial clack of the hinges
signaled the Queen's entry.

Each of the four hundred seats was filled and not one more
word was spoken until the Queen had stepped forward,
surveyed the bleachers and walked tall and slow to the basic
chair in the middle of the room. She looked to the ceiling and
brought her eyes down to a rough-looking woman in the third
row towards the right of the room. Sounds continued to
rumble inside her, the voices brewing.

"You," the Queen whispered to the woman. "What is your
name and complaint?"

The woman didn't budge. This was normal, the first of the
day was usually slow to begin.

The woman's companion elbowed her in the ribs. "Speak,
damn it," she loudly whispered.

"She will speak when ready," the Queen mustered a smile.
"The day's justice will take as long as it takes, and no one needs
to feel rushed in the process."

"Thank you, Your Majesty," the other woman said. She was
stout and simple, but with a gleam in her eyes that the Queen
recognized as her own. "It is my first time to court," the
woman said, "and I am in awes of you, My Queen."

"Your compliments are gratefully accepted," the Queen
said, no hint of her impatience.

"My Queen, I am Doris of the eighth line from the
Western Territories. I have come to request the use of Royal
lands beside my home, not for ownership, but so that the cows
can graze. There is still some fertile land on the very edges of
the region."

"Kind woman, this is court, not the Agriculture Ministry -"

"Yes, yes, Your Majesty. Oh my goodness, did I cut you off? Please continue, Your Majesty, excuse me."

"No, no, go on."

She was nervous now, "The Agriculture Ministry has told me I cannot, and yet I see no justice in their decision since the lands are untouched and yourself, the Queen, have not been in many, many years to this place, so I fear that without demanding more than my lot, I ask for this permission and to overturn on the grounds of justice the decision of the Ministry of Agriculture." She let out the rest of her breath and straightened her back before giving an awkward courtesy, "If it so pleases Your Majesty."

"Kind woman, I see it is your first time to court, for you have been far too pleasant and deferential. Your complaint is justified; you have no need to plead with such servitude. Where do you live?"

"My Queen, you haven't come in so long. It can hardly matter to you. The place is otherwise barren. I speak of the lands on the edge of Rainfields…"

The woman said more, continued making her argument, but the Queen was lost to the present. Lost. Pulled back into a memory at that very moment.

She couldn't stop it.

IN HER MEMORY SHE WAS STANDING ON THE CLIFF'S EDGE, knowing the danger, but denying it. In the distance, she saw a mirage of her mother as she had been all those years ago. The coming storm was a backdrop; dark clouds swirled above her head.

Maeva stood, knowing all the years that had passed;

knowing that this vision could not be. It was only a glimmer of her mother, Idia, just moments before her death.

Her suicide.

Maeva had stood staring at the mirage, too close to the cliff's edge. She felt the danger of her position, and with the Queen Child inside her, so close to birth. Her first child. The Future Queen.

Ariane.

Clouds were so low Maeva felt she was half inside them. She didn't will it to happen, she was sure she didn't but she stepped forward, stepped toward the image of her mother, mother's arms beckoning, mother's arms commanding, the reflection of the memory.

She turned her head and saw the moment her mother flew in front of her, over the cliff's edge. The ghost before her beckoning, the ghost beside her flying. Falling. Dying. Her black cloaks flapped, all of time slowed to a near standstill, Maeva watched her mother's hair flying in the wind.

Her mother's ghost, alter ego of a ghost, called her forward.

When she turned her head again, her mother was back on the top of the cliff, alive, two feet planted. She smiled at Maeva.

And jumped.

Maeva looked at the rocks below. She knew they were sharp, dangerous, deadly. She knew it in her mind, but the water crashing around them called to her.

And the voices inside squealed with delight.

The landing place of Queens.

Her mother stood at her side in the waking dream, and she whispered.

"It is but a trial. There is no true death for a Queen." She grabbed at her own throat. "Even now, I feel my own blood running through your veins. It's better that way, for I cannot stand this anymore."

Then her mother threw her head back, screaming with torture, ripping at her skin as she flew through the air.

Then she was back again on the cliff. The mirage locked her eye to eye. Summoning her forward. Inviting her steps.

She didn't intend to go. And then she was falling.

Falling, her own hair flying now, pulled across her face as she plummeted, nothing to grab hold of. She felt her robes tossing around her, the ground coming toward her and she prepared for the hard landing against rock and coral.

She hardened herself, knowing it would be the greatest trial of her abilities yet.

She did not fear for herself. She would mend herself. She would find a way.

But her fetus.

It had not yet learned the ways of regeneration.

Maeva would survive, but the child -

My child! Listen to me! Stay strong, my child!

Her brain raced for scenarios, any way to avoid the inevitable.

A split second before she crashed against the rock floor, she prepared her body for impact. She had to take drastic measures.

She landed and everything inside her broke, shattered, slices of bone shred her veins. She began her healing immediately, but she knew the child's condition.

The heartbeat inside her had stopped.

She's dead. She's dead. Mother, what have you done to me!

She couldn't accept it. She wouldn't. Not now, not this perfected version of her own code. No.

She would heal it.

Her own body regenerated; freshly reborn cells drove to

her center, to her womb, rushing blood and oxygen and intention.

She started with the heart, healing the Queen Child's heart, to feel the beating lifeblood. She found the broken cells and injected new DNA into the dead spaces.

New life. She pushed with her blood and muscle to revive.

The rest will come, the heart must be first.

Then Archer's arms were then around her, he was panting from the descent as the skies opened up and poured rain down on them. He watched as she healed and shouted through the pounding rain.

"My Queen! My Queen! Why? Why did you jump? Maeva, what have you done?"

She looked at him, through him. She had to heal it. She was the Queen Mother now. And she would not repeat the sins of her own mother. She would not. She felt the walls of the child's skin and forced her way in, sending the cells and blood, pushing inside her in waves of electrical thrill.

Again.

And again.

And again.

And again.

Until the beat resumed.

Beating rain smashed into the Queen's face. She couldn't see Archer in front of her. He was blended with the wind and cloud. She saw only her baby's face from inside. It was red. So red. Red blood. Red death. Red life reborn.

The perfect sequence was no longer perfect.

There would be consequences for her weakness.

Shame grabbed the Queen by the throat and she fought against her own emotion to breathe. She looked up at the sky and let the hail pierce her eyes.

Blinking, she scanned the room, several hundred faces watching her every breath. This Queen of such composure, heaving heavily, eyes stinging from the memory of the hail.

She turned and ran from the room.

"The Queen is displeased by your request," Irene's voice became quieter as Maeva ran deeper into the fortress court-yard. "I will note all requests and bring them to her later."

Slamming into door frames, indifferent to the eyes that watched her moving past, the Queen found her way to her chambers, delicately closing the door, lest she create a worse scene than she had already done.

Rainfields. The death house of royals, a living noose that pulled them in and never let them find their way home.

Irene arrived moments later, stepping carefully into the Queen's quarters. Her eyes scanned the room, landing on the broken chair and cracked bedpost. She waited before speaking.

"The reports have upset you."

"Something is coming."

Irene waited.

"Irene, it's coming, and we won't be ready."

"We are doing everything we can to prepare –"

"Listen to me!" Maeva rushed at Irene, coming eye to eye with her, nearly reaching the same height as the Ganese warrior woman. "No generation has ever known who their true enemy would be. It was never as they thought. Prepare? There is no preparation sufficient for this. Soon. Whatever it is will happen soon, and we will need a leader who is fit for the occasion."

Irene nodded slowly. Maeva counted on her understanding. So few others in Lower Earth would understand the decision she had to make.

"The coronation will not be long away now."

"Are you ready for that, Maeva?"

Maeva looked at Irene. Their eyes spoke between them. She had never intended to have to make such a decision, but her intentions were as irrelevant as the world before the Mist.

The stood for a moment in silence together.

"Let me be alone now."

"As you wish."

"Let no one enter."

"As you wish, my Queen."

"Irene..." Maeva lifted her eyes to look on her Commandante, her most trusted aide. "Send me Archer."

9

———————

An owl called from the trees over his head. Archer looked for it, but it was well hidden in the tall branches of the acacias. He breathed in the smell of the forest at dusk. The air was cool in his nostrils and a shiver came down his arms. He watched the little bumps rise on his skin. At just over sixty years old, Archer had outlived most of his contemporaries. His skin was still taut. His muscles still capable. Healthy.

His own reflection didn't give his age away.

In that way, he had so much in common with Maeva.

Cut from the same cloth.

He smiled. He had always felt the kinship between them, even if it was a near-ridiculous idea. He was her aide. He had complete faith in her.

He loved her.

He was convinced they came from the same original peoples, one of the boats which came over. It was the only explanation why his sequence didn't degrade and why hers kept her so young.

Cut from the same cloth.
Built from the same wood.

A bird flew by, singing to its companion who awaited its arrival in the acacia in front of him.

Notes from the same song.

"What are you doing, Archer?"

The Commandante's voice jerked him out of his romantic daydream.

He clumsily got to his feet.

"What is it, Irene? Why are you interrupting me?"

"Interrupting?"

The Commandante looked around at the trees, grass, birds. Archer fought the sense of shame. He had every right to remove himself for a while, to spend time in his thoughts. What he thought about was none of her business.

They stood, looking at one another, neither moving, neither breaking the silence.

Archer shifted his weight. The Commandante drew taller. He was sure she could smell his weakness.

"The Queen has called for you. And here you are, watching the sunset with the birds."

"I was thinking."

"Get to the Queen. I don't care what you were doing."

He wrapped his fingers around the edge of the door, opening it one inch at a time, waiting for her voice. Certainly, she knew he was there. She always knew.

"Come."

He entered.

"Close the door."

She was stretched out on the bed, the four wooden posts looking like a cell with invisible bars. One was cracked.

"Sit by me, Archer."

He found a stool near the fireplace and brought it to her bedside.

"Hold my hand."

He took her cool hand in his own. Her skin was always so soft. His had been rough since the day he'd been born. Large, rough hands. Hands made for agriculture, heavy lifting, physical work.

He'd never done a day of physical work in his life. He was the Queen's aide. Her most beloved aide; he made sure everyone knew it.

"I will sleep, Archer."

Sleep? Maeva doesn't sleep.

"Everything is changing, Archer."

She always knows my mind.

"Hold my hand until I awake."

If I had any choice, I would hold it until the day I die.

Her eyes closed.

Her cheeks relaxed.

Archer sat at her bedside, her hand enveloped in his, until the dawn threatened to break.

10

Aria's eyes settled on the black horizon. This was the best hour to practice collective thought, when the women of Gana had gone to bed and the only sounds were the pine trees rustling in the midnight wind.

She sat atop the tallest pine in her confinement area, the space allocated for her 'privacy' but which also served as her prison. More than twenty years, her prison.

If only she could be in the capital. Or even the Lakes Region. Or the Central Mass. If only she could truly spend time in communion with those who would become her people. Her blood called at her for it; she felt the longing to be connected with the rest of Lower Earth. It was a longing she'd felt most of her life. A deep-rooted knowledge that in her was the heartbeat of Lower Earth. The dreams of the settlers. The future of all women in her land.

The voices that hummed in her veins whispered words of transformation, dedication, and power. All that Aria would have when the throne was hers.

She inhaled deeply, letting the thoughts cast themselves away. Before the throne she had to sharpen her skills, and she couldn't hear anything when her thoughts ran cycles through her mind. The voices hummed of all she'd ever dreamed, but if she was to master collective thought, she had to quiet them for a while.

She focused on the sensation of the air entering her nostrils, cool air that traveled down the back of her throat. Warmed air then mingled in her lungs. She felt all tension leave her body. She rested her hands on the branches beside her to stay stable.

She listened.

Breath. Breath and blood. Breath and blood and heartbeat. Heartbeats. Breath became breaths and slowly she connected into the sounds of the women who slept a few hundred feet away. Layer by layer, like a pebble in a pond, her consciousness rolled out in waves across them.

A woman started. Lightly choking on her own breath. Did she sense Aria's consciousness? Aria reduced intensity and felt for a change. The woman's heartbeat again slowed, steadied, and her breath became regular.

It could have been a coincidence. But perhaps not. Confirm historical references to collective awareness with Batrasa tomorrow.

She focused in on another woman in another hut. The woman's breathing was labored. A wheeze emerging from between her lips, the sound grated on Aria's ears.

Unnatural. She is in ill health.

Aria stayed with her, following the air in and out again, but the rhythm was disjointed. Blood tumbled awkwardly against its own nature through the woman's veins.

Blood too slow, too poor, oxygen depleting.

Aria stood, surveying the area, trying to locate the hut where the sick woman lay.

Her eyes found it, more than three hundred feet from her location, just as the woman's breathing stopped altogether.

Aria ran.

Long steps, steady steps, quick and sure, but urgent. Aria's own heartbeat began to overtake the sound of the woman's. She had little time. The woman's heartbeat weakened with every second.

She burst into a hut and a woman screamed.

Aria ran through to the room at the back and threw open the door.

She covered the woman's mouth with her own and began assisted breathing, chest compressions, monitoring the lungs, the blood, waiting for the beat of her heart to start again.

She continued. Worried voices rose around her. She heard them and filed the comments, but she had to stay focused on her mission.

The woman was young. She deserved to live. The doctor had not taken sufficient care.

Aria gave a breath, continued compressions, waited.

Then she heard it. Softer than a feather's sound as it floated in the wind, the woman's blood began to travel, taking oxygen, moving it forward, outward, across the woman's body. There were women crying in the room. Aria knew Batrasa was there.

She placed her forehead on the woman's forehead and whispered words, encouragement and praise, life-giving words, and the woman gasped. She took in a deep inhale and her eyes opened wide.

Aria nodded to the woman, stood, and walked out of the hut without a word.

She retook her perch on the pine tree's peak and listened as the women spoke of Aria's divine gifts.

Archer arrived two days later.

"My Aria," he reached out his hands, enveloping hers within them.

"The Queen will have you torched if she hears you still calling me by that name."

Archer pursed his lips. "She's not here. For now, you remain my little Aria."

Aria sighed. "Archer, you have habits that are entirely unsuitable for my eventual coronation."

Archer's face clouded over; Aria listened in. He had news. There would be no other reason for this reaction.

"Don't wish the coronation sooner than it must be."

Aria felt the heat rising from her core and inhaled deeply to keep it at bay.

"Don't wish it sooner than it must be? What is that supposed to mean?"

"It doesn't mean anything, Aria." He touched her hair and she swatted his hand away.

"You take liberties, Archer. What have you told the Queen of my readiness for the throne?"

"I haven't said a thing. That's not my place."

His heart accelerates. His palms grow warm and wet.

"I don't believe you."

Archer looked away. "I have said nothing about you specifically, this I promise. But everything will change, Aria. Don't you see that? This life will end-"

"And the life I was designed to lead will begin. Everything is headed in that direction. My isolation here, my preparation, mental, physical, it's all for that moment."

He knows more than he says.

Archer wet his lips and swallowed hard. He gave a sheepish smile. "Let's just have a nice visit, how about that? Let's go for a walk. Let's discuss the different pines like we used to. The currents, the distance to the Forgotten Islands. Have you been since I last saw you?"

He tried to lead her by the shoulder, but Aria didn't move.

"I think you should go, Archer."

She saw panic in his eyes.

"No, no, Aria. *Ariane.* Listen to me." He looked over his shoulder and took her a few steps further. "Word of your life-saving act reached Geb."

"And?" Aria couldn't contain herself. Finally, more was being known of her. The people's consciousness more aware of her capabilities. Her love for them. Her people.

"And the Queen was pleased. I think she was. You know she's impossible to read. But Aria, so much will change. Don't wish for the throne, please just consider – "

"You've gone mad, Archer. Your words are nonsense to my ears. What omen are you trying to communicate here? Be straight with it or get out of my sight."

"Aria." He closed his eyes. "I look at you and I still see the child you were, though I know you are a woman now. I know your dedication, your commitment, your absolute blind belief in your takeover of the throne-"

He's verging on heretical now. He's desperate. I must hear what he's not saying.

"-but be wary, my Aria. Be wary of false prophets and promises. I've been in the capital long enough to know you will have threats you cannot yet imagine."

He fears for me. Is it as simple as that?

Archer touched her cheek gently and stepped away.

"I won't stay. I can't." He again swallowed hard. "I see that it is me who must change, and not you. It's not so easy, little Aria. I have become very set in my ways."

Aria watched him walk away, out through the main square and out the entry gate to East Gana.

She turned and punched the pine tree.

There's something he's not saying, and I couldn't get it out of him. Damn it. If I can't get information from the man closest to me, then how can I possibly take the throne?

She ripped off a large branch from the tree and threw it

like a javelin before sequestering herself in her hut in self-isolation.

Minimum of one week. I will fast and I will not sleep. I must hone my collective thought or I risk ruining the very thing I've prepared for my entire life.

11

There was always something missing inside her, Uma knew it but couldn't put her finger on it. She was an expert on herself, her own code having been her research project in engineering school. Here she was, designed of the strongest elements, most likely to stand up against obsolete human instincts, and yet there was this sensation inside her.

A void. Something missing.

She knew it because of the dreams. Uma had always been a deep sleeper. It was the only way she knew how. She'd fall in deep to a different world for the hours it took for her brain to adequately rest, and then she'd pop awake, sometimes six hours, or on a rare occasion, seven hours later.

It took a significant event to disturb her pattern, but the dreams did it.

This morning she'd woken up in a sweat, the floating images of tearing clothing, and red satin, and touch, touch across her body, first of satin and then of skin. She had never touched satin, only seen it in the museum. None of the dreams made sense: skin touching skin and rolling across itself, opening and rolling, and pushing and falling, and then, like a smack across her face, she was awake. The dreams came only a few times a year, but the beads of sweat rolling down her back, her temples, the folds of her throat - she couldn't deny it and couldn't explain it.

Desire. It shouldn't have been there. She knew well that sexual desire had been suppressed in her genetic code, just as it had been from all genotypes. That Directive had been in place for generations. It had been one of the first decisions when Central Tower recognized the certain death of men. Passion, yes. Dedication, yes. Even pleasure.

But sexual desire had been scrubbed clean. For obvious reasons.

"Damn it," she muttered, standing from her single bed. Stretching tall, Mary on the screen welcomed the new day.

"Lots of sunshine today in Geb!"

Uma didn't care.

"The Ministry of Reconciliation is preparing a very encouraging statement. I hope to share it with you in this evening's address. Now I will allow the music of the harp to begin your day in peaceful tones."

Eating, dressing, walking to Central Tower, she did it all in a daze, until Adam's voice snapped her out of it just in front of the Tower door.

"Uma! I'm glad I caught you before the review." He stopped, perhaps seeing the look on her face. "Is this a bad time?"

"Yes and no."

Adam looked her up and down, "Rough night?"

"You could say that."

"Then this will cheer you up," Adam smiled, wide and bright, as was his way. "4880 was born healthy. And survived the initial stages of bonding, moving slowly to healthy detachment with no unexpected consequences."

"There are always consequences." Uma frowned; this was not a morning for experiments.

"Relax, relax," Adam continued, "It's good news, see? We anticipated issues with affection and independent thought, and we cut them off at the pass," Adam was demonstrating, acting out a kind of racecourse in front of her. He gently touched her arm and pulled her aside from the arriving colleagues. She wanted to recoil at the feeling of his hand, the madness of the dream rising up again, but she controlled herself.

"Uma, it worked."

She pulled her arm away, hoping it looked natural. "Well, that is a relief."

Adam laughed. "A major breakthrough and it's 'a relief'? You crack me up, Uma." Adam then straightened, a look on his face like perhaps he realized he'd gone too far. "I'm ready to enact the next stage once you've reviewed the file, I've already posted it, but I think within the next ten or so days we should move into the testing phase. I'll bring the report by your office later."

"Very well. I'll let you know when I'm ready."

Adam nodded, paused, and smiled at her before walking tall through the revolving glass Tower door.

A long leash, Uma thought as she watched him go. *Give this man a long leash, the Queen had said. That's what he's got now.*

She momentarily closed her eyes, inhaled deep, and straightened her back before marching into the Tower for Review Day.

Everywhere was a buzz. As Uma entered, she could hear the activity rushing around. She was both pleased by and suspicious of the commitment of her staff. But it was the monthly Review Day, of course, they would be putting on their best for her.

She paused a few paces from the doors and had a fleeting memory of the first time she walked through them.

Exams had just finished, and she'd done exceedingly well. The housemother had been bursting with pride, but for Uma, the exams were simply a means to an end. Central Tower had fascinated her for as long as she could remember seeing it. The sleek glass and rounded walls, how it penetrated into the sky. It wasn't until many years later she would know to call it the ultimate of phallic symbols, though no one knew exactly who had designed it.

"The Tower is one of the first post-Mist buildings to unite the peoples," the woman had said during the grade school tour. Only the fortress reaches taller than it, but that's because of the city cliff. Central Tower is, in fact, the tallest structure completely built by human hands in Lower Earth."

It wasn't just the height of it that drew Uma in; it was what it stood for. No one questioned the announcements of Central Tower. It was the place where truth emerged, and all had to obey. Central Tower was the future, the place where all things were born.

The buzz of bodies rushing into the Tower brought her back into the present moment. With a deep breath, she clicked her heels into movement, putting on her best boss-smile to greet Security.

"Good morning, Ms. Uma." Jan Gillard was their top guard, and it wasn't hard to see why. She towered over everyone as Central Tower did across the city. She won the river swimming competitions year after year. And she was most committed to her job. The Gillard line was especially known for its physical superiority, large circulatory system, and powerful muscle regeneration.

Uma was one of the few who knew that Jan Gillard would likely not live past the age of thirty. Very few in the Gillard genetic line had surpassed it so far. Marion Gillard lived on, but in a sad state. A shocking thing, really, considering all she had done in the Queen's Guard.

"Good morning, Jan. Anything to report?"

"No, ma'am. People have their heads down today. Do you know it's Review Day?" Jan smiled, a little too innocently.

Not the brightest line, Uma thought. Everyone knew that Uma was the one who established Review Days in the first place.

"Very good. Review Day, it is."

Jan gave a little laugh, pleased for having gotten the right answer when no question was asked. Uma took another deep breath and moved into the building.

Ground floor - logistics.

This won't take long.

"Ground floor report," she announced as she burst through the double doors, catching the workers by surprise. A collective light gasp and the Room Head was rushing forward with the mandatory papers showing accounts received, supply lines, alerts to potential power outages during anticipated rainstorms that week.

"Prepare the generators, make sure solar panels are covered twenty-four hours before the potential storms, not like the last-minute scrambling I saw you do last time. Understood?"

"Yes, ma'am."

"How long have you been in charge of logistics, Laure?"

The woman was surprised to hear her name, names were not a favorite of Uma, everyone knew it. "Seven months, ma'am."

"You're doing a good job. Watch out during the storms, there's more to anticipate for those, but otherwise your management of supply lines is good."

"Yes, ma'am, thank you."

Without any goodbye, Uma turned slowly on her heel, watching the faces of the others in the room as she went. She squinted her eyes to hide a smile. Logistics staff especially feared her. They were right to - the last head of logistics had been a betrayer. They'd all seen it - and then seen her absence.

Uma smiled to herself.

There won't be another betrayer there. Not with the look on those faces.

Moving behind the logistics room, she found the cleaners, most of whom came from Cork Town, all of whom were not allowed above the eleventh floor. They could be trusted with bookshelves and bathrooms, but to put the delicate chemical equipment in the hands of a Cork Town misfit, that was asking for catastrophe.

They were always friendly and simple.

Anna led the team of cleaners. A basic designed sequence. Intended for dedication and contentedness with most basic provisions. Uma had overseen the expansion of that program herself. There were some drawbacks, susceptibility to outside influences, and the like, which made their Cork Town accommodation somewhat worrying. Conspiracy theories had a tendency to thrive there.

"Ms. Uma! Well, we're glad to see you today, we've been making extra sure to cover each corner with this being Review Day."

"No doubt, Anna."

"You know you can count on me, Ms. Uma."

"I do, indeed."

"Ms. Uma?"

She took a breath to find a little extra patience. "Yes, Anna?"

"About the number of cleaners - "

Anna cut herself off. Somehow even she was able to see that this was not the moment to ask for any favors.

"Never mind, Ms. Uma. Sorry." She lowered her head and re-joined the line of cleaners who waited to be dismissed. Uma watched as one of the others, name tag saying Rhonda, gave Anna a dirty look.

Uma took her time looking them over. They each looked like they expected to be chastised, and Uma let them believe it, making a show of inspecting their buttons and folds of their hair.

Without word or courtesy, she turned and left the room. She heard complete silence behind her, knowing they were waiting for some kind of sign of dismissal. They waited while Uma looked at her checklist in the hall. Thirty seconds went by before slowly and silently they took half steps back towards their duties.

Uma continued, eager to get through the first eleven floors and make her way to where she needed to be. Floor fifteen. Something wasn't right and she couldn't put her finger on it. It had been weighing on her since the dream. Something there, something in it. There was a file she needed to review.

The file had caught her eye months earlier. There was nothing special about it. Another report on the incubation program that had been dismantled, something about the retrieval of the equipment, something about vision capabilities, and something about the skin. All subjects should have been terminated; the mosaicism of the genes had been pervasive.

But it wasn't adding up. She waited until floor twelve to start asking questions. Most of those she asked couldn't offer any information.

"Incubation was abandoned more than two decades ago, ma'am."

"I know that, of course, and where is the remaining equipment?"

"I wouldn't know that, Ms. Uma."

"But you are responsible for all equipment, historical and current."

"Yes, ma'am, but the dismantled programs were royal-led."

"So you have no reports on them?"

"Of course not."

Uma frowned. Her questioning might raise suspicion, especially amongst those for whom the answers to these questions looked painfully obvious.

She softened her face. "Good. I'm glad to see you have not extended beyond your current responsibilities. I have at times been concerned that your enthusiasm might be a result of off-strategy activities."

The researcher shuddered.

"No, ma'am," she replied quietly. "I wouldn't do that, I'm not one of those. Thank you for enquiring. I am within my limits, ma'am."

"Yes, I see that now. Be wise to those around you."

"Yes, ma'am."

That would put her off her scent for a while. Uma knew well that gentle accusations in Central Tower were a useful weapon. Hidden agendas were a necessary *modus operandi*.

However, she was still no closer to understanding why there were anomalies in the equipment management.

Royal-led.

The project had been managed from higher up than she had expected.

With incubation abandoned, some pieces of equipment had been kept for learning purposes and for the animal programs. It was all relatively well documented. So it had seemed. Lucius had been the overseer of the project; no less than the Great Geneticist would have been allowed such freedom of implementation.

She set her thoughts to a different problem.

Adam.

Adam and the new birth, 4880. What was it that she sensed in him? Not deception. Not Adam, he wouldn't need it. But it was nagging at her. Too many things nagging at her and this feeling that her control was slipping away.

Just like what had happened with Lucius all those years ago.

Has it really been nearly twenty years? Where has the time gone?

It had been right here, on the fifteenth floor, that the Primary Overseer, Roman, had burst into her office. She was only Mid-Grade Overseer then, though everyone knew her promotion was imminent. At that time, Roman reported to her. She never would have ever guessed how high he would go.

It was right there that Roman had told her the outrageous idea that Lucius had been tinkering with files.

His accusation was unfounded. Uma knew it because she herself had always accompanied Lucius to the file stores. She monitored him closely at every moment. For each review of each genetic layout, she had been there. Sure, she was surveying the files, as was her job, but she had also been learning.

The wisdom and ability of the Great Geneticist were unending. To accuse him of tampering with the files was borderline unethical.

For every piece of information the public heard, there were five more of which they knew nothing. The experimental fetuses. The genetic coding challenges. The amplification, modification, and life expectancy alterations. All held in tight circles of Central Tower's elite. Floors seventeen and above only.

It wasn't a question of secrecy, but rather of scientific inquisition. In a program as personal as Willing Women, which was in fact even more invasive than any of the Male Program had or ever would be, the subject was delicate, treated with respect, and unspoken outside the walls of the Tower. It was contractual; breaches were punishable with imprisonment. More than once, even in the last five years, violations had been treated with an efficient disappearance before the leak could cause further harm.

"Uma."

Roman's voice pierced the air. She was pulled out of her memory, back into the present moment. Back to her desk.

"Yes?" She blinked.

"I've interrupted you."

It wasn't a question.

"Just considering the impact of some new results Adam brought today."

"He told me."

Damn it, Adam. Again crossing the line. Roman is my *line manager.*

Uma forced a smile.

"I want to discuss it. First thing tomorrow. I want us to review the material closely. I'll be gathering all the senior members."

Uma tried to hide her surprise.

"Lucius will be there?"

"Come on, Uma. Lucius hasn't attended a senior member's meeting in years. What's wrong with you today?"

She quickly shook her head. "Just distracted. Sorry."

"In the meantime, make sure the previous tests are cleared. If we're going to run this through to implementation, then we will need all the resources available."

"Understood."

She couldn't tell if Roman believed her. He turned and pushed the button for the elevator.

She thought again of Roman accusing Lucius, and how she felt like so much more was happening under her nose than she knew.

Adam's jubilance this morning over 4880 shouldn't have anything to do with that.

It shouldn't have.

And yet it did. But Uma didn't know how.

The feeling was the same, and she didn't like it. She felt – uninformed. Out of the loop. Excluded from something that seemed important.

She broke from her routine and headed straight to her office. Floor reviews could wait, this could not.

Before she could go any further, the report on test case 4957 sat heavily on her desk. Uma sighed. It had been a particularly difficult one. She opened to the inside cover and recalled the circumstances. She just had to stop it before it was planted in a Willing Woman.

Clear it, Uma. Roman wouldn't be pleased about this one anyway.

"Willing Woman clinic 5. I need 4957 pulled." They would terminate it with the others. The risk wasn't worth it.

She didn't wait for a reply; the Receiver in the clinic would know how to handle the call. She took in a deep breath through her nostrils and exhaled, not in relief. But at least that was a definitive action. It felt good to make a decision.

4957. Uma flipped through the report again. The blend of hormones had been risky - they had known that going in. But 4957's condition was both stable and alarming. It was the sex organs, the internal systems. She'd never seen anything like it before.

She lifted the x-ray film to the light. Yes, in hindsight it was all there, but in their initial assessment, it had appeared relatively normal. The angle of the image hadn't given away the severity of the condition.

Uma sighed again. It was her job to prevent these cases from advancing. She was particularly sensitive since the Western Coast incident; the combination of wrong Willing Woman and experimental sequences could almost give rise to mutiny.

Uma put her face in her hands.

She heard her office door click open and click closed again. She sighed. Only Adam dared enter without knocking. She lifted her head.

Of all people, she did not want to see him now.

"I said that I would tell you when I was ready." Uma looked back down at the report.

"I see this morning's luster has already worn off." He leaned over her desk. "4957?"

"The time has come to terminate."

"Shame, really."

She wasn't sure if he was talking about the project or her mistake in managing it. "Yes."

The discomfort grew in the room.

Why isn't he leaving?

Adam wasn't one to linger. His presence made her uncomfortable.

"Is there something else?"

He looked away, and she immediately knew there was. She found her skin getting prickly, and her breathing slowed. Involuntarily she lowered her head and looked at him from the side of her eyes.

"Yes," he said after a long pause, looking at the ceiling.

Yet another long pause and Uma rested her hands on her legs, not knowing what else to do with them.

"Given what we saw today with 4880 and knowing what we do of 4957's anomaly, I wonder if there might be hope in it."

Ah, she thought, *now he's coming to it.*

Adam was brilliant with statistics, numbers to him were like colors, simple and apparent, self-evident. There should be no reason for him to hesitate.

He is hiding something.

He started, "If we figure in the chance for survival -" and she was sure he already had "- then the risk could reap some unforeseen rewards."

"Unforeseen?" Uma wasn't sure she was hearing him right. Unforeseen was not a part of the policy that guided their work.

"Yes, I know it is an anomaly, but that's why I wanted to

bring it to you. I'm reporting it, honestly, and -" he stopped for a moment. "So that's it."

She looked him in the eye, unwavering. "You are not convincing, Adam. Report taken, but this appears to be a freak accident, and we both know I'm the culpable one, so let's acknowledge that here. If I'd been doing my job, 4957 never would have come this far along."

"I know, I know." He filled his lungs, appearing at a loss. "But could you reconsider for - "

"I've already called it in."

"Ah okay, sure. That's probably the best choice. There will be another opportunity. 4880 still gives us a lot of hope."

She gave a forced smile, intended to close their interaction.

Still, he didn't leave.

What does he want from me?

The muscles under her eyes tightened, almost imperceptibly. "And?"

Adam paused, but then just gave a slight nod, and left.

What to make of that?

She couldn't imagine that 4957 could be any cause for concern. But what did he see in this failed case that was different from the others? Perhaps he was encouraged by 4880 and wanted to press on. She granted that the deformity in 4957 could be more cosmetic than critical. Cranial malformation and genital irregularities to put it lightly. But they had not conducted all the normal tests of viability yet. It likely was not as severe as other deformities they had managed.

Still, it was the fact that it had caught them by surprise.

Uma winced. Surprises were clearly outside her remit. No one in Central Tower appreciated a surprise, and certainly not one following otherwise normal fetal development.

Adam had spoken with hesitation, but that could come down to the sensitivity of the matter. He knew about the Western Coast. He wouldn't want to see a repeat of it either.

More likely he knew I was unlikely to agree.

She looked up at the clock.

"Damn, I've got to go," she said to her desk. The Queen would be preparing to speak.

All else could wait. She pulled the office door behind her, turned the double lock, and rushed to the main square, hoping not to be one of the last to join the Tuesday Briefing. She never liked to be last.

12

____

Adam examined the file again, wondering how he'd missed it so many times before.

The chromosomes are viable. It's unbelievable, but they're viable.

Would it survive? He didn't know. Probably not. Certainly not if Uma went through with the termination. But there was a chance, small though it was. He just had to take it a bit further, and then he could tell Isaac.

When he first started studying probabilities, it was to see whether he would live past the age of forty. At the time, that felt like a very long time away, so the burden of a probable death didn't hold the same fright as it now did.

Ten years and counting, he thought. *If I can just clinch this now. Or at least in the next few years.* Without thinking, he touched the amulet, even though he despised what it stood for.

And then what?

In fact, there was no magic number; probabilities were only as good as the paper they were written on when it came to organ decay. Between the parasites, the bacteria, the viruses that the Final War had ushered in -

In some ways, it was a miracle he was alive at all. He had already beaten the probabilities.

Maybe this little one could too. Maybe this line will be the beginning of a new Male Program.

No doubt it would be a horrid looking thing, you can't have that degree of mutation without consequences. But perhaps the mutations wouldn't be so bad. Perhaps they'd be internal, or at least relatively invisible. Or able to be covered up. Would it be more like a boy or a girl? Would it even survive childbirth?

The prospects were starting to weigh heavily on him.

There was no pushing Uma any further than he already had. He knew he'd been pushing the limits as it was.

The ticking of the clock suddenly bore into him.

He took a quick detour to the holding room, found what he was looking for, and slipped it into his bag before walking quickly to the clinic. He didn't have long before the Briefing.

At the clinic, he gave Rita the biggest possible smile. He knew she liked that sort of thing.

"Adam! How unexpected!"

He acted surprised. "Didn't you get the call from Uma?"

"Well, yes, I was just about to pull the file."

"You haven't pulled it yet? Rita! I'm shocked," he tried to chastise just enough to throw her off, not enough to make her defensive.

"It's been busy around here, Adam, I know she gives twenty-four hours -"

"Don't worry about it. I've got to add the closing remarks to the file, so how about I pull it for you."

"Oh, you're sweet!"

"You can do the verification after the Briefing then."

He winked and walked through the door. Dropping the big smile, he couldn't believe his luck. His heart was beating out of his chest.

Yes, the luck of his life.

He slipped the new documentation into the file. No one would be the wiser, not at clinical level. It was enough. That would be enough. It would be fine that 4957 would be terminated.

"4957, let me introduce you to 4880." He made the switch.

Adam just had to wait now for the right candidate to try again.

13

Grimacing in dark silence, Uma was unconvinced. Something about the whole exchange was haunting her, but she couldn't place her finger directly on it.

What is it? What am I missing on 4957?

She had been through the file again, and again, and again. Tossing and turning in bed, she went over each piece she could recall.

Vitals were normal, even if it was disfigured. It was the same as the others, I'm sure of it. There was nothing even in that dossier. It was incomplete. So why does it matter so much to him? What does he see that I don't?

There had been no indication of viability, no hint of promise in the file. And yet, Adam wanted it.

Staring at the ceiling, she ran her fingers over the lava amulet she slept with every night. She didn't care if people thought her an extremist for it. She watched the cracking concrete as the steps above her slowed to a stop. Just her luck to have a neighbor who had been modified to need less sleep than average.

Maybe she could ask Carole from the fifteenth floor about the situation, in hypothetical terms.

Don't be an idiot.

Of course, she couldn't talk to anyone about this. All she had were hints of an idea, barely more than a fleeting thought. She would need more than this if she were going to consider escalating it to Roman.

But she had come to trust her instinct. While Adam wasn't one of the backroom men, that didn't stop him from having ulterior motives. He could be looking to expand the Program, get more Royal support for it perhaps. But Adam didn't have direct access to the decision-makers. Any of that would have to come through Uma anyhow, just as it always had before. Adam knew protocol and he wasn't one to defy it or find workarounds at that level. His history of openness with Management was the reason why he was allowed to be a direct report to Uma. Otherwise, he could have been stuck in an off-shoot unit. Like Isaac. Had it been Isaac who brought 4957, that would have been a completely different matter altogether. Isaac and his backroom buddies were hardly subtle.

But this was Adam.

Would Adam try to manipulate me? Could he even, if he tried?

She ran over the details of the dossier again in her head.

She had been frustrated by the initial results. It should have been terminated much sooner, that was clear. She didn't like it when the program bordered on near implementation only to be revoked at the last minute. It had only happened a couple of times in her tenure, but when it did, she had been equally disappointed. Like the Western Coast. She would never forget the look on that woman's face when they told her they would have to terminate. The Willing Woman had somehow built a bond with that thing inside her. Perhaps that was one of the side effects of its condition, for the mutual reliance was excessive from fetus to mother and they had almost lost her in the procedure. Their vitals had become interconnected.

Uma took a deep breath, eyes still fixed on a distance through the ceiling.

Lost in a meditative space of non-thought, Uma's consciousness suddenly hit her in the face.

This isn't even up to me.

This wasn't for her to decide. This was up to Roman. If she didn't report suspicion, she would be equally culpable. And if there was nothing to hide, then Adam would simply explain, and it would all pass.

I've been overestimating my position. What if I didn't report it?

She shuddered. There had been more disappearances of late – Uma personally knew at least three over the past few weeks.

Nansy is back but just look at the state she's in. She would never say it was because of the disappearance, but she's practically comatose.

Uma grasped the lava rock around her neck and closed her eyes.

This is all on Adam. This one isn't on me. This is not another Western Coast. This isn't on me.

Although she tried to ignore it, a blanket of guilt lay softly across her, despite her predisposition for duty. She started planning the conversation with Roman in her head.

The night continued in an internal battle. The voice of obligation, the voice of reason, the voice of self-preservation all fought with each other.

And if you're wrong? What's at stake?

Adam won't bring the findings forth to you anymore, you know he won't. Years of building trust with him and Roman. But don't you remember when the Queen was at your door?

The Queen. *At your door.*

And now you want to bring Roman in, after that command from the

Queen? And you don't even have more than a shred of cause? What will the Queen think of that?

You idiot.

She rolled over, pressing her face hard into the pillow, letting out a low moan.

Just sleep. Sleep, sleep, sleep.

That little voice kicked in again, kicked her in the side, it felt. She cramped up and thought she might be sick.

You want the Queen to find out you've taken the little project too far? That you've gone beyond the limits she laid out?

She hardly even said a thing! She hardly even brought you in! The Queen didn't spend more than five minutes briefing you, and that was nearly ten years ago. You're going to put it all on the line for a ten-year-old half moment with the Queen who simply said, "Give him a long leash, and make no scenes."

What does that even mean? No scenes? You don't even know what's at risk here.

She flipped back over, eyes ceiling-ward, trying to force the voice out of her head.

"Sleep. Sleep. Sleep."

Her shoulders grew tenser and tenser. She couldn't seem to weigh the risks for this situation the way she did on a thousand different subjects during the day. The wood platform dug into her hip she rolled to the other side. She thrust herself back flat and the sheet wound her ankles together.

This shouldn't be so hard.

But she knew. She knew from instinct, and years of experience, and from watching the quiet contact between the eyes of those she knew were backroom men. Her instinct wouldn't leave her alone.

The backroom men thought they were so covert, so invisible.

Not to her, they weren't; she could smell them out like cockroaches on a cooked goat. The records were clear, their responses predictable. They could try their hardest, but they were no match for Uma, no match for her at all. She reported them without hesitation.

But with all those cases – the backroom men, those who would betray, those who couldn't keep their work confidential – in all those, she had only ever been the one to make the report. She hadn't been the one to make the final judgment call.

Why did she come to me? Why, of all people, did the Queen come to me?

It didn't matter now, Uma had to admit. The Queen had come. Now it was Uma who had to make a decision, one that could reflect on the rest of her career. And the rest of her life.

It's my reputation in the middle of all this. There is no easy way out.

Every decision would have blowback; all had consequences she couldn't anticipate. She let the hours pass, trying not to think. Finally, she accepted she just wasn't going to sleep at all.

She watched with wooden dread as the red sun rose through her old cracked window.

14

———————

"**R**ainfields is a horrible place," Marian Gillard drawled out, spittle bubbles running down the side of her mouth, the paralyzed side, the one that only partially spoke, partially smiled. "I've been there, you know."

"We know, Marian, we know."

"Aye, not everybody knows, I'm not a fool telling stories for the wind, you witch."

"Carry on then, Mari-girl."

Marian snarled in the direction of Trudith, the serving woman. "Trude the Prude, you can shut up and mind your own business."

Trudith winked at Rhonda as she served her a beer.

Turning back to the young ones, Mari continued.

"It's horrible. Wet rock that you slide across, sometimes not knowing if you'll ever stop. You glide along the moss cover to the next rock, and never mind the sharp edges tearing up your soles in the meantime. But it's not just your soles getting ripped to shreds, it's your soul."

"Geez," a little voice said.

"Mari, you calm down now, you'll scare them."

"They should be scared!" Mari stood from the stool, stomach dropping down around her. She was mammoth in proportions, top of her head just grazing the wood ceiling.

Trudith looked back at the scene; even Rhonda was now wrapped up in the storyteller's weave. She paused, remembering the first time she'd caught sight of Marian Gillard. She had towered over her, just as she did now, but then every ounce of her giant ogre body had been muscle. She had been dexterous and quick even with all the bulk she brought along with her. Imposing wherever she went, she had been a memorable sight. Her wide face was almost man-like with an imposing square jaw, and some wondered whether there was a genetic secret behind it.

Trudith didn't wonder if there was a secret, she knew there was. No one had to tell her. Despite being born half-blind and finding her way out to Cork Town, Trudith had her head about her. She saw, and understood, what was happening around them.

But even she couldn't explain Mari's transformation. It seemed almost overnight. She had been growing upward and outward, and then suddenly it seemed she grew outward and outward only, fatter and fatter. Her face started to droop, and over the course of a shockingly short period, it looked like Marian Gillard was going to drop dead in front of them. She'd been a guard at the fortress, one of the Queen's Guard, no less, and within seeming moments she was reduced to this, a blabbing obesity, she hardly shut up - the dignified giant now a pub junkie in Cork Town. Her fall was astronomical, her tragedy visible to all.

"Are you coming to the blowout this weekend?"

Rhonda's voice broke Trudith out of her memory. Rhonda was fresh out of school, but was bright. Trudith wondered whether she'd become a Willing Woman. They needed more women like her as Willing Women.

Can't attend the blowouts if she's a Willing Woman, though. I don't know if she's ready to give that up.

"Probably," Trudith mustered up a smile. "After a week like this, it'll do me some good." An easy way to blow off some steam, Trudith loved the beating of the drums. She felt it like seven heartbeats and the ancient rhythms would take over her body. There was nothing like dancing in one of the underground blowouts.

"Just when you think you have your way about you, bam!" Marian's voice overtook the pub. "A massive storm will hit. The hail will poke your eyes out and imagine crossing that kind of terrain then! Wa-ho, it's a mess, and you're a mess in it. But the hail will stop and the sun will emerge from the blackest of clouds, just to burn the flesh off your face, just like that!" and she snapped her fingers, the sound echoing through the pub, her fingertips still more powerful than most peoples' thighs.

"What're you staring at, girlie?" Mari caught the red-haired girl-woman with the deformed face poking her head around from the kitchen.

Trudith had told Rose to stay out of sight. She tended to poke her head out to hear the stories told by the patrons, though most folks were put off at the sight of her. When Trudith took over the pub a few years earlier, Rose came with the place. She swept and washed up, asking for nothing more than her meals. Trudith figured she was a teenager, maybe even in her twenties. Though she looked pre-pubescent. Her horrible face and stunted body never seemed to age.

"Well? I asked ye a question?"

Rose backed away slowly, vigorously shaking her head, keeping her eyes on the floor. "Not, nothing, I - "

"Get on then, get back to work."

The girl-woman scurried away, as she always did. Rose never liked to be called out for watching.

"And then what? And then what?" Fred, always an eager

audience, simple and sweet, he hung off every word Marian dribbled.

Mari smiled, her charm pulling the small crowd closer, increasing the dramatics.

"If you have to spend the night there, that's when the real darkness sets in, and I don't mean the darkness of night, no, though it is a kind of blue-black of the sea that swallows you whole. But no, I mean the ghosts. When you find some little space to lay your head, inside a shelter or not, you can't sleep. Hell no! You can't sleep with the voices of the dead and disappeared running across the wide expanse. You can't see them, but you can hear them, clear as a bell, the pattering of their feet, the insistence of their decaying dead breath, it heats the hair on your neck, they breathe that close on you."

"Ghosts of who?" a little voice in the crowd asked.

"Who? Oh, child, I won't be the one to tell you, no, not me. The nightmares you'll have, the horrors, the sights - no, not this one, I won't tell you that. What I'll tell you is this. Rainfields is a horrible place, has been for generations, perhaps since the earth itself vomited up the black rock that those horrors call home."

The girl weaved her way through the little crowd, coming eye to eye with Marian, her face delicate and her skin translucent, but her gaze fixed. Her dress dangled on her, not too large but appearing so. This girl's shoulders were just bone jutting out of her paper-thin skin. She was, as far as could be seen, the exact opposite of Marian Gillard.

"I want to know who they are," she said without fear, turning her shoulder to Mari in an almost provocative way, something exaggerated about it. Something Marian seemed to recognize.

"I will not say. Who are you, girlie?"

"I will not say," the girl mocked. "But you will tell me." The crowd began to back away, sensing something raw, something not quite right was happening there.

Even Mari was starting to falter, "Why would you want to know, little one?"

"I am not so little. I only look that way. Now tell me."

Mari looked even more unsure, but she had been the Queen's Guard. Trudith watched as Mari pulled back her shoulders and sat taller, setting her face as though she would not budge.

"I will not. You tell me why you must know."

The girl leaned in and whispered in Mari's ear, then stood back and smiled with darkened teeth, before backing away and turning out the door into the day. Mari's face dropped.

Trudith felt she had to step in. Mari was going from grim to worse before her eyes.

"Go on then, all of you. We've got work to do here," Trudith shooed the crowd off, giving Mari some air and time. The pub could reopen for dinner, no need to entertain now. But even Trudith's curiosity was getting the best of her. She massaged Marian's shoulders from behind the stool.

"What did she say, Mari? What's got you so upset now?"

"I cannot say."

"But - "

"I cannot say!"

And with that Marian stood and rushed out the door, unhinging it on her way.

Outside Marian tried to shake it from her head. She violently shook herself, hoping the sounds, the words, the memory would fall off her.

She wouldn't repeat it, couldn't repeat it. But the words kept circling in her head.

She is as real as I am. Can her words be true?

Mari was haunted, would continue to be. Even with all she'd come up against, all she had done in the name of the Queen. The disappearances, in the hundreds by the time she retired. And then there were the more serious offenders. Marian had been skilled if brutal, but that had been the Queen's command.

But this. This was driving somewhere deep inside her. The child's rice paper skin of veins. The child's cruel smile, knowing the menace she was causing.

The child's whispered words whirlpooled, unceasing and grating in Marian's head:

"You once disappeared me there."

15

———————

Fire to water to earth and to wind. Some of the Cork Town girls called her a witch, but she wasn't a witch of any kind. They only said it because Rose tried as much as possible not to be seen, ever. A heavy hood hid her deformed face from view even in the hottest seasons. But despite their taunting, Rose still felt connected to them: to each person, each living creature, to the earth itself, and she was grateful for her existence. She knew how much it had cost.

Her one-room hut in Cork Town, the last commune before leaving the capital altogether, was her little haven. She loved being so close to Papa and she felt safer being far from the center of Geb. It didn't matter that she was nearly thirty years old, the dizziness of urban life was often too much for her. She took it all in like a deep breath, the sounds, the colors, the people, and their directions. It was overwhelming and made her brain move in so many directions, processing plans and would-be plans and pains and fears. She read them like a book on each passerby's eye.

She felt everything.

Their blood. Their breath. Their heartbeat.

Sometimes she could feel a child's eyelashes as they blinked. Or so she thought. Papa said she was empathizing too much.

It was she who named herself Rose. Roses were so pretty, so hard to grow, so soft and so red. She loved red. Red like her heart. Red like the blood of every being in Lower Earth. Rose.

She retired her old name at the ripe age of four, conducted a ceremony in the back ally of Cork Town after the pub had closed for the night. The glasses were clean and the women had moved on for the night, so in the back alley, she buried her name and gave birth to a new one. Rose. No one ever asked her for any other name. No one cared to know. She was Rose, the woman-child of Cork Town who smiled warmly under her misshapen face. The neighbors had grown used to it, becoming at ease with her, forgiving the accident of her birth. No one there knew about the circumstances leading to her defects.

For the rest of Cork Town, kindness was not naturally given to her. The hood helped, both saving herself from prying eyes, and avoiding discomfort for those who might look upon her.

Eyes too big and too far apart. Nostrils that stretched too far from the bridge. Only her mouth was right-sized, though her tongue could stretch to the length of her elbow if she willed it to be so. Her ears gave her shame, beast-like ears that ejected out from her head, as though they would depart at any moment. She kept her soft red hair full and long, its natural wave creating a forest in which her ears could hide, and to dull the sounds that invaded her brain. Angry sounds hit her like batons, voices shouting or glass breaking or children shrieking. She would stuff her ears with cotton wool to sleep.

Whimsical and fairy-like she floated through the night-time streets, comfortable in cold midnights, humming sad melodies that existed only once. She never remembered them or tried to.

It was well past sunset when her work at the pub was done. She stepped into the night air, the street mostly clear. The blowout would have most of Cork Town's women in the caves by now, so she could move freely without fear of being seen. She inhaled deep and then felt a call, a desire, or a wish. The words in her mind molded emotion into thought.

She had to go to the fortress. She didn't want to go to the fortress. But she had to. This was not a question of choice. She never particularly wanted to go there, but she understood the power it held over her.

It was her birthplace, after all.

This was not the first time that the unwanted desire came. Sometimes she resisted, shrugged her shoulders, and found a chore to fill her time.

But this night, she couldn't resist. There was something so crystal clear in the silent call of it. Soundless but alluring. Beckoning, but suspicious.

Something wasn't right.

Rose pulled her body inward, shutting out any sound but that which didn't belong. She tried to find it in her mind, moving her ears through the streets while she stayed still. Seeking out the disturbance.

A few women scurried in the direction of the caves as the blowout would soon commence. Rose paid them no mind.

There was an intrusion. A discord.

A stranger.

SHE BEGAN TO WALK. THROUGH CORK TOWN, THROUGH THE old power station. The sensation of night air on her cheeks was silken. She didn't feel the cold.

She entered Geb.

The fortress waited for her. It was eight miles in the distance but visible atop the hill on the city's most eastern edge. It didn't look big or small, dark or light. It was simply there.

She heard her name. Her old name. But the voice who spoke it was not calling to her.

She stopped, suddenly less sure.

All went silent again.

The sound of water and fabric. The familiar sound of washing, water splashing, and woman. A woman sighing at the effort.

Rose heard it immediately on the woman's breath.

Tiptoeing in movement that barely touched the earth, Rose kept silent in the shadows, an act she had perfected with time.

She heard the woman's chest expand, the air transform in her lungs, the heat of the conversion, and her exhale. Her heart.

Her smell.

Sickly sweet.

Rose knew the smell of treachery. She had smelled it in her first moments on Earth.

This woman was not from Lower Earth. She did not belong at all.

A scout was living amongst them.

Again she heard her old name in the distance. If it wasn't calling to her, and yet she was there, should she go? Or should she keep her eyes on the stranger?

Frustrated at the double pull to watch the scout and follow her name, she stood paralyzed as the traitor finished hanging the laundry and went back inside. Rose backed away, staying close to the shadows, moving as silent as the night.

With each step, the fortress grew closer. Rose began to feel less sure. The scout had shaken her fragile resolve. A question began to form. Rose did not often allow these questions. She rarely liked the answers and so she did her best to avoid any thought of them at all. But this one was growing like a cancer, dormant, a small cyst in a back recess of her brain, she had shut out soon after her birth. Now it rose up, silent and toxic, and Rose again heard her old name. Her name, like a clap of thunder, coming closer with each step.

A longing rose from somewhere deep inside. Under her lungs, deep in her core. Hardly anyone had spoken that name to her, nearly no one in her whole life. She had tried to forget it, to be reborn, but a name never hides when it is your name. Her name, spoken on the lips of one in the fortress. Her name, echoing down from the far-off hills, from the far-off mountains beyond that. From beyond and behind the fortress, from the distance beyond.

Rainfields called to her again.

Rose shook her head to release herself from the pull.

The voice in the fortress spoke, "Ariane. Come, come."

Sounds of the city began to die out behind her. Hissing light posts and cat steps on windowsills faded away. She had a sensation she might have called fear, if she had known what to name it. A rising wave of questions with no answers.

She saw a glow in the upper window in the south wall of the fortress.

Rose took three steps and had crossed the square. Another step and she was at the base of the south wall. Three steps up and she was under the window of the third floor, fingertips holding between the stones, toes resting on the accidental ledge between rows.

She listened.

She knew this room, its dark walls glowing warm in candlelight, and nothing had changed. She had been born here, the place between birth and the rest of life. She knew these walls well.

From her perching place, she could see perfectly into the Queen's quarters.

The Queen had her back to the window.

But the young woman across from her caught Rose's eye.

Her skin glowed in the moonlight and her deep green eyes were no color Rose had ever seen before.

Rose had spent the last five years avoiding a moment like this. Ever since the Future Queen began to make appearances in the capital.

"Ariane," the Queen uttered Rose's original name, but she spoke it not to her. The false sister stood across from the Queen, the discussion deep and intense. The green eyes narrowed as the false sister stood taller, speaking harsh words, words no Royal should speak. Words about disappearance, who should be gone, who had no right to live.

The Queen spoke again, Rose's name of old slapping her ears. The name that should have been hers. But it was now the name of a Future Queen.

She watched the Queen's face twist, dismissing the Ariane before her, chastising and mocking. The Queen's words were silent to all human ears beyond the Queen's quarters, so low was her voice. But Rose's ears weren't human.

Hers were the ears from the design of Queens.

"You do not understand, Ariane…," her mother snarled.

The Queen - her mother - and the code they shared made Rose's blood curdle at the sound of her former name.

"Hush, someone is listening to us," the false sister and her green eyes walked to the window.

Rose had to get away; it was more than unbearable. She leaped and ran. She ran in tripping spurts to leave her mother's voice behind. Anything to get away from the fortress that should have been hers to lead.

Anything to forget again all that should have been.

Her former name echoed in her head as she tumbled away, running in spurts back into the depths of Geb, not caring about the scout or anyone else who might see her. She had to get home and crush herself into her bed, under the pillow, muffle the sounds away. Shut out the voices of former Queens inside her that lifted to the edge of her hearing.

Even as she ran away, she felt her mother's heartbeat intensify within her own. Her mother's voice whispered gently over the city, speaking what should have been her name.

"Ariane."

16

———

The first drummer was only just beginning her set when Rhonda arrived. Just in time. She loved to be at the blowout from the first beat.

The rhythm grew and Rhonda felt it against her ribs, the echo in the cave was harsh, bouncing the sound back at them. Everyone stood still, only a finger twitch or neck tilt was appropriate.

It was only just beginning.

The blowout was not a place for folly. A few had pushed the limits too far, and that's why Don Women were instated. Don Women made sure that participants regulated their behavior during a blowout. That way the mystic nature of the event was respected, and nothing untoward took place. They couldn't afford to have the royalty cracking down on them. These nights were too important. They were their only reprieve.

The beat moved into its second set, the speed not faster but the sounds growing complex. The drumming woman's hands were hardly visible in the cave wall's candlelight. Rhonda listened for the pattern.

The rise and fall, there it is.

It wouldn't be long now, not long until the beat kicked up and the second drummer joined.

Yes, yes, there she is.

The beat moved on, moved on strong and simple, a clear hit, left and right and left and right. Pause.

Oh yes, yes, yes it's coming!

The first drummer did the quick successions, fingers flying as the second drummer watched, the third, fourth and fifth awaiting, eyes tracking each hit, each slap, and swipe.

Oh yes, come on, let's have it! Rhonda felt it more than thought it. Her hips were still and ready.

But the downbeat. She was waiting for the downbeat. Eager for it.

The others were feeling it too, the rumble in the room growing, ready, anxious for it.

There it is, the second drum, on the hard rhythm now, steady... steady...and...

The downbeat kicked in and the bodies began to sway, shoulders left, shoulders right. All bodies in the crowd swaying.

Rhonda saw others she knew around the cave. She thought she saw Edna, her neighbor and fellow cleaner, near the entrance, but it didn't matter. None of them would speak this night. No one ever did.

Here it comes back. I hear it now. The pitch. The slap.

Yes.

The sounds were older than Lower Earth, the beating from days before Mist and before men ruled the whole planet. The sounds filled the women's feet as they stepped in place, legs bracing, they moved wider, hips left, hips right, the movements subtle, a warning, a hint cast out, though they didn't dare anticipate it before it came.

Rhonda felt it rising in her, in all of them. That's what the blowout was for, this feeling, this old feeling that was "mother walking as we were inside, before we knew what a step was". The steps left, right, hips swaying the steps up and down through fields, through forests and cities, through life. The unborn walking through mother's feet, through the world. Through life.

"Through life!" the drummer called to them and the second drummer thrust into the beat.

Hips and shoulders, bounced, moving in time, all ears felt the echoing of the sounds off the walls as the third and the fourth and fifth drummer kicked in. That was the moment. All bodies moved as one with the beat.

"Through life!" the drummers called out and the bodies jumped in organized chaos, into each other, into the walls, into every boundary.

This is it!

The beats ran, they grew, they swelled and then, there it was, the moment.

Yes, this is it. Rhonda felt the energy compress as the bodies slowed to a stop.

Only one drummer played, a single slap, and slap, and slap.

The bass joined.

Boom, slap. Boom, slap. Boomslap, boomslap, boomslap-boomslap and it was building again, and again, and again and Rhonda couldn't think of anything but the sound against her ribs, and she was jumping and rolling into it, into the others. They were all doing the same, moving the same. The blowout grew, exploded, as the bodies moved faster with the beat, the beat with the bodies, the running, and jumping, and rolling against the cave edges and Rhonda was with them and in them. A great explosion of them all.

"Through life!" she called out.

"Through life!" a voice echoed.

"Through life!" two more, and then more, and more voices join in the call.

Her body took over. She closed her eyes, lost in the darkness as the hundreds of bodies jumped into a single beat, forgetting their world, forgetting the fear, the disappearances, and death, the imposed ritual. The amulets bounced against their chests as the bodies flew into the night and danced until the coldest hour died out.

17

"Go, let me prepare." Irene stood in the doorway of her chambers still in her nightclothes. The messenger had woken her with panicked pounding on the door.

"Any reply, ma'am?"

"It will come. Stay near the fortress. Speak of this to no one, you understand?"

"I never would have, Commandante."

Irene closed the door and let her eyes shut for a moment.

She pulled on her uniform. Buttoned the cuffs. Flattened the collar. Thread her belt and pulled it tight.

Pinned her medals.

Slicked her hair back.

In her reflection, the Commandante saw the picture of dignity and poise.

But inside her head was panic.

The news had come via the Guard to a messenger; thank heavens it was a Lania of the ninth line and not one of the others who might have felt compelled to leak the intel. The guard had stumbled upon a scout without knowing at first. The giveaway, so reported, was the underclothes. A scout not like any scout they'd captured before.

A female scout.

A female scout from Upper Earth. The tides are changing. Whoever would have guessed they'd send a female?

The foreigner must have stolen garb on arrival in the dark counties, for that was just about the only place in Lower Earth where people wouldn't report something unusual. They were used to strangers arriving there. After all, it remained the haven for many of those who had been disappeared. Some couldn't bear the idea of returning to Geb, shame on their names as it was. The dark counties, as far away as the West Strangelands, were a perfect hive for those otherwise unwelcome in the other, more loyal, parts of the country. The Sisters who lived there were always ready to welcome a traitor in their midst. The Queen hadn't listened to Irene's protest about the Sisters being allowed to continue the way they did.

And now, a female scout.

It was impossible to know how long she'd been there. Even the guard who discovered her reported being shocked by the sight.

Elen Gillard, the Queen's guard who had arrested her, was known for her dedication and her physical abilities, but not her intellect.

Irene would be the first to interview the Gillard guard, though hours passed and she hadn't yet arrived. No other soul was permitted to speak to Elen during the journey. Irene had been clear: not a soul to say a word, the voyage in silence. Elen Gillard would recount the details to the Commandante. That way Irene could brief the Queen before news spread.

Maeva is not going to like this at all. She's been in such an unusually fragile state. This better not put her over the edge.

"She's here Commandante."

Irene stood from her desk and controlled her pace, hoping she was hiding her desperation well.

Elen was seated on a bench in the corridor, waiting. She was such a different specimen, designed for her vocation. Her block of a body was an oversized visual mistake. Buzz-cut scalp that had no symmetry, parts of her skull were shaved flat over lumps of bone. Her broad shoulders and thick chest held no breasts, her ribs to waist to hips were a brick of muscle. There was nothing beautiful in Elen except her desperate loyalty to the Guard. She was third rank, responsible for the raids and night watches in the outer territories.

Irene carried herself according to the Ganese priestesses principle of bodily preservation. She kept her hair long, dark, and healthy, according to the Ganese traditions. Her curves were at once feminine and powerful. The Ganese had long been against genetic modification. Irene's code was as natural as the original people of Gana who had inhabited the island long before the settlers came. Long before it was called Lower Earth. The old tribe never would have guessed that the refugees would become their rulers. Nor would they have guessed that Irene would lend her code for the first genetic copy of a Ganese.

Irene gently shook her head and focused in on the woman before her.

Elen stood from the bench and saluted.

"Tell me everything." Irene had no patience for customary greetings, not now.

"I couldn't believe my eyes," Elen Gillard's eyes widened at the memory of it. "I was just going by, doing my normal rounds, the reasonable route and saving the tough line for later, you know?"

Elen paused for a reply but didn't get one, so she continued. "I would be seeing people about, this and that, here and there, completely in the usual. But then this. The fabric was wrapped-like around her upper thighs. I wouldn't normally be looking like that, you know, the rules on privacy and all, but I was on duty and she was by the water, beautiful lady, somehow sparkling against the river edge, you sees, and -"

Elen stopped herself.

Irene could see it was on the tip of her tongue to confess to something shameful. Elen was known for it, these unusual sexual outbursts. If she wasn't so good at her work, they would have been done with her long ago. Flaw in the design.

But Elen's instinctual response to threat had resulted in the apprehension of some of the country's worst traitors. So they kept her.

"Go on, don't worry about those details. They are irrelevant for now." Irene added, "You have done well."

Elen's face relaxed.

"So, there she was, and her underclothes, the fabric was a sort of burlap, the kind we learned about in Past Ages classes, and I don't have much of a mind for that, but the treatment from times gone by fascinated me, you know? During the menstruation time? We learned about this custom, the wrapping from torso to thighs. And it stuck I guess because there I was and I was watching it unfold in front of me, like right there, unrolling from her thighs, the blood dripping out and damn, I knew, I saw it, and thought 'Oh no!' because we'd been hearing of the scouts and blending activities they'd be doing, but damn, here it was right in front of me, one of them, hads to be because we don't use those old ways here, being advanced and all."

Elen straightened her spine. She leaned in close to Irene's face.

Irene tried to focus, but her patience was running thin.

The Gillard line. All bulk. I'm going to explode if she doesn't hurry it up.

"Madame Commandante, I swear to you that the moment

I realized, I had her by the throat. I made sure she wouldn't talk, but I didn't go too far this time. I'm still living the shame from the Ganese woman you so rightly made me aware - "

"Shut up, Gillard, this is your chance to redeem yourself." Irene took in a deep breath. She needed more detail. "Now go further back. Tell me everything you saw her do before you apprehended her."

"I was cresting a hill, the big one to the east of Longor Town, on the eastern edge of the Dark Counties, and the first thing I saw was her hair. It was wild-like. She kept brushing it out of her eyes while she hummed something that I had no idea what it was. And then I thought maybe she was from somewhere deep in the dark counties because they have lots of habits in those places that I could never understand, having been born in - "

"Focus, Gillard. What did you see her do? What did she have?"

Gillard raised her eyes upwards, remembering. "She had on a normal long brown skirt, standard issue from the fabric drops, nothing unusual in it. She was carrying a kind of satchel type thing, I hadn't seen it before, looked like maybe she'd made it herself and wasn't a pro at it. "

"What was the satchel made of?"

"Standard issue."

"Okay, go on."

Gillard's eyes looked left and right as she pursed her lips. "I'm not sure there's anything else to tell, Commandante."

"Of course, there is. Think it through, what else did you see?"

"Well, I saw her react, you know, when she saw me seeing her."

"What did she do?"

"It was kind of animal-like. She crouched down, hands on the ground, only because I stepped on some kind of stick and it made a snapping noise. She could have thought me an animal or something, given the time of night it was, but I'd already seen her blood wrap and her knees pushed out-like from her body in that crouch, and her hands were kind of like this - "

Gillard held her hands out in front of her almost like claws, one lower and one higher with her shoulders at an angle. It was the defense position Upper Earth was said to teach. It apparently extended to their women as well as the men.

Gillard held the pose and continued her story. "That's when something just went click in my head and next thing I knew it was my instincts - I ran at her and neutralized her by the neck, putting her out so I could carry her back to the city."

"And where's her satchel now?"

"Uh," Elen eyes darted around, looking for an answer, "Must be by the river, Commandante."

"By the river," Irene sighed. They'd have to send someone out now, and chances were it had already been picked up.

"Sorry, Commandante." Elen lowered her head and cursed at herself under her breath.

"It's fine, Gillard. You only did as we would have expected."

Gillard gave a quick smile, not hearing the insult in Irene's tone.

Irene spoke quietly into the Queen's ear, "We've found another one. A woman this time."

The Queen hadn't yet risen from her bed, despite Mary's morning voice having already awakened the city. Irene could see the Queen's bare shoulder cresting the silk sheets. She knew she was awake. The Queen hardly slept.

"We'll need to interrogate." Irene approached the bed. "I suspect she's not alone. They wouldn't send just one. Their women aren't up to it. Still, this development, the use of female scouts is - " Irene chose her words carefully, " - disturbing."

Still, the Queen didn't budge. Irene knew she'd heard every word, so she waited.

She saw the Queen's side ribs rise and fall with a sigh. "Sit."

Irene sat on the side of the bed, the Queen's body facing away from her.

"My Queen, I think the time has come for us to expand the Willing Woman program, as I recommended. We are going to need warriors in the coming times."

The Queen did not respond.

"Maeva, we can start with the Ganese. I think they are ready. And they come from the stock of warriors." She cleared her throat. "I mean that *we* come from a stock of warriors. Going back generations. And we were one of the few peoples to survive the Final War - "

"Yes, yes. Hush. I'm thinking."

Irene waited.

She was sure the Queen's mind was moving faster than a comet. She had this way of appearing sullen when in fact there were a thousand firing pistols in her brain, each one spreading to another until a fully formed idea would emerge. And it was always something greater and bolder and wiser than Irene could have imagined.

So she waited.

The Queen sat upright with a shock.

She looked possessed. Her eyes widened, the whites of them shining in the early morning glow. Irene jumped back off the bed. The face of the Queen contorted and froze, horrible, almost disfigured. Slowly the muscles in her brow eased. Then her cheeks, and finally her jaw slackened.

Irene was held in limbo, a rabbit before the fox, struck dumb. She couldn't will herself to move. She couldn't even will herself to think.

What's happening to her?

She watched the Queen's mouth open, silent, inhaling across her tongue in almost a wheeze.

Then a sound emerged ever so quietly, hardly above a whisper, and yet banal. Raw. The pitch was inhuman and the depth of it so profound that Irene felt punched and all the air burst out of her lungs. She cringed, the cry filling her head, ricocheting against the inside of her skull.

Finally, the wail stopped. She waited for a sign the Queen was herself again and tried to regain her breath.

The Queen's shoulders relaxed. Her breathing was labored and quick, but constant. Sounds came out, words, though her lips barely moved.

"It's nearly time. Someone stronger than me. I cannot manage them anymore. The time has come to arrange a meeting, pave the way, prepare the new leader." The Queen inhaled. "Clear the past."

Irene waited for more, but the Queen fell silent.

"Maeva?" Irene's voice trailed off. It was always best not to interrupt.

"The Future Queen must have a reign clear of conscience."

Irene hesitated. "What conscience?"

"I'd had faith that the passing of time would have made this easier." She heaved a heavy breath.

Irene's mind was racing. She couldn't keep up. "My Queen - "

The Queen glanced at her, annoyed, then looked off into an unknown distance. "It's time for the two to be set aside. Ariane must have a clear reign. I won't let it be for her the way it was for me," the Queen whispered.

Irene's head was pounding. Her heart sunk into her stomach. Now she understood.

There can only be one Queen.

"Yes, my Queen. I will take care of this."

"Don't be an idiot."

Irene took a step backward. If there was to be only one Queen, then it was her responsibility to oversee the culling of any other who might threaten that right.

"You are a warrior, Irene," the Queen's tone sounded nearly ironic, "but this is beyond stratagems and sheer force. You don't know what they are capable of. I do."

"But if not me, then who?"

"I don't know." The Queen's nostrils flared. "I'm going to consult Lucius."

Irene froze.

Lucius? What does he have to do with any of this?

The Queen seemed to read the question in her eyes.

"He designed them. Lucius. He's the only one who'll know how to kill them so they'll never come back."

18

"We'll need to interrogate. I suspect she's not alone."

Irene continued speaking. She felt it, but inside Maeva's head, everything had gone black. The day she was dreading had arrived, and she had barely sensed it was coming.

"Yes, yes. Hush. I'm thinking."

Lower Earth was being penetrated, and this time by a female scout. A female. This was too far. It was only a matter of time. Upper Earth and their pre-Mist ways were coming. The oppression, the rash violence. Everything the settlers had demanded that Lower Earth end. The voices within her blood screeched; her brain snapped into mad action, visions and memories and screams from the past, the threats of so many generations rose up inside her.

They're coming. Oh settlers, mothers of the past, quiet, please let me think! Do not interrupt me now. Let me think.

But it was too late.

Words, clear and articulate, rang at her, bouncing in her brain, deafening her. The voices of the old Queens climbed over each other into her ears.

"You've been playing at this for too long."

"It's the Future Queen who will pay for your weakness."

"You must pave the way for the Future Queen to reign. The others must be gone. You must cull them now."

"Or else you leave Ariane with no choice but to do as you did - to kill her own genetic kin. And you know the price of such an act."

"You can't let her become like you."

Maeva didn't want to listen, but she had no choice. They held her consciousness hostage, pulling her deeper inside.

"You let this go on for too long, your genetic experiment. It ends now. You must have them killed. They must be killed."

No. Their skills will be necessary during dark times -

"You will be the undoing of Lower Earth if you let it fall into civil war."

"Civil war will erupt. You know it. Loyalties will divide."

No, no, no. I don't believe it and I won't do it. I won't.

She was dead upright in bed. The sound of the voices echoed against the walls, though Irene sat, mute, clearly innocent to the war inside the Queen's head.

"You must cull those which remain. There can only be one Future Queen Ariane."

There must be another way.

"Then listen. Listen to what you already know."

"There can only be one."

"They were each born for a single purpose. Their blood rings with the call of the throne. They do not know any other life. You know how it will end. You saw it with your own eyes and you killed with your own hands."

This isn't the same.

"It's exactly the same. You've been lying to yourself for a very long time."

The rush came. Maeva felt it first in her bowels, and then in her chest, rising to her throat and on to her face. It was all she could do to stifle the sound, but her whole face was on fire and the cry burst out face first.

A cry of mother's love, a cry of Queen's fear, a cry of hate and grief for the act she had no choice but to take.

The voices inside pulled themselves inwards, quick as they came, skittering away. Cowardly voices who taunted, but who felt nothing.

She spoke in half-awareness, needing aloneness, needing Irene gone.

"Lucius. He's the only one who'll know how to kill them so they'll never come back."

She was hardly conscious as she dressed and ran to the hilltop. A few minutes to think. Time to be sure of what had to be done.

TIME. THERE IS NO MORE TIME.

The sights and sounds of the city dulled as she meditated on it quietly from the hilltop behind the fortress, just past the city limits. She breathed in deep through her nose and out fast through her teeth, willing the world to be something different, for it to change before her.

I am Queen. I create. I destroy. I decide. There must be a way. There must be some function they can perform. There must be a way they can be of service to Lower Earth, even if they are not declared Queen.

But she could see no other way.

They were born from the blood of Queens. A Queen is born to lead. Nothing less.

There was no other way. They would only become obstacles, or worse, to the new Queen. She knew all it too well herself.

They have to die.

The balance in which they hung was too precious, too delicate. It was all her bloodlines had fought for. So many she had killed already for their world to be saved - it would come to nothing.

She had to go to Cork Town. A small part of her clung to hope that Lucius would tell her something different. But her hope was thin and fragile. Eighteen years she knew this moment was coming. But how to do it, how to cull the failed models, the previous methods she'd considered all faded to black. The code of Queens was strong in them all.

Only Lucius would know.

Eight miles in short minutes, she crossed Geb to the gateway of Cork Town. The gate stood wide open, the Queen's Guard at their posts.

I cannot see anyone now. No one must know I'm here.

She swung around, north of the city, approaching from Power Hub, the hum of the generator low as the city slept.

She scaled the perimeter wall, passed the power conversion plant, and scaled the second wall, landing on the asphalt of Cork Town's far north border. She closed her eyes.

Thumping of drums in the distance reached her ears.

A blowout. Good. I can move without fear of being seen.

The women wouldn't emerge from the caves on Cork Town's southern edge until near sunrise. She had more than enough time.

As she strode through the commune, she sought out any sensation of Rose. A gentle wave, like a benign current of electricity, washed over her. Rose was there. Somewhere.

Don't think about her now. Not now.

She passed women on opies passed out in the streets, none the wiser to the Queen's presence beside them. Maeva shook her head.

Get to Lucius. The rest will have to be addressed later. Cork Town is descending. We have to invest to bring it back to level. Or else it will become a ghetto worse than in the pre-Mist days.

Maeva laid her face in her hands for a moment.

Remember why you're here. Go straight to Lucius. Perhaps there is a way - perhaps there is a purpose for the others. Perhaps the culling need not be a culling at all.

She banged on the door hard enough to wake Lucius and then climbed through the open window. She sat on the single chair as Lucius muttered in the separated sleeping area. Finally, he emerged. The look on his face made it clear he didn't yet know why she had come.

"Maeva. I don't recall inviting you for a middle-of-the-night visit."

"You're going to want to sit down, Lucius. We have much to discuss and I don't have much time."

"You want them dead? You want those designed to anticipate and sense any danger in a five-mile radius, you want to have them killed?"

"It's not that I want it."

Lucius huffed.

"Come now, Lucius, you are not so naïve." Maeva stood. "You knew this time would come, and you would be doing the same thing in my position."

"Oh, Maeva, there is so much I would have done differently, had I been in your position." She watched Lucius catch his breath. His heartbeat quickened. "And Rose?"

Rose. So she called herself now.

Rose. Can a half-wit, disfigured, nearly disabled woman-child pose any threat to the new Queen?

Maeva inhaled slowly.

She too was born with the code of Queens.

But Rose had been broken and repaired with the genetic

equivalent of mud and guts. She was the deformed mosaic of a Future Queen.

She may have some version of the code, but she is no Queen.

Maeva didn't lift her voice above a whisper.

"Does she show any signs, anything, of what she was supposed to be?"

"Maeva, she's a twenty-eight-year-old frightened child. She hardly speaks. She hides in shadows. She may have been designed for – " he swallowed hard, "but she does little more than mop floors, pick flowers, and hum at the moon."

As expected. There is no threat from a would-be Queen who was broken before she lived.

Maeva sat on the edge of the bed. The studio in which he lived – though what he did could hardly be called living – was stiflingly small. "Then the others. Tell me, Lucius, how can it be done?"

Lucius sat back in his wheelchair, the draping fabric of his nightclothes sticking to his skin as sweat soaked through. Maeva still couldn't reconcile the body he'd become since his degradation began. And yet he still lived. He knew something the others didn't. In fact, he knew much the others didn't - that's why he was the Great Geneticist.

Lucius looked her straight in the eye and lowered his voice.

"A knife through the heart," he said. "It's the only way."

The Queen flinched. "So violent. There must be something more dignified."

"Certainly, but the method would take longer. They might sense it coming. They might be able to block the effects of any poison, and you'd risk their fight response if you went for strangulation or another type of physical attack."

Maeva closed her eyes. Lucius was right.

Lucius cleared his throat. "I'm not finished."

She opened her eyes.

"It has to be you."

"Me?"

"You."

"Don't be ridiculous, Lucius."

"Anyone else will fail. You can get close. They have no choice but to trust you. Their future, as they know it, hangs on you." He looked at the ceiling, "They have no idea." He brought his eyes back to hers. "You must go for the heart. They'll hesitate, and then it will be too late. This is how you had me build them."

She lifted her hand "But there's - "

Lucius cut her off, "You come to me for advice for this gruesome act. You dare to ask me. And then you challenge me? I designed their code for any such eventuality. As you commanded, I'll remind you. You and your offspring experiments. I designed them to be even better than you, and you know it. I designed them so they wouldn't be throwing themselves off the edge of cliffs." Lucius jutted his chin forward. "If they are to die, then they must be dead. If you are going to kill what I have created then it's you who must kill them. That is the only way."

She turned and walked to the door.

"You, Maeva. Do you understand me? It must be you. Anyone else and it will fail. It will. It's the betrayal that will kill them as well as the blade."

Impossible, this mad world speaks in impossibilities.

Lucius had never been wrong. But she was the Queen of the ages. The ages!

And Lucius had betrayed her before.

He's exaggerating. He's overstating it, just so that I will be the instrument of the act. No, I will not let him control me.

Yes, she would see them dead. But she would do it her way. Lucius didn't have to know.

She looked Lucius in the eye and stood taller.

"So be it."

. . .

SHE LEFT CORK TOWN, HER FEET MOVING FROM UNDERNEATH her as fast as they could. She'd kept the voices at bay but they were boiling inside her now. Hot lava of voices threatening to burst any second. Maeva had to get away, run, far, and fast to the place she knew they were taking her. Back to Rainfields.

She had to plan this out. Lucius only described the lock, she had to find the key to culling. She would work out every single detail before moving into action. It was for the sake of all of Lower Earth. To avoid an otherwise certain civil war that would arise when future queens felt cheated out of their promised reign. They couldn't understand what she'd had to do. They would fight to the end. That's what they were designed for.

Just like her.

I will win this. For Lower Earth. Nothing must go wrong in the culling of the Queen's design.

She ran and ran, voices screaming and visions across her eyes of the coming slaughter as she went.

19

—————

He had her. Lucius knew this was her weakness, her only soft spot, her Achilles heel.

She won't kill them, not with her own hand.

He knew it; he had created her too, after all. For all the fierceness that was encoded in her, she wouldn't be able to do it.

He was counting on it.

The Queen left, running on those deer legs as she did, away before peering eyes might catch glimpse of her in Cork Town. She was a beautiful sight to watch go. He stood from his wheelchair, frozen, watching her do all he couldn't.

He, barely living. She, what he had made.

Oh, but she is beautiful.

He waited for the girl to come in the morning, as she always did. He sat awkwardly in the rolling chair, nerves pinching and flaps of fatty flesh sweating but his mind raced through it, calculating the chances, having to take the risk. There was no choice now, he'd guessed this day would come, though secretly hoped it wouldn't. He'd spread his bets a little too thinly in the end, and now he'd have to find a way out. They were his creation as much as Maeva.

Rose could do it. At least he was pretty sure she could.

He heard the quietest of steps on the windowsill. She insisted on entering from the alley, just to avoid the main street. Her shame pained him, but he'd grown used to the sound of her fingers lifting the window.

He always wanted to call her by her true name. A Queen's name. But perhaps it was just as well, her birth name seemed cursed.

Her face was red as sunset, hesitant, sensing his heartbeat and fear. She was more sensitive than any of the others, of this he was certain. She read others from the inside. Perhaps a consequence of her life ending while still inside the womb. She read more than blood and breath, she read feeling and weakness and, most of all, intention. She was the reason Lucius had been able to keep up with the advances in Central Tower.

He looked her up and down, realizing how close she could have been to death had the Queen wished it so. The body of a girl and the face of a child. She would never age any more than this. Two-thirds the height of the rest of them. Her hair the flame on a body that would never develop beyond this adolescent sprig. Yet she had the resolve of the ocean.

The thought occurred to him that she might outlive them all. *Wouldn't that be ironic?*

"Come, come child. We must talk. You are going to have to do something very important."

He felt torn, unsure about his right to ask, unsure she could even do it if she wanted. She was, after all, a compromised version of perfection, perfect though she was to him.

Her eyes grew wide and stayed large as light bulbs as he took her through the plan. She hardly moved but for an occasional quick nod.

"You have a choice here - "

"I have no choice."

"It's to save them."

"It must be done."

"Yes." Lucius wiped his brow. "What do you think of it?"

She looked in the distance. "I knew it was coming. And that it was my time to do as I was born to do. They are my kin. I will protect them."

"It will demand more from you than you've ever experienced."

She looked at him with resolve. "I can do more than anyone thinks."

"But can you do this?"

She paused, and he watched her drawing up from within the years and histories and generations that ran through her veins, this would-have-been-Queen who never aged, this mistake of a moment's agony. Her lips moved in silent words as she sought deep within, asking the question of the Queens of long ago, firing through pathways and veins, blood rushing with the answer.

"Yes."

20

Aria reviewed the DNA sequence before her.

Her eyes cast over pages of sequence, her earliest lessons telling her to seek the message that sat behind it all.

Proteins align but the connection remains weak. The gene specifying resistance to the viral treatment is not on these pages.

She sat back against the chair. The latest virus infecting wheat crops was causing havoc in the West Fields. If they didn't find a cure for it soon, they could be without for several years.

The sequences are standard, so why is this strain so robust?

Apple fungus, the seed-borne rice disease, the recent rotavirus in the water: she'd conquered them all. Each had its own weakness. But the wheat streak mosaic virus was a new threat. They had evidence of its existence in the old world; the texts spoke of it, though it had never been in the island continent where Lower Earth was established. The wheat streak mosaic virus had belonged to a continent now uninhabitable. Back during the Final War, the Mist had adapted and attacked their soil.

Now the virus was invading Lower Earth. She had to find

the weakness in the strain so that they could treat the crops. And fast.

The RNA, where's the account of the RNA transcribed from the DNA?

She shifted through the papers, but it was missing.

Its key must be in the RNA; where's the sequence?

The page was missing from the file.

How could they be so careless?

Aria pulled together the papers and gathered them into the file. She emerged from the hut to the surprise of the priestesses who were walking past. They lowered their eyes immediately in deference.

Aria sighed; this wasn't the time for games of collective thought. If the West Fields were at risk, then two-thirds of Lower Earth's population could come close to starving.

She marched towards the center of the village; the trek was more than a mile from her hut, but she needed the rest of the sequence or her efforts were useless.

"Aria!"

She turned; Leadon jogged to catch up to her.

"Up to something important."

"Wheat crop killer."

"Oh yes, those ones are especially bad right now."

"But I don't have all the material!" Aria threw her hands up in the air. "I don't know why Habana would send me on this genetic goose chase, unless she's really that irresponsible with the files."

"Shh!" Leadon looked around. "You can't talk about the chief like that."

"I can. And I will. If I'm to be Queen, then I have to be able to resolve these agricultural diseases. Don't you see, Leadon? Lower Earth will be run over with crop killers if we aren't careful. Disease. Bacteria. Viruses. All these are the remaining gifts of the Final War. And here I am trying to solve the structure without the RNA sequence!"

Aria looked over to Leadon, but Leadon's face said it all. She had no idea what Aria was talking about.

It's just as well. If Leadon knew everything we were up against… she has it hard enough already. Being the Commandante's copy won't do her any favors.

"Look, Leadon, I have to speak with Habana. I'll explain it to you later, alright?"

Leadon shifted her weight. "Alright. I'll wait for you."

"No, don't wait."

"I don't have anywhere else to go. You know they don't let me conduct the warrior exercises with them."

Aria's face softened.

She may be the Commandante's double, and yet who knew two women with the same code could be so different.

"I'll see you soon," Aria squeezed Leadon's shoulder and then ran towards the village center.

"Habana," Aria called as she entered the sacred woman's hut.

"I am here."

Aria pushed aside the streams of cut leather and entered Habana's prayer room. Habana sat in front of a small fire, burning leaves on the end of a stick.

Aria began by kneeling on the altar.

"Lassa Habana weh."

"Pona sebana weh" Habana replied.

"Lassa mokha wanna weh."

"Haffaah."

Aria stood. There was no more time for custom. "The file is incomplete. I cannot assess it without the sequence of —"

Aria didn't finish. Habana had lifted her hand, a page of code between her fingers.

"Are you testing me?"

Habana looked up from her burning stick.

"Part of the training."

Aria let out a terse exhale and snatched the page from Habana's hands.

Habana smiled.

"You will be the Queen of Central Tower as well as the Queen of the people."

Aria scanned the page of code. The sequence rose from the paper, the weakness apparent before her.

"It's right there," she pointed at the page. "How could the great minds of Central Tower miss it?"

"Your mind is greater than theirs."

"But Lucius – "

"Lucius doesn't concern himself with crop viruses."

"If the Great Geneticist doesn't concern himself with the viruses that threaten Lower Earth's most basic needs, then what does he concern himself with?"

Habana pursed her lips at the burning rod.

"Now that you'd have to ask him yourself."

"Oh, I will."

"I have no doubt." Habana looked up at Aria, her eyes glazed. "Ariane, I will soon be gone. My days left in this world are few. Come."

Aria sat down beside her.

Habana whispered. "The women of Gana were meant to be free. You know that has always been my belief. One day, we will be free again, all peoples. But not in my lifetime. Ariane, if you are to lead this land, lead from freedom, and let us all thrive as we once did. Long before the settlers came, the Ganese were a rich people. We can have peace between us without an iron rule." Habana stopped. She looked away. "I know I could be disappeared for these words, but my life is over soon anyhow. So, take these as my dying words, and use them as you must. Lower Earth is not one land. Lower Earth is a mosaic of its many peoples. We can govern ourselves and still have peace between us. It was once that way on this continent. Once upon a time. Before the Final War, before the Mist. I know that much has changed, but humanity, at its core, has not."

Habana inhaled, deep but labored.

"Don't say a word, blessed Ariane, just find a place for these ideas in your superior mind. I know you are running the probabilities already."

Aria didn't deny it. The scenarios ran through even as she tried to focus on Habana's voice.

Habana's wrinkled fingers came to Aria's cheek.

"You will be a good queen, Ariane. I have seen it. Now leave. Tomorrow I could be gone. I won't ask you to remember me, only the words I have spoken to you. Go now."

Aria stood and slowly backed away from the little fire. Habana's eyes stayed fixed on the line of smoke that danced from the embers of her burning rod.

The following day, Aria received a note that Habana had died. They had buried her in the night with silent warrior priestess custom. They hadn't invited Aria to join.

21

———————

Rhonda was eating her stew with a few of the other Central Tower cleaners, and it was bland as ever though they'd been told it was being fortified to meet nutritional value minimums. She was still riding the high of the blowout the night before. She hardly noticed another one had joined them until the woman spoke.

"Edna is gone."

Rhonda felt her head furrow as others around the table gasped. "Gone where?"

"I think she was... I think she's disappeared."

Rhonda choked on her food. "Edna? Why?"

"I'm sure it was something she said about last night."

Edna had been a little loose in the lips, but Rhonda couldn't believe that it would be sufficient for this. The blowouts were well known, an accepted secret that wasn't so secret. But Edna was always so chatty, chatty, chatty.

The woman put her tray down on the table and tucked close beside Rhonda. While the lunchroom in Central Tower was nowhere near full, she was pressed against Rhonda's left shoulder.

"Why Edna, why now?" one of the other women asked.

Rhonda couldn't figure it out either. The blowouts violated no Directive, though many had wagered on whether there might one day be a call against them. Nothing obvious happened in them that could be labeled treachery, though any who attended knew boundaries were pushed right to the edge. They didn't know what that edge was, but in the searing underground heat, as they danced and rolled against the dirt walls, they felt it on each other's breath. An unnamed desire. They would grab at each other in neither love nor violence, pulling into the other bodies and pushing away with the beat of the drums, their only music. That's why the don women had been put in place, after all. The beat of the seven drums rising and swirling around them and steam turning to sweat, and they danced and pulled and rolled and pushed until the sun threatened to rise on their walk home. There was no night watch in Geb city limits, that had long been abolished during the unification of cities, but Rhonda was sure there were eyes on them.

"Maybe there's an explanation," a woman said, jerking Rhonda out of her thoughts. "Maybe Edna's just gone away."

Rhonda shook her head. "There's no other explanation, you know it as well as I do."

"Then what do we do?"

Nobody was eating anymore.

Rhonda paused wondering whether she was being alarmist or realist, "She's not coming back. There's nothing we can do." Rhonda turned to her food and forced a mouthful of mashed potatoes and parsnip down her throat. It felt like a boulder inside her, scraping and scratching as it went down and she had to rush a gulp of water to keep it all from coming back up.

"What we can do," she continued, "is make sure that during Uma's review we look like absolutely everyone else. Nothing different, not stand out, our work has to be good but not too good. Get it?"

The heads of the cleaners all nodded slowly. One of them asked, "Do you think someone from the Tower told on her?"

"Shut up," Rhonda hissed. "It doesn't matter. Someone obviously thought something of her, and we might never know who or why. It doesn't matter anyway." She stuffed more food in her mouth, and this time she swallowed it easily. "Don't speak of this."

"I won't."

"Me neither."

"Me too."

"Good. Now finish your lunches." Rhonda stood up sharply and unwound herself from the bench. She had to get away from this place, away from her thoughts. Away from Central Tower, if just for a few minutes before the review would begin.

Bursting out of the service doors into the garbage lot, Rhonda didn't care that the smell from the dumpsters was overwhelming. She sat down on the curb and tried to clear her mind.

So this time it was Edna to get disappeared. And how many before her? Rhonda had lost count. When would it be her turn to disappear? And where did they go anyway? Were they living well, wherever they were? Were they living at all? Rhonda figured there was only one way she would ever know the answers, and she hoped that day would never come.

In their world, there were those women who died in hospital, those who degraded at home, those who died of freak accidents, and then there were those who disappeared. Their absence created a vacuum. There wasn't one person in Geb who hadn't known someone who disappeared. A cold rush always ran down Rhonda's back during the Tuesday Briefings when the Queen made reference to the care of those who had been "moved out to other shores" according to the Directive.

Where is that shore, Rhonda wondered as the wafts from the bin overpowered her senses.

She took in a big breath and thought of her former neighbor. It was when she disappeared that Rhonda started noticing just how pervasive the disappearance had become. The neighbor woman had always been so kind, quick to smile. Rhonda thought perhaps she'd seen madness behind the woman's eyes, for they would open so wide that the whites flashed at her, and she rarely spoke a word above a whisper. She'd vanished on a perfect summer day. Something must have been wrong with her. She must have been taken for her own safety. But Rhonda wasn't sure.

Rhonda had always been content with her situation. Being a Central Tower cleaner came with perks: good hours, a sense of contribution, extra time off after the week of productivity. Before she'd started questioning what she saw around her, Rhonda had been perfectly happy to continue her days in a comfortable routine. She used to feel a sense of pride and awe at how far they had come since the settlers first came.

But not anymore. It was like a veneer had worn off and Rhonda was starting to see what was underneath. The settlers couldn't have wanted this for them, they couldn't have wanted to see members of their society cast away just because they danced a little too long in the night, or because they had an exclusive friendship, or because they questioned the direction the Queen was leading them.

Save me, settlers. But the Queen cannot be justified in this. She has no right to pluck Edna away like a common criminal. How can this possibly be right?

The question plagued her and there was no one to ask. Even if there were someone, the risk of asking hardly seemed worth it.

A shiver ran down Rhonda's spine and she grasped at the amulet.

This is not the time, she told herself. *I've got to get to my position for the review. And I've got to keep my head down.*

A flash of Edna's long brown wavy hair popped up in Rhonda's memory. Edna had the loveliest hair. It always had this waft of spring flowers when she'd turn her head and it would all fly around her face. Then she'd break out in a wide smile and laugh at you for being completely transfixed in the vision of her. She had been beautiful. Edna had been exceptionally beautiful.

I'm already thinking of her as though she's dead.

Rhonda didn't let this thought last another second. She whipped her head up from her crossed arms so quickly that her eyes saw stars. Not allowing another word to enter her mind, she silently opened the service door and walked to her station with the other cleaners.

22

It was the same dream. It came in seasons. The first few times it came, Isaac didn't understand. It was during his training that it all came to light, the instincts that, in *his* design at least, hadn't been as successfully repressed. Most scientists believed sexual impulse had long been tamed by the Mist and by intentional design in genetic code to suppress. But they were so very wrong.

Isaac was the proof.

His recurring dream never let him forget it. In the dream, he's in a warm place and everything is good. It all feels good. The air, the sun, and there's water, an ocean or sea or maybe a large lake, it doesn't matter which it is. Life is good and he's feeling good and the world has that glow like it only does in dreams.

She appears, this apparition with dark hair and green eyes, voice like honey and she smiles at him.

Like every time, it gets erect, it's inevitable - she's beautiful and they are the only people on the planet and she's smiling just for him. There's no Mist, no Final War, nothing. And there's no one, except them.

She's in his arms and they do something he doesn't even know how to do, his face against hers. He takes her and he feels her and finds everything as he must, and she's beautiful and she loves him, and he loves her. She wraps her arms around him, logistically impossible given the size of his gut.

But this is a dream, and in a dream everything is possible.

They lie entwined and he knows, he just knows that at last he has planted in her the child, the boy child, the one who will turn it all around.

As happens in a dream, it's months later, and she's giving birth and he's there and it's coming, the boy is coming, finally, and he has pride bursting out his ears, his eyes, the top of his head. The baby is coming, he's arriving!

No.

It's a she.

It's a girl. Impossible.

The green eyes laugh at him, pitying him.

"Oh, poor thing, this baby was planted long before you took me. But I still cared for you, don't worry, you did well. It's just that - procreation – poor thing, you'll never be able to do that. And certainly not a boy. You know that." And then she whispers, "Reckless man. As all men ever were. Reckless."

Reckless.

It echoes in his head even as he awakes in sweat.

Maybe I should be satisfied I get to dream of it at all.

But then, in real life, he still hadn't figured out how to make his body work as it should. All he had to do was figure out how to code it. How to make a male body, any male body, work as it should.

That was his scientific imperative, his *raison d'être*, but he was still so far from any kind of success.

It's finite. All finite. And we live the effects from generations ago.

He poured himself hot coffee and burned his tongue.

It goes much deeper than that. Come on, Isaac. There's a sick riddle in this. A targeted biological attack from generations ago. The riddle is that the Mist never killed desire nor sense of biological purpose. Only the ability to make it happen.

He took out the toast, burning his fingers on the scalding half-black bread.

Another day, trying to make this damned thing work.

He took in a big sigh. Isaac's optimism never let him down. The dream reminded him of why, one day, he wanted to see that child. It could come out of anywhere, he didn't care. It didn't have to be his own gene matter, just a boy that was all his doing.

One day, just let it be before I degrade completely.

He pulled out the cold fried chicken from the previous night and ate it in his shorts.

The doorbell interrupted him, startling him out of his thoughts. It had only ever rung twice before, and that had been in emergencies.

Work emergencies.

Hardly anyone cared where he lived, only those who watched and documented his every move as a member of the backrooms, and that didn't count.

He opened the door, his heart pounding.

"We've got to move fast," Adam's voice pierced in a sharp whisper before Isaac could even say hello.

"I'm coming." Isaac threw the day-old chicken into a paper bag, the paper bag into his briefcase, squeezed into a pair of trousers, and was out the door in less than a minute.

THE CONVERSATION WAS NOT GOING WELL. ADAM HAD LAID OUT all the code across his desk, but Isaac could not get a sane answer out of him.

"Why this one, why now?"

"It's different."

"They're all different, that's why they are experiments."

"This one has a variance."

"We've seen that before. It's called a disease, damn it."

"No, not like this! Isaac, Isaac. I'm telling you. I think we should get the backroom men involved."

"You're not telling me a damn thing. I don't know where your head is at. Or maybe I do, don't think I haven't noticed what's been happening around here."

Adam paused. "What do you mean?"

"You know what I mean. Do you think you're suddenly going to break through?" He stepped closer to Adam, trying to look through his eyes and figure out what was going on behind them. "Do you think you're the one who is finally going to have the right answer when everyone, every single one of us has gotten it wrong so far?"

"No, that has nothing - "

"You think this will make you some kind of hero, Adam?"

"No."

"And what about Sara?"

"What about her? Isaac, this is crazy."

"You're the crazy one, Adam. You want to birth a freak, if that's even possible, if it can possibly survive until full term, and you want to do it in secret? You can't bring the backroom men in for this, you'll get us all disappeared."

"Isaac, it's viable." He waited. "It's the first time it's viable. Isn't that what we're here for?" He got closer to Isaac. "Isn't this the whole reason for any of this? And more than that, I've already swapped out the sequence. We can get a Willing Woman for it."

"How do you know?"

"Crynal phenotype."

"In the Willing Woman Program? I doubt it."

"We can get one."

"Only if someone is looking the other way."

"Someone will. And now that we have the gestation period to fewer than four months, we can make this work."

"This is reckless, Adam." The word echoed in Isaac's brain. *Reckless man.*

Adam crossed the room to the window. The morning sun was just breaking over the hill behind the fortress and the light streamed in. Isaac stared at the back of Adam's head, trying to figure out what was going on inside it.

Adam turned around, his face red. "By your logic, why do we even bother? Ultimately, we're just running hamsters on wheels waiting for our time to die. Do you want to die, Isaac? I don't, not yet. This is our chance, Isaac." He walked close to him and whispered, "We're not the only ones. Lucius is operational."

"Lucius?" Isaac shook his head.

"He is. He's been in his own makeshift lab in Cork Town, but he hasn't stopped."

"The Great Geneticist won't be interested in our little project."

"He will be interested. In fact, he wants intel. From us."

"How do you know?"

"There's a girl who told me, a Cork Town girl with red hair."

Isaac didn't ask; he didn't want to know what a Cork Town girl was doing by coming to Adam. The Cork Town oddballs were unpredictable on a good day.

But Lucius – this was an advancement indeed. They hadn't seen the Great Geneticist in Central Tower in years, but Isaac should have guessed that he had just gone quiet. Lucius had always been eccentric. There was no predicting his next move. Certainly not since he'd degraded so badly.

"Lucius. Fine. And what does Lucius have to say about 4957?"

"That's what I'm going to find out. But I'm not going to

have long. There's no time to do any of this. Uma will know, she'll double-check, above all, on 4957. I've already switched it out, but we've got to find the Willing Woman and have the other sample prepared. I can't do it. Too suspicious. I already sorted out the former dossier."

"You want me to get in the way of Uma's reputation? Does it look like I have a career death wish? Never mind career, she'll have me disappeared."

"You have to do it quickly, sometime in the next few hours."

"You've gone nuts."

"Do this, Isaac. I'll set it all up. You just have to make the call. Call it a paperwork delay or mix up on an assignment or I don't care what! Figure it out!" Adam threw down the file on his desk, grabbing the single page of code sitting on top. "I'll leave in twenty minutes. I'll be back before lunch. Then we'll have our answer."

"You're not giving me much choice."

"Of course I am, it's just that there's only one choice you can make."

Adam didn't wait for him to reply, he was gone.

23

A dam couldn't hide his shock when he saw Lucius, spread out on the bed like a carcass, naked but for the wet sheets sticking to his living corpse.

"Who's there? I'm not expecting any visitors and I don't want any."

He stood silent, the lump in his stomach was getting bigger.

"Who the hell is it?"

"Adam, sir. Adam of the first line, from Central Tower."

"Ah, Adam of the first line. Well, this is a surprise."

Adam noticed a shock of red hair that was peeking out from behind the bathroom door. She backed away, having been caught watching.

"It's okay, sweetheart," Lucius told her, "You remember Adam. Just as well you pay this man no mind. I have important things to discuss with him." Adam glanced at the folder in his hands, and when he looked up, she was gone. Adam looked around the room, sure there was no exit but the door behind him.

"So, Adam of the first line from Central Tower, you are a long way from home."

Adam raced ahead, "You were the only one I could come to, with all we've got moving ahead, and I didn't know if I could trust anyone, so I - "

"Hey now, hey now. You've only just arrived."

Adam felt heat rising up the back of his neck. This had to go to plan, and he was blowing it.

"What makes you think I'm the one you can trust?" Lucius sat up in bed and Adam watched the rolling fat glide down his chest, creating waves that bounced into each other as sweat glistened in the movement. He tried not to stare.

"Don't you mind all this," and Lucius threw off the sheet, his legs touching from hip to knee in wide angles, the head of his penis emerging from somewhere between stomach and thighs, the shaft of it abnormally large, but the rest was still hidden deep underneath it all. "Tell me what you've got."

"I've found an anomaly."

"You don't say."

"I think it could be viable."

"That's not very likely, or if it is, it's likely not very important."

"I think this one could be."

"Why would you think that?"

Adam pulled out the summary sheet of sequence and passed it to Lucius, noticing suddenly that his shallow breath was echoing in his head.

Lucius tossed the sheet to the floor. "What do you want me to do with this?"

"Can't you just look at it? Tell me what you see?"

"I see a bunch of work that isn't mine to do anymore."

"You're the Great Geneticist!"

Lucius laughed. "What age are you living in, son? Look around you! Look at me!"

Adam dropped his head shaking it, slowly. He had to move the conversation on.

But Lucius insisted. "I said, look at me. Don't you see what I see when I look in the mirror? A giant slab of what used to be a man, don't you think? Look at my tits, look at my chicken wings of arms-"

"Lucius - "

"You come to my home, asking for help, and the only thing I'm asking in return is that you look me in the eye, that you see what I've become – what we all become. What you'll become, Adam. Look at me and control the panic rising in your throat. I'm asking that you look me in the eye, with all of this, and still say, 'Lucius, I need you.'"

This was going all wrong, all wrong and the panic of it squeezed at Adam's lungs. He couldn't breathe. They were so close, just on the edge of it. But Lucius was the key.

He raised his head, catching Lucius' eye. What was it that he saw there - yearning? Lucius was begging him. The Great Geneticist, he'd been tall, dark, broad-shouldered, and admired across the land. And brilliant. Lucius had been the one to turn the Tower onto the right path. Everyone in Lower Earth knew it, though no one knew what had become of him. Adam now understood that even the Great Geneticist could not stop what would happen to every man in Lower Earth. Decay, degradation, death.

Here they were, each begging the other. One begging for acceptance, the other for help.

It didn't seem much a price to pay.

"I see you, Lucius."

They held each other with their eyes for a good while, two men sweating in the heat of the day, the hum of the generator, and a single fan between them. They stayed this way while the moments passed, both settling into each other. Adam felt it was so close. He was so close.

Lucius dropped his eyes.

"Let me see this sequence."

Adam let out a long breath and collected it from where it had blown to in the corner of the room. He didn't have to go far; the apartment was stiflingly small.

Lucius glanced it over.

"I can't tell anything from this."

"The sequence is all there."

"Are you listening to me? This sequence is useless."

Adam felt the heat rising again up his neck. "Do I have to point it out to you?" They were going in circles. This man whose reputation had once been as the most capable, the savior of the people of Lower Earth, and all Adam could think about was how infuriating his decaying former hero really was.

24

———

"Are you listening to me? This sequence is useless." Lucius tried to hide his mockery, layer it over with genuine disdain, give no sign of the amusement underneath. He had to get Adam to the threshold.

"Do I have to point it out to you?" Adam shouted at him.

I can't let up on him, not now. Can't let him see that I'm egging him on.

"There is no point, Adam of the first line from Central Tower." And again Lucius tossed the sheet into the fan's breeze.

"Please, Lucius, please! I've never begged for anything, not like this. You've got to consider this, at least." He whispered tightly: "Please."

And there it was, what Lucius had waited for, taunting and tempting. Adam's fear rose from deep within him, and his brown eyes flashed blue. Bluer than the sea, bluer than the skies, a shifting blue that Lucius had never seen in anyone or anything else. Lucius pulled in the corners of his mouth to hide his glee. God, this boy was beautiful. He'd gotten it right when he planted that anomaly. He did not doubt it. He hung suspended in that momentary blue beauty before breaking his own trance.

He let out a false sigh. "I see what you see, but you need to learn something here, Adam. Context. This is meaningless without context. Have you got the full file?"

He watched Adam's eyes grow wider. His brown eyes, now settled.

"I'm working on it right now."

"Come back here with the full file."

He watched Adam close his eyes and exhale. "Okay." He took in a deep breath, nodded gently, and turned to leave.

"Adam - "

Adam stopped, the door open, halfway between worlds, and Lucius wanted it to last just a little longer. He sought a reason.

The idea struck him. Perfect opportunity. Adam could make it happen.

"I want to see the Green Files. Bring them with you when you come."

Adam again nodded, seemingly unsurprised, only an eyebrow raised. Lucius guessed his motivation was transparent. The Green Files had been his idea after all. It was only normal he'd want to know how the Male Program had progressed.

Lucius pretended to be resting when Adam came back. He muttered something to Adam about leaving the files on the table and he'd contact him later. Just as well, he wasn't sure what to say to him next. So-called 4957 was an easy analysis. It was the Green Files he needed to see.

Flipping through the pages, he felt like he was running into brick wall after brick wall. On the surface it looked simple enough, it all looked to be in place. And yet, Lucius couldn't put his finger on it.

"They're missing something here," he muttered to himself. "Where are the reflections reported?"

It seemed almost intentional, this omission. It was just complex enough that a beginner could conceivably skip it by accident. A more senior researcher might gloss it over, dismiss it as erroneous, or just let it slide.

But Lucius knew how pivotal it was, could tell just by looking. It screamed at him from the page.

Letters and numbers blended into a story, he moved from file to file, desperate, the despair rising with each passing minute now, the absence too glaring for him, like a bridge that crosses half a river.

The papers were flying through his little apartment; he didn't bother trying to keep them in order, he flung one after the other into the air, mounting frustration, he scanned each string of code with the eyes of a fox in the night. Homozygous dominant, homozygous recessive - none of that mattered. What mattered was missing.

"Something, there has to be something here."

On and on, the pages flew. Night passed and morning rose, and years of work were reduced to fire starters, for all the good they were. Manically grasping at the next green file, and the next, and the next. Casting away the first page in the seventeenth file, it hit him straight between the eyes. He fell against the back of his chair like Goliath, the code in front of him his David. He felt the air crushing his chest.

"And there it is."

Just a few letters held all the secrets, perhaps generations-worth of them. Forgotten in one line of code, misplaced, intentional or not, the effect was the same on a global program for the survival of man.

Perhaps no one knew it but him. It was possible; he'd always been able to see what others missed. The code could have been an accident. It could have been unintentional. It could have been mistaken direction, focusing on the wrong isolate.

Or it could have been a choice.

Planting a time bomb in the male sequence, messages that passed from line to line, from generation to generation unnoticed.

Yes, it could have been a choice. And had he not found it now, no one else would have until long after they were all dead.

A dormant message that intensified with time. A death warrant. A line of code that could not be changed. A line of code that would kill them all.

He nodded his head slowly, knowingly, for hours as he ran the predictions and the possible explanations through his mind.

When did I first know? I somehow always knew. The creation of Rainfields? Perhaps it goes back as far as that.

Lucius pulled his rolling body up from the chair, just long enough to drop over on the bed.

Have I been in denial all this time?

Denial.

I was a pawn, or worse -

Insignificant.

Defeated, he waited for the sun to rise before summoning Adam.

ADAM HAD ARRIVED WITHIN AN HOUR OF HIS CALL.

So close to him, Lucius felt Adam's breath move the hairs of his upper lip.

This boy. Now a man. And he is here in front of me, as chance would bring us back together.

Not chance, Lucius stopped his thought, *perhaps there's such a thing as destiny after all.*

Everything felt raw in him. He searched Adam's eyes, pleading with them silently.

"You might remember me from a long time ago - " he started quietly but stopped short.

There was nothing. No indication in Adam's face that he had any memory of those early days.

Seems his design is more naturally human than I thought. The Ariane design would remember almost everything from the time their eyes could focus.

"I looked different then," Lucius continued, hiding the note of shame, just barely. "I wasn't in all of this," gesturing to his rolls of flab, "I was a picture of what a man should look like."

"Of course. I knew of you, Lucius. We all did, your reputation preceded - "

"No, no. Never mind then."

There was a sting of sadness, but it wasn't so bad. He'd always known the consequence of the choice he'd made, and even now he knew it had been the right decision.

But, well, it would have been nice to see just a flicker of recognition.

When he'd handed the infant boy after his incubation birth to Myra, the Willing Woman, she held him close and cooed. But Lucius knew she would never give him what he could have. There was something to this sense of filiation after all. It wasn't blood - but it was a deep and heartfelt passion for life. For his life. For Adam's life.

He'd turned out well, this boy of his. Lucius smiled inside, felt fire lighting his eyes.

It wasn't just pride, it was hope.

It only takes one. Adam is my one, and he is good. Look at him. Healthy. Smart. Brave. Even if he doesn't know just how important he is.

Lucius knew he was beaming. The tragedy of the code was mellowing in him already.

There will be another way. With Adam, there will be another way.

He took a deep breath and relaxed. "I've read it."

25

"I've read it," Lucius lifted the orange file in the air before dropping it on the table like it was nothing at all.

"So?" Adam approached, eager. This was it, it all hung on Lucius now and whether he saw if it could be done.

"I read the Green Files too."

"You think they're related?"

"No. No, I don't."

"So then why the Green Files?"

"Have you read them?"

"Sure."

"And nothing struck you?"

"There have been a lot of gaps despite best efforts."

"Despite best efforts," Lucius repeated.

"Please, Lucius, I've got to know. The file on 4957 - do you see it?"

"See what?"

"The potential."

"Yes, I do."

"You do!"

"Yes, but it's delicate."

He felt Lucius watching him, but he couldn't stop staring. He waited for the next words out of Lucius' mouth. It was like they would never come.

Lucius straightened in the chair and his body made a noise, rumbling deep. Adam tried to stay focused despite the din of bodily fluids rising above the hum of the generator. "What you're trying to do here, Adam, it's risky at best. It will be impossible to predict whether this pseudo-human would even come out viable, take a breath at all. There could be consequences."

"They seem worth it, don't you think?" Adam needed Lucius to get further into it. He didn't need a rundown of the ethics; it was about possibility.

"Worth it? Worth what? Your career, or more? This would be more than enough to get you disappeared, if not permanently, then long enough for you to have no more value in the scientific community."

"Value, huh. I'll tell you my value," he turned away. "I'm barely more than an experiment. My Willing Mother would stare at me in shock. Sometimes it was like she couldn't look at me at all. Like you, Lucius, I'm a walking fossil. I'm already dead."

"That's not true."

"It *is* true!" Adam pulled back his voice, noticing the sharpness in it. He still needed Lucius. This wasn't the time to patronize the patriarch of modern science. "I just don't want to go out thinking I hadn't done everything humanly possible to find another solution. In my decades of research, in your double or even triple the years, have you ever seen anything like this, like 4957?"

"No." Lucius looked him straight in the eye. "I have not."

Adams gently bounced his head. "Then we must. We can, so we must. It only takes one."

Lucius looked off to some distant place, and it seemed hours before he spoke again.

"You can't just use any womb. You're going to have to identify a carrier that is more robust than common. Most of those aren't in the Willing Woman program."

"I'm getting one, Crynal phenotype. And we've reduced the viable gestation period to 3.6 months."

"Crynal. Yes." Lucius nodded before resting against the back of the wheelchair. "You'll have to figure out how to move the planned births across to different carriers, but frankly I don't care about politics. You can handle that part."

Adam was elated. That was easy by comparison.

"Don't be dismissive, Adam. This is neither easy nor safe. You are treading in very dangerous waters. Have you understood that?"

"Lucius," Adam approached even closer, the stench of the chair was powerful, but he had to look deeply in the scientist's eyes. "You really think it's viable?"

Adam saw something soften in the man. The corners of his eyes dropped lower as Adam felt the hot air whistling out his nose.

"Yes." Lucius' eyebrows rose in recognition. Adam couldn't read this gentle change. It felt intimate, personal. Suddenly Adam felt he was intruding on a private moment, though he was a part of it. He wanted to ask, but something in him kept him quiet. He didn't know what to say, all he could think about was telling Sara.

26

I'm a traitor, Sara said to herself, her eyes fixed on the sky out her bedroom window. She grasped the amulet around her neck, praying even though she didn't believe the stories about the settlers being omnipresent. Still, she found herself pleading for forgiveness.

This is it for me. It's only a matter of time.

When Adam had arrived at her door with the news, she'd thrown her arms around his neck, a wave of joy and gratitude and wonder overcoming her.

And then it happened. His lips on her lips and they were devouring each other like the world was at its end.

You're going to be disappeared, Sara. They'll see it all over your face. They'll read you like a book. They'll know what you've done. And that you wanted it.

She rolled over onto her side and looked at Adam's sleeping eyes. Those eyes. This feeling in her gut wasn't supposed to exist. She knew they had scrubbed it out generations earlier. And yet there she was, living proof that love wasn't just for the collective. She loved Adam until her heart twisted inside her.

Adam's eyelids fluttered but didn't open. His shoulders lifted and fell, waves of his breath washed over Sara's skin.

How is he so at peace?

The Directive of the fourth generation repeated itself in her head. They'd memorized it in sixth level. It reinforced that there was no place for what she and Adam had between them. The words echoed in her brain as she watched the rise and fall of Adam's chest.

"We shall be as one, across land and sea, a humankind that is kinder than all those who came before the Mist. Kinship is not within individual relationships, no sister is our sister alone - these exclusive ties weaken our collective bond and demonstrate a lack of commitment to the greater family. Love does not belong in its diluted state between two people. Our family of humanity will be respected with reverence, our relationships deep across boundaries and geographies. We will not accept the violence of our past; we will hold peace in our hearts and through our swords. We will slay no other in anger but breed love in our acts of survival."

She hadn't understood what it meant until now, even if she had dutifully studied it, memorized it, and accepted it as rule of law. Sara had always wanted to serve through Central Tower. She knew it was written into her genes. If commitment to the greater laws of Lower Earth meant she could achieve that dream, she had been ready for that. She had left the home of her first Willing Mother without looking back.

The disappearances were the answer to this Directive. Ripples of stories where those who disappeared in the night had committed some treacherous behavior. Betrayal. Sometimes against society, sometimes against the Queen herself and on a rare occasion, against oneself, for which the disappearances were intended to be a sanctuary of healing for those minds that were troubled. Suicide was a known epidemic, they had learned of it in the sixth level, but Central Tower had been able to address that through tweaks to the code. A predisposition for contentedness with their situation.

But Sara was now anything but content. Ever since she'd been told to shift her focus from crop killers to improving the common code of women, she had been suspicious. It wasn't right for their human resources to be so distracted from their natural resources. And yet, across the Tower, more and more researchers were being pulled off the very programs that had been the reason they joined in the first place.

Sara was losing faith.

And then there was Adam. She didn't have words to describe what she felt when he was near her. She tried to balance it with her fear of disappearance, but the feeling was more powerful even than her need to self-preserve. Whatever it was, it had a hold on her. And she wanted more.

She'd known it the moment his lips were on hers.

When finally their mouths had separated, she had seen something deep in his eyes. They shone like crystals, like sunlight on the northern seas, undulating color underneath the brown veneer. She felt it then and knew he felt it too.

Fire.

It was deep in her and it was hot. They had sat at the table for hours in conversation, their hands clasped. It felt more important than it ever had. The stakes suddenly higher, their own lives on the line for it.

"I can make it happen, Sara, I know it. 4957 will be the new human."

"I believe you."

"I can't do it alone."

"I'll help."

"I'm scared." That blue again, it blinded her.

"Me too."

"Sara - "

"Yes?"

He stopped, mid-breath. The tears began to well in his eyes, she watched the little waves inside them grow, until he blinked and they came down, two perfect parallel paths on his cheeks.

"I think this might be it."

She nodded. She believed it. The timing too perfect, the conditions were just right. This is what they had been working towards for so long.

He stood, grabbing at her, his arms tangling in with hers, clumsy and urgent, they crashed together, bodies and faces, their mouths breathing each other, drinking in each other in mad bursts. The table fell over, the chair fell over, they lurched together and landed against the wall in hot breath, so fast she thought her heart would explode.

They passed several minutes there, bodies against the wall. Just breathing, his chest heavy against hers.

She led him to the bedroom, they sat side by side on the edge of the mattress. He spoke facing straight ahead.

"Please hold me."

Sara took him in her arms and brought him gently down to lie on the bed. Fully dressed, with their shoes on, they spent the rest of the night in silence, his hand tightly clasped to hers, even in his sleep.

We're as good as dead, Adam.

She turned her eyes back to the rising sun.

27

The Queen woke in the dark, already almost at Rainfields edge, and she cursed her blood for what it did to her in the night. She had been caught unaware more often these past weeks, in deep sleep, which had never been her way.

Now her legs carried her miles away before her consciousness even caught up.

Of course, she thought, *of course, it would be this place. Today of all days. Of course, it would call me to it.*

She slowed for the final steps, approaching the edge with gentle feet, softer than cotton in the breeze, as slow as the earth turns, displacing only a few pebbles as she went.

The moon glared white. She stared at it as in the periphery of her vision. She remembered in vivid color the time she jumped.

Jumped, I jumped. I didn't step. They called to me; Mother beckoned me. Oh, my child. So much I owe you.

Ariane, her first. The disfigured infant, the Queen's own face reflected in the horror of the child's.

Other memories, faces, of those she'd loved and of those she'd hated, floated across her sky. Into her peripheral vision.

Into her line of sight. Faces were everywhere. Maeva shook her head.

Focus, Maeva. This is the moment you must focus more than you ever have in your life.

She fixed her eyes on the moon, on her intent.

We're in such a delicate balance. So many who have come before, so many who fought to survive. And now it's on my shoulders. But my own offspring? How many must be born and die before we get this right?

She asked the question knowing part of the answer. She had created this. She was responsible for it. There was only ever supposed to be one; their multiplicity was her own doing. It had seemed so right at the time. Assurances, for Lower Earth.

She would see them killed, but she would not fall for Lucius' trap.

"They'll see it on my face," she called to the moon, "They'll know exactly why I'm there. They'll see right through me."

Panic rose in her gut. She looked through the sky for some answer, any answer.

"What would I do if they know what I've come for? What would I do? I'd falter, I'd fail. Can I possibly leave it all to fall in ruin? Incite some civil war, worse than Lower Earth has seen since the Mist? No! I can't let that happen. It's not going to happen in my time. I know what they'll all say. It will all come back to me, the destroyer, the Fool Queen. The one who ruined it all!"

The sky gave no response.

"Mother! What is this life you have put me in?"

All was quiet.

Even the voices were silent.

"How is this what I've become!" She ripped at her skin. The pain eased her mind. She tore at her arms, her neck, her chest. Welts rose, flesh folding on itself. She didn't stop, not yet, she needed some response.

And still, all was quiet. No sound but her blood rushing to heal. She held it back, forced herself to feel it. To feel the pain.

The Queen stood, skin flapping and flesh seeping, her ugliest self and she felt it was right. She was right to be ugly in this of all places.

She inhaled the sea spray, letting it sting in the wounds. Waiting, her world on hold, for just a moment longer. Everything inside her was desperate to heal, but she held the blood in place.

And then she let her biology react. The blood rushed into the gashes wasting no time, running like rivers pulling air and time inwards, splitting cells at breakneck speed, turning wrangled veins into petal-soft cheek, lips, eyelids like butterfly wings.

And she was back in her body, the Queen's body. Solid, healed. She glowed in the moonlight.

Turning her back on the night, she started slowly across the damp moss on black jagged rock, not feeling the cuts, mind clear and focused.

"No, Mother. Not this time. It will not be my hand," she spoke into the night, resolved.

She set her course for Archer, to steady him for what he would have to do.

"It will not be my hand."

Her foot slipped on the moss.

She had never before missed a step. She found herself on her back, staring at the black sky. Her head struck, she was shaken, forced to go to the very place she didn't want to revisit.

Her mind drifted back, back to her first-born child's birth. And how she had made such a great tragedy of her.

Back to the one whose life she destroyed.

Ariane, the first, the true Future Queen.

The moon above her became the moon of her memory, twenty-eight years earlier.

THE FULL MOON SHONE BRIGHTLY INTO THE ROOM AS SHE began to give birth.

There was the shock of red hair emerging from her body. She hadn't yet seen the face. She was exhausted and in pain. The babe was clawing at her canal, resisting being born, demanding to return to the womb.

"Come, child, come! Queen Child, come!" Maeva had pushed from the nape of her neck to her ankles, all muscle and ligament twisting to close the path from which the child came, leaving no choice but the light.

The child screamed from inside as if she knew the world she was about to greet would offer her no solace. Not for a Queen Child like her. Not after dying in the womb and having life pushed back into her by her mother's force.

"Please, child, please," Maeva had pleaded, and at last the head crested, with hesitation, inching into the world with the reluctance of a lamb to the slaughter. The babe turned as if to look back, but indeed the gate had closed. She would never return.

How the child had cried.

"Please, Ariane, hush now. You will be a queen, born from my own body. The pattern of queens born through detached incubation is over. You come from my blood; my blood to yours." Maeva coaxed as she clipped the cord with gentleness, the love of generations suddenly alive in every pore, a need to protect, a need to hold. "Come, child, you are with mother, you are the only one, and I, your only mother, child, come to me and see how I love you."

The already long red hair on the newborn covered her face. Maeva caressed it aside and at last, their eyes met.

Maeva froze, consumed in an instant by the guilt of what could be only her fault.

The child's face. Disfigured. Ears that began too low on the head. Eyes that could see forever but placed in the wrong spot. No symmetry. The code was perverted. Everything in the wrong place and the hair of fiery sunset across greener eyes than sea and pasture, greener than the depths of space. Dark and sad, and ready to love.

A Queen Child brought back from the dead while still in her mother's womb.

A Queen Child deformed.

The collapse over the cliffs. The death that should have been final. The life-giving that wasn't natural.

She should have let the baby die.

"Oh, my Ariane. I am so sorry."

On hearing the words, the child stopped weeping. Maeva laid her down on the sheet in the middle of the floor, covering her with blankets and blocking her face from sight.

"For all you will live, and all I can never give you, I am sorry."

The babe looked her in the eyes, and they shared the memory of the fall.

The child knew it all, she could tell. Another victim of Rainfields.

Not the first and not the last, the voices of old within Maeva spoke.

The child of no more than a few minutes looked at the Queen. Maeva looked back her deformed Queen Child, her Ariane. She felt the silent babe do what no queen had ever done since the Mist.

She's forgiving me.

Maeva was washed over with a sense of release, felt it rushing up from within her. The gift of forgiveness from the newborn's eyes, given to her who was least deserving of it. The child's strange eyes softened.

Maeva couldn't look away.

"Irene," she whispered, hoping she'd be heard from the other side of the door.

"Yes?" Irene replied, opening the door just a crack.

"You will swear to silence for what you will see."

"Yes." Irene had only been a few years in the Queen's service, but she had been sought out from Gana years earlier. Maeva felt a magnetic pull to her. Her dark complexion and intense eyes captivated her from the start. Maeva trusted her implicitly at first sight.

The door creaked open a crack and Irene closed it silently behind her. She was the only one in the fortress who knew of the Queen's implantation of the Queen Child. The pregnancy had been hidden for the full six months under robes and frequent travels to the outlying counties.

On turning from the door, Irene's eyes widened at the quiet bundle on the floor.

"My Queen, you've had the Queen Child in secret?" Irene approached cautiously, as Maeva sought Irene's eyes. Maeva kept the child's head covered just enough to hide her defects.

"She is innocent," the Queen said.

"Of course, she is. She is just a baby."

"No," the Queen choked back. "She's not. I killed her."

"She is alive, my Queen, I see her breathing under the blanket. You are confused by the labor - "

"I'm not confused. I killed her once, Irene." The Queen inhaled deeply and barely spoke, "At Rainfields. I was weak then. I fell. She died, and I brought her back. But now she's been punished for it. No one can know, no one can ever know, no one can - "

"Shhhh, now, my Queen. The Queen Child will - "

"She is not the Queen Child!"

Irene gasped as she unfolded the sheet and saw the child.

"It's my fault."

"I understand, Maeva."

And with the slowest of movement, slower than time itself, Maeva looked one last time on the child's face and embraced her through the space with love, unseen and powerful and fleeting. Still, the baby did not cry.

Irene took the bundled babe, and slowly moved the sheets away to fully reveal the mistake of a face. She inhaled deeply, moved by the child's smile who knew no anger, moved by her forgiveness of Irene's fear.

"Ah yes, little one," Irene whispered, "You were loved, remember that."

"You have to - "

"I will take her, my Queen."

"You can't harm - "

"There will be no harm, my Queen."

Maeva suddenly knew what must be done.

"Take her to Lucius. He'll know what to do with her. He'll take care of her." Her voice trailed off. "He's as much as her father. He will love her. He will know what to do."

The perfect child he'd created.

What will Lucius say? All the gifts he designed in her — what will he say when he sees what she's become?

"Mama?" The babe spoke clear as day.

"My child-" the Queen looked on from the floor of the bathing room.

"Come, little one," Irene coaxed, "Leave your mama to her world. You will have a new home."

"Mama?"

"You no longer have a Mama, child. We must go." Irene moved towards the door.

The shock of red hair looked up from Irene's shoulder with a start, meeting the Queen's eye with question and fear and loss.

"Ariane," Maeva whispered, "Your name is Ariane, and you were once very, very loved."

The baby's eyes welled, reaching for the Queen, confused.

Irene slipped out of the room saying only, "I'll take her to Lucius."

The door closed.

Maeva sobbed silent tears in the corner of the room, still surrounded by her waters and placenta not yet delivered.

Her world would never be the same again.

SHE LET THE MOON OF THE PRESENT NIGHT COME BACK INTO focus, her body completely drained by the memory. She stared up at the sky as the weight of all she had to do pushed down on her chest. There was no choice anymore, the path was paved. The back of her head throbbed. She didn't want to move.

There was so much yet to come. She needed a little reprieve from it all.

She lifted herself.

She let the cool air brush across her body, and then she started for home.

Nearly eighteen hours later, she closed the door of her bedroom behind her. She collapsed in bed. And she slept.

28

———

The sound of the flutist came on the screen. Rita loved living close to the screen. It was like she had a friend beside her even on the coldest nights. The gentle hum of the screen was soothing to her, and mornings were always the best. The wood flute filled her heart with joy, and she smiled, her head surrounded by the soft white pillow.

She paused there. Another morning and another day. She would make toast and drink orange juice, prepare her chicken sandwich, and take an apple.

Oh, a pear! It is pear season after all.

Rita loved pear season.

Rita knew what she was born to do. She was born to love life, to wake with love in her heart. She took on the day with zeal, she closed it out with zest for the next day and she felt it all in the glorious morning flute. The sound was gentle; the vibrations in her chest made her smile. She was so close to the screen she could actually feel it.

"Oh day," she declared and popped out of bed, eyebrows high and lips curled up in a smile. Sometimes it felt like Mary on the screen was talking straight to her, only to her. The green eyes of the image sideways out the window perked up as they always did at this hour. Mary was her friend, everyone's friend, reliable and true, and something in her always felt familiar, like looking in the mirror from a new angle or catching your reflection in a gentle wave. Like a sister.

The shower was hot, her coffee was hot, the bread from the day before more delicious in its crust than when she picked it up from the market stall.

How can that be? she wondered and then simply accepted it as fact.

Rita loved her design. At the clinic, she mulled over the others and was grateful for the traits infused in her. How much was design, how much was simply nature or daily nurture, she didn't know, and it didn't much matter. Hers was a good design, one meant to endure, just like the others, and she had faith in their system. She had seen the little lives emerge - stronger, abler, smarter. They would survive, they would, no matter the conditions that Lower Earth threw at them.

Shame about the boys. But the time is what the time is, so why spend time worrying about it?

She gathered up her things for work as quickly as possible, a quick brush of the hair, the teeth, and general daily hygiene.

This day will be as great as yesterday. And the day before that, and the day before that. Yes, it will be a great day indeed.

Rita's life was an unending chain of days as great as the one before it. She sighed in wonder at her luck. She heard Mary announce the coming hour for departure to positions, but Rita wasn't yet ready to move. She was held in place by the beauty before her.

Across the table, the red sunrise cast daggers of shadows more striking than the imagination could create. The flutist played on in the background.

29

The woman's cheery smile was both inviting and off-putting. Lucy watched how time and again she greeted each arriving patient with the same giant, full-toothed smile, same sweet melodic voice asking them how they were, have they been well since the last visit, how was their child, how was their Willing Mother, how was their job. At first, Lucy thought she was robotic, but as more than forty minutes passed in the waiting room, Lucy caught glimpses of her talking to herself or her paperwork or the coffee machine. She was always the same. An inexhaustibly cheery woman. Even when she kicked her toe against the doorjamb it was followed with "Oh gee, gosh, darn!" and a flurry of giggles as she shook her head to herself and walked back to her desk.

"I'm looking for Miss Lucy?" The voice of the cheery woman sang through the sliding glass square in the wall. Lucy almost didn't recognize that it was her name.

"Hi, hi, sorry, that's me."

A tilt of the head and a big smile. "Why hello, Miss Lucy. Your first time heeeere?" It was drawn out almost mockingly.

"Yes." Lucy touched the lava amulet around her neck. She realized she'd done it and became self-conscious. She dropped her hand to her side.

"I'm Rita. I'm the greeter, and it's great to have you here! I'll take you in now. Did you have any trouble finding us?"

Lucy was led into a simple room, white but not too impersonal, with a big window that looked into a green yard that was kept up with potted tropical plants. It made the room feel warmer, though it was a standard clinic room like she'd seen on other doctor visits.

Rita dramatically dropped a magazine called "Growing on the Inside" on the little table beside Lucy, which she flipped through. Articles talked about well-being, fertility health, meditation, and balanced eating during pregnancy.

On the wall was posted the declaration on Willing Women. Lucy scanned it.

Now, why didn't they tell us about this more in school? I can't be the only one in this position.

Waiting for the doctor, she had time to read it from start to finish, twice over.

DIRECTIVE ON WILLING WOMEN

"DIRECTIVE, SO PASSED IN THE AGE OF THE SECOND establishment of the Willing Woman Program.

That the child born to said woman will remain with said woman until such time as either the health status or state demands require otherwise.

Expectation is that infants and young children will be best cared for by mothers who carried them. Emotional attachment is probable in first days and is a helpful aspect of the Program for the purpose of building relationships within the broader

Lower Earth population. Movement into homes will be enacted as deemed preferable before adolescence.

When appropriate, according to Program requirements, children will move out of the first Willing Mother's home into either a group home or the home of another Willing Mother. Such transitions enable relationship development across different attachment figures.

Exceptions will be applied as warranted, particularly in the cases of insufficient capability on the part of the Willing Mother. In these cases, homes or women listed as available caregivers will appropriate all rights previously held by the Willing Mother.

The Program recognizes the importance of relationship, with both the advantages and disadvantages it brings. The State will operate as mediator in situations deemed necessary, or by the Royal Court, if so escalated.

Participation in the Program is a privilege, not a right. It is based on capability and competence, genetic conditioning, and other social factors. Women not accepted may appeal through the Common Process of Objection.

Campaigns will be set at regular moments through the course of the year; potential participants are encouraged to attend. Specialized campaigns will be mobilized according to need: social, scientific, or otherwise.

The practice of Willing Women will continue until the Royalty deems it no longer necessary for the continuation of Lower Earth's population. At the time of writing, no such termination of the Program is expected."

Lucy knew The Directive was posted in all clinics, a legislated requirement, but it provided little insight into what it all meant, and what happened behind the scenes in the several thousand strong workforce. It was the second-largest cross-county employer in Lower Earth after the Education Ministry.

Everyone knew someone who was connected to the Program through the genetic conditioning teams, the recruitment groups, the clinics, and the post-care workers. The screens explained that the Program provided much more than just the ability to keep the population figures steady - it was a way for society to remain connected with their humanity, a side that was deeply at risk in their post-Mist reality. The Program was acknowledged, explicit, discussed, and debated - but only with regards to its application.

No one questioned whether the Program needed to exist.

When Lucy was younger she had attended one of the regular community meetings held across Lower Earth. They were supposed to provide accurate information, as rumors were always rife. It seemed many people had a desire to disband or completely rethink the Program - which the Queen dismissed out of hand across the screens. There had been a Tuesday Briefing specifically on this subject. "Of all our challenges in this generation, I am not about to question the one solution that is working." Lucy had found it hard to disagree, all the more so now in her current position.

The seat in the little white room was the kind designed not to be comfortable. The lines of the chair were sleek and the wood well varnished, but after a short time, Lucy felt her legs going numb. The article on ideal diet for fertility was hard to focus on, so she ran her thumb over the lava stone to calm herself. The edges of the rock had already softened at her young age, she'd touched it in so many anxious moments. She let her mind take her back to the rally she'd attended a few weeks earlier. It was there that she'd decided to do this.

It had been in the Central Meeting House. The place had been transformed into a conference center of sorts, tables set up and with women at each - some former Willing Women, some pregnant, some who were reps from the Ministry, there to give administrative advice. Every visitor was assigned a number. All names were held anonymously on a list at the Ministry, confidentiality guaranteed. Lucy was thankful for that; she wasn't ready yet to tell her mother of her decision.

Lucy remembered how one of the Willing Women, Janis, had been particularly friendly with her. Janis had nodded with understanding when Lucy explained her situation and said she'd been in a similar position herself. Lots of ambition, but also a struggle to get through the final levels of school.

"So have you given up everything else now that you're a Willing Woman?" Lucy had asked.

Janis laughed. "Absolutely not! I'm still doing my studies on the side, now that Anee is older. I could see myself doing urban engineering implementation, or perhaps agriculture implementation planning since I'm not meant for the countryside. But in the meantime, I also focus on Anee's studies, making sure that she can get that leg up that I didn't. You know, they've reduced the gestation period, so you might even have it easier than me." She smiled at Lucy.

Lucy had been reassured. She was still young, and even if right now her progress in algebra had slowed, she still felt competent. Janis had inspired her. So it was possible to be a Willing Woman and not lose everything she'd worked for so far.

"It's a sacrifice though, don't forget that," Janis had cautioned, "but one that is not only for yourself, as each child is a gift to Lower Earth, and Willing Mothers are at the soul of it. You can see your future in your child's eyes, your history in her as she discovers the world. But it does come at a cost. And remember, at some point, your girl will move away from your home. It's both a blessing and a challenge."

Lucy was pulled out of the memory by the awkward seat in the examination room which was now cutting into the underside of her thighs. She was adjusting herself when a pair of legs approached her. She was absorbed in the tingling sensation of her backside when the voice spoke.

"Hi Lucy, I'm Doctor Lydia Easom, of the Easom line. We are procreation specialists," a stately woman of around fifty entered, closing the door solidly behind her. "I am your Accompanier. I understand that you attended the recent rally for Willing Women."

"Yes."

Doctor Easom looked up from the lenses of her glasses, "And that is how you decided to sign up for the Program?"

"Yes."

Doctor Easom continued to look at her expectantly. Lucy didn't know what she was supposed to say next. "I met a very nice Willing Woman there." Doctor Easom nodded but still said nothing. Lucy felt her neck getting hot. "I found the Willing Women passionate about their status."

"Many are," Dr. Eason finally interjected, but speaking quickly while flipping through pages in the folder in front of her, "It's both a calling and vocation. An advancement of Lower Earth. You're a part of something bigger when you're a Willing Woman. What else do you know about the Program?"

"It's a four-month gestational period and a total five-year written commitment."

"Five years is average. It could be shorter or longer depending on circumstances. The minimum is the gestation period plus six months of mandatory breastfeeding."

"Right, of course." Lucy was starting to feel like she was back at school, and not getting the correct answers.

"Have you ever undergone any fertility testing?"

"No, ma'am."

Dr. Eason semi-smiled. "No need to ma'am me, I feel old enough as it is." She began writing in the folder, then paused, staring at the page.

Lucy couldn't bear the silence. "Were you a Willing Woman?" she asked.

Dr. Eason looked up at her. Lucy sensed it was a more personal question than she had thought. "No. I wouldn't qualify. My vocation is in medical, they require my commitment here."

"Oh yes, of course." Lucy felt stupid.

"Here are the next steps. First, you go for a questionnaire and testing. Blood, tissue, vitals, a few others that are non-invasive. One vaginal review. From there you have a psychiatric assessment to ensure strength of character and assure that there are no aberrations. Finally, you and I will meet again to discuss parameters. You will likely be faced with some difficult questions. That is intentional. Do you have any questions about this?"

"No ma'am. I mean, uh, no."

"In that case, at this stage, I will move you into an interview room and Rita will be right back to go over the questionnaire. You will have an opportunity to ask questions when you and I meet again. But not in the meantime. I need to make this clear. During the testing and review process, you forego the right to discontinue. You may withdraw only after all of the testing is completed. Do you understand?"

"Yes."

"Does any of what I have said to you here today give you cause to withdraw at this point?"

"No, no." Lucy shook her head more vigorously than she intended.

Doctor Easom nodded in Lucy's general direction and left the room with her folder. Lucy waited what felt like a long time before Rita came bouncing back and invited her to join in another room, one more like a living room than a clinic.

Rita offered up that glittery smile again. "Would you like a coffee? Tea? I believe we still have some biscuits. They are delivered at fourteen hundred hours every day. I just love working here!"

"No, thanks. I think I'm ready for the questionnaire."

"Well, look at you, getting right down to it! I like your energy! Let's jump right in then, shall we?"

The initial questions were basic enough: name, birthdate, family grouping, blood type, siblings, school results. The next set got more personal: successes, failures, dreams, goals. Then what Lucy thought ought to have been the first question:

"Why do you want to be a Willing Woman?"

But before she could answer, Rita was reading out a checklist.

"Tell me all that apply: to experience childbirth, to keep the population of Lower Earth healthy, to contribute to Lower Earth's future, because you have failed in scholarly activities (Lucy winced at that), because it is your calling, because your Willing Mother sent you, because your friends have joined, to see a reflection of yourself in a child's face - " the list went on a little longer, and Lucy quickly said it was for the future, intentionally leaving out her exam results from the story.

There was a written portion to the questionnaire, which Lucy assumed was used to assess literacy as well as suitability. The essay style questions varied from "What kind of Willing Mother would you want to be?" to "What value do you see in a Willing Woman Program?" and "If you were selected to be a Willing Woman, what would change for you?"

It took the better part of an hour before Lucy could return her completed questionnaire to Rita. It was starting to get dark outside.

"Don't you need to finish up soon?" Lucy had never thought to inquire about opening hours.

"Nope, I work through dinner. I just love this place."

To be fair, Lucy found it a pretty nice place too. People were happy to be there. Those in the waiting room smiled or glowed with their pregnant bellies. The walls were colorful with pictures and drawings, except for the clinical rooms, which each opened onto the luscious green garden. The staff were friendly enough, and all went to extra trouble to make her feel welcome. She understood why Rita was willing to put in the extra hours.

Rita explained that the testing would require her to return the next day. Lucy was disappointed; she'd hoped to get it all done in one shot and then have time to consider if this was the path she was going to take. But the decision would have to wait another day.

In the meantime, she'd have to lie, if only by omission, to her mother.

Her mother had taken good care of her since she'd been moved to her in her fifth year. She'd always been gentle and encouraging, if not overprotective from time to time. Lucy could get irritated by how her mother would tout Lucy's accomplishments like she'd done them herself, but her experience at the clinic somehow put that into perspective and she had more patience than usual that evening.

Except when the topic of summer school came up.

"Mother, there is no point right now, you don't seem to understand. I can't keep up. I want to keep studying, but it can't be this way."

"If you put your head down, you'll be fine. I'll help you, don't worry about that."

"Advanced geometry, mother? You're going to help me with that? Please."

"I'll keep you motivated. Look, it's only one summer, you'll

be caught up in no time and then you can seek admissions for
any - "

"You're not listening to me. I can't do it. It's not a question
of taking another summer, I need to go a different direction."

"A different direction? What in Lower Earth does that
mean?"

"There are lots of options out there. I'm just looking into
what else could suit me."

"What could suit you better than a tenth floor Central
Tower job! You came to me with this plan, I didn't force you.
This has been the plan all along."

"It's not anymore, mother! That's it! I can't talk about this
anymore tonight." Lucy flew up the duplex stairs and slammed
her bedroom door shut. She stared at the ceiling.

What am I doing? Worse, what else could I possibly do now?

She had no answer. So she closed her eyes and accepted
that tomorrow would be the day for answers. Not that she had
a choice. She was still in the middle of the review.

The clinic seemed somehow less sunny on her second visit,
but Lucy chalked it up to poor sleep. The whole thing had
weighed heavily on her in the night, and she felt less sure.

Rita seemed to sense this when Lucy came through the
door. She had a more soothing tone for her on arrival.

"Well, hello again. What a delight to have you back. I'm
sure yesterday was a lot for you to take in."

"You know, it was."

Rita smiled. "You're not the first. This is a big deal, a huge
opportunity, a major change. It's okay to feel uncertain." Rita
sweetly scrunched up her nose, "You'll know what feels right
when you finish going through the process."

Lucy didn't have to wait. Rita ushered her in, passing Dr.
Easom, who noticed her going by.

"Lucy, I'm looking forward to chatting with you later. We

have some things to discuss, but first, you have to finish the tests."

Lucy didn't know what to think of 'things to discuss', so she just gave a small smile.

The tests were not quite as simple as Doctor Easom had made them sound. Blood was one pint, not just a small sample, and Lucy felt lightheaded. Rita brought her biscuits. The tissue samples were also an uncomfortable trip - Lucy felt like she was being surgically carved in four different places.

"Where are you taking it from now?" with her legs in the air, Lucy couldn't understand what the nurse was doing.

"Your cervix. It's standard procedure."

She'd never felt anything like it and hoped that wasn't something she'd have to do again.

Lucy realized that while she knew a fair bit about the administrative process of becoming a Willing Woman, she didn't know anything about what would happen to her, physically. She asked herself the questions to distract her mind from the poking, prodding, and scraping down below.

Once I'm planted, will they have to take blood and tissue again? How often will I have to come to the clinic? Will I have to take drugs? Will it hurt?

Still, on the stretcher with her legs in stirrups, Lucy got the distinct impression that this was not what she came here for. Second thoughts flooded in.

Are all women treated the same? Are they planted the same or were there different processes? Do all bodies accept and adapt to the plantation? Just how do they plant it in there anyway?

Lucy was frustrated at how little she'd researched in advance.

How many women go into this blind?

Waiting for her psychiatric evaluation, she sat beside another young woman, who Lucy assumed was going through a similar process. She was reading the "Growing on the Inside" magazine, and Lucy couldn't help but interrupt.

"Excuse me? I'm sorry, I'm just wondering if you know what they are going to do in there?" She gestured to a large wooden door that stood out against the other plastic ones.

"Oh sure, she's going to ask you lots of questions about what you remember from zero to five years old, the health of others who were in the household then, what it was like when you moved into your next mother's house, or if you were in a girls' home, that sort of thing. Nothing too strange, don't worry." The woman smiled.

"You've done this before?" Lucy didn't think the girl was much older than her.

"This will be my third."

"Third! Wow."

"Andrea of the sixth line," said a voice from behind the door.

"Oh, that's me, but don't worry, you'll be great, regardless of your rating." She walked off into the room with the wooden door. Lucy didn't get a chance to ask her what a rating was.

Bruised and bandaged from the tests, Lucy was running through possible lies she could tell if her mother saw them. She would try to keep them covered up, but just in case, she thought a backstory was important. So it would come out naturally.

And then it was her turn.

The psychiatric evaluation was painless enough by comparison. Lucy was surprised by how basic it was, even though she knew the woman was evaluating her every word. She'd been honest when asked if her mother knew she was there.

"That's pretty normal," the psychiatrist had told her, "I'd say about half who come through the recruitment process haven't told their mothers before getting their rating."

"What's the rating?"

"Doctor Easom will explain the process."

And so Lucy waited, six hours into day two of her Willing Woman application, finally at the last step and eager to go home. The free lunch had been good enough, but she was ready for her mother's spaghetti. She needed comfort food.

"Lucy, come in."

Doctor Easom got down to business before Lucy had closed the door behind her.

"I'm not going to mess around with you here, Lucy. I'm going to get straight to it. It is uncommon for us to see someone from your rating joining the Willing Woman Program."

Lucy was confused, "But my genetic mother was a Willing Woman."

"Yes, but she was a carrier Willing Woman."

Lucy didn't understand.

"You see there are different types of Willing Women. There are Willing Women who are recruited into the program, and there are Willing Women who are carriers. These carrier women are of huge importance to Lower Earth. I don't want you to misunderstand; there are many different elements to how we run the birthing programs. Your first Willing Mother had something in her that called her to the Willing Woman vocation. We could read it in her DNA sequence. All carriers have it. You, however, come from a different line. Different enzymes, for example. Your line has different capabilities, and therefore different callings, different objectives. And so it is surprising to see you here today."

"Called her to this vocation? I don't understand."

"When I say called, I mean that there was something in her genetic code that gave her a strong predisposition to successful birthing. To put it simply, we know that the Mist affected different family lines in different ways. And where we have found strong genetic code for successful birthing, we have also found that these women were drawn into this vocation, usually without needing to be recruited, or even asked. But you are Crynal. That means you have a specific phenotype, an elite group. And your group has other advantages."

Lucy thought of Andrea, being on her third child and still so young. But Andrea was built for it, had the right 'type'.

This was the most interesting history lesson Lucy had ever learned. And she was amazed that these simple facts were not in the national curriculum. They somehow seemed important.

30

I rene tapped on the Queen's bedroom door with her fingernails.

Days had passed since she'd last seen the Queen. While that wasn't necessarily cause for alarm, Irene had a strange feeling in her stomach and couldn't shake it.

She put her hand on the door handle. Turned it. Dared to open in a few inches.

She pushed her head through to see the Queen's sleeping body on the bed. Her skin gleamed in the last rays of moonlight before the sun rose. Her chest lifted and lowered, ignorant to Irene's eyes.

Irene couldn't believe it.

In her more than thirty years based at the fortress, she had never seen nor heard of the Queen sleep like this. She waited, expecting the Queen to sit upright at any moment and chastise her for breaking her privacy.

But the Queen didn't budge.

Irene saw that her arms had rays drawn along them, like new skin cleaving between the old. She craned her neck a little further and saw the rays extend up her shoulders to her neck.

What's happened to you, Maeva?

Irene had underestimated the impact of the decision to cull the others. Irene had no other name for them. The other queens. Maeva was culling the excess of queens.

This day was one we had expected – but I feel less sure now that we are living it.

Lower Earth relied on the Queen for all direction. If she couldn't see Lower Earth through the transition to the next Queen, they were going to be in great, grave trouble.

31

Maeva dreamed, vivid and palpable. She knew it was a dream, but she threw herself into it with unbridled abandon. It was too captivating to deny.

In the dream, he is beside her, the king of old in this new man's body. Archer's body. The warmth of him like waves against her skin. They are reclining on stones, dark massive slabs that are cool to touch even in the midday sun.

Rainfields. Rainfields of old. Rainfields, the greeting place of new peoples. Rainfields, the landing place of hope.

When she looks down at herself in the dream, she is nude. Her breasts rise and fall heavily with her breath, and she is covered in a layer of sweat.

She feels ashamed and vulnerable. She tries to cover herself with her hands, to at least preserve some dignity before he turns his head and sees her in this state. In the dream, she prays.

Archer, don't see me this way. Don't turn your eyes.

But though he is in Archer's body, he is not Archer. She, however, is fully herself.

He is all of them, all the old Kings from over the years, embodied in this moment just for her. She reaches for the lava stone but it's gone, disappeared with her cloak and underclothes. She is only herself before him.

Her breath quickens as she watches his eyes turn.

Her heart is beating in her ears and she desperately tries to hear his blood rushing, his accelerating heartbeat at the sight of her. But he has gone silent.

How is it possible that he has no reaction, and here I am in this condition?

Only then does she see it - he is nude, too.

She takes in the shape of his shoulders, his arms.

How have I never seen him like this before?

The sides of his body, the line of muscle that curves from rib to hip to groin.

He is unashamed of his nakedness, of that part of the man that had been the target of the Mist's attack. The core of their history. There it is, just in front of her. Vulnerable. She feels her power over him; she can finally cast him away, as the queens before should have done, the lament of the voices of ages past. At last, she can make it right. She can make him pay for the many before him and all he has come to represent.

She raises her eyes to meet his.

How his eyes beseech her.

Why doesn't he speak?

She looks deeper into him, through his eyes to his soul.

Why does he look so despairing? Why does he look at me so?

His left hand lifts in the periphery of her vision and comes to rest on her shoulder. Skin to skin, there is a rush through her.

Electric.

This is dangerous.

She knows it, but she cannot articulate why. Not now, not in the safety of the dream.

The back edge of his hand runs from her shoulder to the shelf of her chest. Still, he does not stop looking deep into her eyes.

Speak, she thinks to him, but she too is silent.

A shock runs through her when his hand passes along the side of her breast, the feeling inexplicable. Old and new.

They are together, watching his hand trace the curves of her body in the stillness of a moment that sits between the seconds. It is almost not lived at all. They both watch his hand come to sit on her thigh.

His head snaps erect and she meets his gaze, his eyes now panicked, his mouth opens a sliver.

A line of blood gathers at the corner where his two lips join, and wordlessly, breathlessly, it falls down his face, a single drop landing on the lava rock cliff beneath them. It's then she sees the point of the knife protruding from his chest, pointing at her like a finger of death. Pointing at her, for she is to blame.

She wants to scream. She wants to hold him as his body goes limp. But she is stuck in this dream world where she is frozen and her body won't respond to her commands.

He falls. Backward, headfirst, without sound, he is over the Rainfields cliff and into the sea below. She scrambles to the edge to watch him.

A head crests from beneath the water.

He is not dead! She declares to the stone of the cliffs. *He is not dead! He will rise from the water!*

His head raises toward her, his body still in the water, though it lifts him. The water itself raises him up, swirling as a platform, bringing him back to the place where she sits in her nakedness.

He is coming back!

The water falling over and across, she cannot make out his shape, but only that he is there.

He's nearly upon her, the rising swirling sea, and she can hardly wait, hardly contain her beating heart.

The waters slow as he approaches her, this immortal king of her dreams and of history. She stares unblinking, and his form is there.

He, too, is unblinking, his face frozen in love.

His face frozen in death.

Blood pours from the wound in his chest. His dead-love face grows grotesque, the shame splashed in blood smears from the water's madness.

She vomits. Vomits all the love, all the humiliation, all the things she should have known, and didn't. It projects out of her onto the dead man's body. He crumbles under the weight of it, he falls off the water's platform back to his grave below, and standing before her, bloody knife in hand, is the one she knows is her mother's mother's mother. Or even of the one before. Perhaps this is even the first queen shaking her head at her, it doesn't matter now.

This Queen of Before just shakes her head, slow and deliberate, eyes unforgiving on the Queen's naked body.

"You will kill us all."

Maeva awoke, the cold of night descending. Her flesh was torn, she'd been tearing at her body again.

Lifting herself, healing herself, she dressed in her long, green velvet robe.

It was time to call Archer.

Archer stood at the window, looking out into the square. She couldn't take her eyes off him. Even with everything she knew, everything that went so far back, she was nonetheless transfixed under his gaze. His jaw was as strong as the first day she'd seen him, of special note given how young they both were at the time. It came down and set hard in a square to match the line of his shoulders, leading the eye down the gentle curve of his neck, which contrasted harshly against the lines of his chest. But somehow even this jarring was perfect in itself.

The old King's code lived well all these generations later. He had hardly degraded at all.

His hair remained full and his gait was bouncy, even youthful. He was one of the few men who had crossed the invisible line of time and come out the other side. The rest of them began their slow or quick declines, but Archer evaded age. The skin on his cheek was smooth but not soft, showing his experience but not his years.

He'd been protected from the worst of it.

He'd have been suitable for the Queen's Guard, except for the women-only policy. She could have changed that. She could have given him a military position. She could have offered him greater leadership, Commandante even, but she didn't. Most simply accepted that Archer held a favored role as an aide to the Queen, even if they didn't know why. He had the code of Kings, but never their authority. He was not to be trusted with even an inch of power. Never.

She'd always had his movements closely monitored. "Exceptional visits to the outlying areas" were the only anomaly ever in the Green Files. And she knew why he went there. East Gana and West Strangelands. Perhaps it was just as well he was going to be the one tasked with the act - he'd always been too drawn in by Future Queens that lived in the protectorates and their perfect duplicity.

Despite her warnings.

Archer stood across from her, waiting for her to address

him. Patient and silent. As she stared at him, something began to flutter in the bottom of her stomach.

Stop it, Maeva. It's just the code, the affinity you feel is just the code.

But she wasn't sure. Her heart accelerated and her eyes wouldn't lift, wouldn't turn away. Archer stood there, unmoving, gazing off somewhere far in the distance. There was such softness in his face, something so familiar in the way his cheeks relaxed. Something warm.

Comfort, that's what it is, comfort. He's nothing special. Just a man. A man with the code of Kings.

He turned and looked into her eyes. She sought the code out from within them, a heat rising up her neck.

Where are you, King?

The first King of Lower Earth, the direct descendant of the settler King. The king who'd changed the game - the king who'd altered the course of their modern history.

What is so special in this DNA after all? Take the crown off the king and all that's left is a regular man. And yet this man survives when all the others are degrading around him.

She knew there were questions about why she held him in such esteem, why she kept him as though he were kin.

For her, the answer was simple.

Keep your enemies close.

Yet, not only did Archer seem to be the most loyal of her aides, he did not seem capable of the level of deceit that the voices of the old queens' warned her about.

Still, the history of his code was too well known. Her own mother's words had been stark in their reminder.

"When he seems calm, expect rage. When he seems kind, expect menace. This is how we know him to be, and one day he'll live out his history. There's no doubt of that. Will it be now? Will it be with you? That remains to be seen. But what you can be sure of is that despite any effort you make, his blood lurks at the beginning of it all. Tweaks of him are across the Male Program. No matter how you try to shut it down, that self-preservation will supersede, just when you aren't looking for it. I won't pretend I know how, Maeva, but you keep your eyes open."

Standing before him now, she didn't see it. Could it be that this version of the man was somehow lesser? He looked on her with such adoration, such deference. She found it hard to believe this line of DNA could have ever been responsible for all it was claimed to have done.

Just look at this man. He will follow my every word, simply because it was me who said it.

This task would put it to the test. She inhaled deeply.

"Archer, there's something you must do."

SHE DIVORCED HERSELF FROM HER BODY AS SHE EXPLAINED IN detail his mission ahead. She watched him with detachment, not allowing the chaos in his eyes to dull her to the violence. She observed it with curiosity.

"You will use the discovery of the female scout as a ruse. It is believable. Ariane would be expected to seek out such an enemy. She will think she's killing a scout who has disguised herself. If you're lucky, they will cull one another in the fight. If you're not lucky, you will have to ensure she dies as painlessly as possible. I will arrange for the weapons and poison."

Archer's eyes shut gently, remarkably gently, the lids sitting just so in seeming absolute peace, though she knew all that was rushing through him.

He has to understand. He must own the act. I must make sure he will follow through, despite his affection for them. He is human, but I cannot let his humanity distract from the necessity of the act.

"Do you understand what you must do?"

Archer swallowed hard. "What you are asking of me, my

Queen," and now it would come, the excuses and fear. His voice quivered. "I just don't see it, I don't understand - "

"I'm not asking you to understand the reasons. I imagine -" she sought a little bit of sympathy inside for him but found none, "I imagine this must be difficult for you to comprehend."

Archer pulled back.

"Difficult? Difficult? This isn't a question of difficulty, Maeva. This isn't even betrayal. Betrayal is glorious besides what you are asking me to do." He grabbed a chair and pulled it closer. He sat and put his face in his hands.

She closed her eyes. "You're overreacting."

"Don't you get it, Maeva?" his eyes searched her, she felt them burning across her skin, and it felt good. "What you're asking of me is to put a dagger in my own heart. These girls, they are the very center of -"

"I do not ask you to understand, this is not for you to understand. I am not asking anything, but I command that you obey." Her voice cracked.

I must control my temper. He cannot object and he cannot dissent. If it's the last act he will ever do for me. This must be done. He must believe that it is the right thing to do.

"You do not know what is on the line here, Archer. You have only ever had a sliver of awareness of the world in which we live. Nothing more than that. You've been privy to more than most, but you must see," she walked to the window facing the west square, "none of this happens by accident. The world is changing and we are changing with it. Lower Earth needs more than you and I can offer it. This must be done for all the world to carry on."

"But they are just girls."

The voices rumbled within, her patience was running low. She couldn't bear to reflect on it further. It just had to be done. "They are women, Archer! And they are too many. We must cull the crop to only she who will stand forth as Queen. Don't you see what the consequences are otherwise? I will have them brought to the same region. The guise will be arranged. You will need to see the act done quickly. I cannot guarantee how they will react once the first one is dead. This is about pragmatism now, Archer. The remaining one could respond in a multitude of ways. This is where you must use the trust you have built," Archer winced, "to ensure you can execute the other one. Use the lines I have given you, they must believe they are killing the scout, the scout in disguise. They must not know who is under the cape across from her."

"But they'll know."

"They won't know."

"THEY'LL KNOW!"

Maeva was thrown aback by the force of his body rising to stand, the chair falling behind him. He continued in whispers.

"You are asking me to do an impossible thing. Even if they don't know at first, the moment they look in my eyes, they will know everything." He lifted his head, looking beyond her. "I'm not strong enough to do this."

He might be right.

"Perhaps not. But you are not doing this only because I say so. Archer," she came close to him. Their forearms touched and the heat of his body rolled over her as she looked up into his eyes. He seemed to be growing taller before her. "You are the only one I can trust to do this, and you must do it because you love them. Because only you can do it and be sure they are killed dead and without pain. It's not only for them, but we have a world of people looking to - " she hesitated, "To us. Archer, they are looking to us to lead them. This farce never should have gone on so long, and I do regret it but here we are and I'm not sure I could have done any different. It is not their fault that they were destined to this - but it is indeed their destiny."

"I cannot believe that."

"Believe what you want, Archer, but don't be so naïve as to say you can't at least see what's happening here." She walked to the window, her eyes fixed on him. "I cannot bear to look on you now. This is the moment I have most needed you in my life. Do you hear this? I need you, Archer. They trust you. They love you. Let them die with the dignity they deserve."

Archer's face twisted and the Queen couldn't stand it.

She opened the window and stepped onto the ledge, another step to the roof. She would not let him see her this way. She was at a loss.

How to convince him. How to make him close his eyes and do the act?

She'd been foolish to think he'd blindly commit it after the years he'd spent with them. She never should have let him set eyes on their newborn bodies.

Their newborn bodies in his arms. Their beautiful bodies.

Do not let those memories in now.

She looked out over the night from the rooftop.

Just some air. I can't bear to look at him.

She let out a violent breath. She felt like her guts were being compressed.

Focus.

It was too easy to be pulled into history. She hardened herself into the now and waited. It was only a matter of time. He would come to join her. She pulled her knees into her chest, perched comfortably and easily on the roof's deep slanted edge. Her robes cascaded around her like the midnight sky against the darkness above and the single light of the square below. She couldn't see how the thousands who converged there found any space at all. From above, the square appeared no larger than a tree leaf, the buildings along the edges cutting into the open area, interrupting and jagged. In the nighttime light, it shone as something mystical. She observed the cobblestones, their uniqueness, the trodden parts more visible closer to the fortress, the outer edge in remarkably good condition. Made to last. Destined to see so much more. The thousands and thousands of feet that would trample them in rushing to briefings to announcements, to the good and the bad. And the terrifying. They would all come, and they would all be communicated here. Mouth to ear to mouth to ear, a cancer spreading as the news reached everyone.

When will it be? When will Upper Earth finally make their move? Will we be ready to meet them? Do we even know how?

The female scout had so far proven useless. Upper Earth clearly arranged it so that no matter the pressure, she had nothing to tell. So far the Guard hadn't used the tactics of the old world, but that wasn't off the table.

Maeva would do as she had to, just like those before her had done in the face of yet another attack on their very existence. Hadn't that been what all of the regulation had been for? All their efforts, all the separations, the disappearances -

All the controls had been put in place.

Only one star was in the sky. She stared at it, willing just a small respite, time to figure it out. The weight of it all made her body sink deeper against the roof.

Archer's head finally emerged from the window below her feet. She heard him sigh before heaving his large body out the window. For Archer the ledge was perilous; she prepared her muscles in case she needed to grasp at him in mid-air. She'd done it before. She shifted herself a little lower, thinking how childish she must look to him, balled up on the roof.

Why do I care what he thinks of me on the roof? I've just asked him to kill our kin. My kin.

My children.

His eyes rose to her, and it was he who looked childish. Those sweet eyes she remembered from so long ago. They had barely been of school-going age when he'd smiled at her. He'd been hiding behind a building on the corner of the very square below them. Sahna had let it happen. She had known it was important.

He had aged, grown stronger, perhaps even a little harder, but his eyes still gleamed in the moonlight like a little boy.

He's been crying.

She tried not to succumb.

So this is what heartbreak looks like.

"Come, Archer, come sit with me." She tapped the treacherous rooftop beside her, cold flat stones with sharp edges. Archer delicately made his way up. The balcony ledge gave him enough leverage to pull himself over the rain-worn gargoyle.

He set himself down heavily and inched in his seated position toward her, eyes set on hers. "I'm sorry."

"There is no need."

"Yes, there is."

He seemed larger than the world somehow, beside her. His broad shoulders filled her view. His breath was quickened and shallow. She heard the flurry of his heart, but his voice was calm. "You know as well as I do that I'll do anything you say." His shoulders rose with a long inhale. He whispered, "But I know this is breaking you as much as it is me. You can pretend, you can shut the voice out, but it's there for you as much as it is for me. I know it, Maeva. I just don't know how it isn't breaking you in two."

He enveloped her with his arms, strong arms. She felt him slip and so she solidified herself against the roof to hold him in place. He held her as a friend, a father, a man. A lover from an age past. He pulled her in closer, closer, and she fell against him, fell into him, his face in her hair, and breath on her ear. She was so little in his arms, curled up in a ball, a little ball of the woman on whom everything sat, and just for a moment, she wished for freedom.

Settlers, just let me be a woman who means nothing to the world! Let me just live and breathe and not be responsible for it all. Why, why can't that just be me? After all these years, just a little moment's peace. Why can I have no peace?

She didn't fully register his hands on her waist, turning her from facing the square to face him straight on, their shoulders and chest brushed against each other. He brought her into him, into an embrace on the rooftop. She didn't register his cheek against hers, nor the heat coming off his body. She was lost to her freedom, lost in silence as she pushed the voices farther and farther down. She was deaf to the sound of his heartbeat pushing harder and harder, his hard body pulling her, firm and slow. She was lost in it and lost in the midnight moonlit sky, blind to the fire in his eyes.

His breath caressed her lip.

The alarms sounded and madness boiled up like lava from that deep place of her mother and mother's mother and so on for what felt like forever and the voices were then upon her like gaslit flames.

GO! they screamed and her body convulsed with the power of their voices.

GO! NOW! YOU ARE THE PREY AND YOU ARE FAILING AGAINST HIM! GO NOW! NOW! NOW!

She was convulsing on the rooftop, completely out of control but watching it happen to her in passive observation. An active electric pain rode her as the voices scraped and scratched at her insides. Archer desperately gripped the steep roof as he looked on her with horror.

Blood trickled from her mouth.

What have I done!

MAEVA, NOW!

DO NOT THINK!

HE'S POISON!

GO!

And she was up, she was off. She hurtled forward from that

place of the ages, tumbling and trembling, smashing into trees and breaking them as her vision tunneled. She saw nothing but the distance ahead, thought of nothing, and couldn't stop moving, knowing she would run until she reached cliffs. She would look into the water below, and she would again fight the Rainfields pull, to keep from throwing herself over the edge into the dagger rocks below.

32

Aria prepared her satchel. Every cell in her bristled. Everything had come to this moment. Every promise, every preparation. Every ounce of her soul was focused on the singular goal.

Kill the infiltrator.

The throne would be her reward. The Queen had been explicit. She had only one more test, one final trial.

I cannot be fooled. I cannot hesitate. The infiltrator looks just like us. Just like me. They have perfected their disguise. To think the scouts are across the country, masquerading as the women of Lower Earth. I must trust in everything I have invested, all my training. It was all for this moment.

She left in the middle of the night, throwing the gate to Gana wide open and beginning the trek to the Great Rainforest. The two-day journey would crystalize her resolve.

For Lower Earth.

For all women who rose from the ashes of the dying men at their feet.

For the land which is our only comfort.

All I must do is kill the threat to our very existence, the way of life we struggled so deeply to create.

Upper Earth will not win. Upper Earth would make us as we once were. Upper Earth would see us slaves to an obsolete doctrine.

I will not let it come to be.

She stepped forward, steadfast, and committed her way to her people. Raising her fist high she sang an old warrior priestess prayer for victory.

33

Archer's every movement was unbearable. The weight of his clothing hung heavily on him. The simple act of dressing was more like working in a quarry under water, desperately trying to move boulders uphill and against a current. Every move strained him. The fabric of his shirt set his skin on fire, like needlepoints tearing across his chest.

All time slowed almost to an absolute stop. Pulling on his socks and boots felt eternal. He had to find the courage to stand up and plead with himself in the mirror.

"Anything but this. Do not allow me to do this. If only my body would rebel. Don't let me do this. Not to my girls."

But already the momentum was pushing him forward, packing his hunting bag, his human hunting bag.

Two daggers, cloths to wipe them down. Two daggers - one for her and one for him. And the other would have a spear. Each aspect of the plan had a backup.

Water.

Rope to transport them after and to mark the place for collection.

The rest would be supplied by the checkpoints on the way. The Queen had assured him as much. It seemed she had accounted for every detail, leaving no room for him to err.

All reality was conspiring around him to make it so.

No matter what, he would see them dead.

Culling. Maeva calls it culling. It is bloody execution, treachery. Treason. She won't believe me for a second when I tell her she has to kill a scout. She'll read it all over me. The stench of it will be unmistakable.

He checked again that the daggers were there, careful not to disturb the vial prepared for the deed. He would treat the tips with poison.

Then she would be the one to take that final step. Ultimately it would be her hand.

He checked again that everything was there. He was in a state where he could very well leave it all behind and not miss them until the critical moment was upon him, and then –

No dagger. No poison. No murder.

But indeed, they were there. Nestled calmly into the folds of his satchel, they were waiting, dulled, and dirty. Archer did not allow himself to linger on the thought of what it would do to her insides once plunged. The dagger looked grotesque to him, and he fought the urge to wash it down, shine it, buff it until it was the picture of perfection. They deserved that much.

The thought dropped away as the overwhelming wave of duty overtook him. He stepped forward as time resumed, a thrust of momentum at his back. He slammed the door of his modest apartment as he went.

"Don't stop, don't think, just move," he whispered to himself.

"Archer!" A voice from a floor above pierced through him and his numb, dreamlike state shattered at his feet. He tried to pretend he didn't hear.

"Archer! Archer! Listen, I've got something for you!"

He tried to push on, rushing down the stairs, as the voice became more distressed.

"Archer! Please!"

The desperation in the voice stopped him cold.

"What is it, Wilma? What can be so important that you absolutely must have my attention right now?" He looked up and saw her head poking over the sixth-floor railing.

"It's a note with your name on it."

"I'm coming up."

Taking the steps two by two his feet were feeling heavy again, and he wondered if he would ever leave this apartment block, never mind all that lay ahead.

"Who is it from?"

"How would I know?"

He clenched his teeth. "I assume someone dropped it off."

"You assume wrong. I found it slipped under my door with your name on it. Must have confused the apartments."

Not likely. More likely someone knew that Wilma would make sure I received it. Someone who could ask afterward if the note had been delivered.

"Thanks." He tapped the banister, turned, and fled, ready to ignore any protest behind him, but there was none. He paused in front of the door and looked at the note in his hand. The heavy dark writing inside was apparent but he couldn't make it out through the folds.

If I open it now, I might not go.

Involuntarily, he unfolded the paper with the simple dark scroll, knowing it could only have come from one person:

"She is waiting for you."

He crushed the note tight in his fist and pushed open the heavy door without waiting another moment.

The sunlight accosted him. The dim corridor had given no indication of the blinding light outside. It took his eyes a few moments to adjust from the blanket of yellow-white in front of him to the quiet near-abandon of the streets.

Where is everyone?

It seemed too vast, this quiet. Even on a Sunday morning, there would be those already up who did the shift work, at the very least some movement around the center of town. He felt like he was in some kind of time vacuum, where everything was on hold, waiting for him.

He pushed ahead, left foot, right foot, concentrating on moving, going forward, going ahead, not allowing the note in his hand to burn his resolve for another second.

The fortress stood in his peripheral vision, but he couldn't see Maeva now. Even the smallest glimpse and he'd again be a cowardly wreck, begging to be freed from this duty.

He had no choice anymore, not even in his own mind. If it had to be done, then it would be him and his hand to see it through. He would carry it out with the greatest reverence and love he could find within his soul. That much he owed them. That, and so much more.

Night had descended by the time he reached the first checkpoint. He was greeted with a silent nod by the woman who led the Queen's Guard in that region. He could not be sure what she had been told, but an array of meats and fruit were laid out for him, and the regular cot had an extra mattress. After being shown to his room, he sat in the dining tent and began to take in the surroundings.

There was not a man among them, not anywhere that he could see. The eyes on him were suspicious despite their defer-ence. They had all been prepped for his arrival, to make him comfortable, but also to keep their distance.

An arm reached out, offering him cured ham. He took a

few slices, but the woman's face reacted as though he was supposed to decline.

Another arm offered wine, which he declined. Again, he was met with distrustful eyes. He could not do anything right here.

"I'll take an early breakfast."

A nod.

"Just before sunrise."

A nod.

"I'll not be any further inconvenience after that."

A nod.

He couldn't wait to get out of there and on with the task at hand.

HE SWALLOWED DOWN THE EGGS AND PORK AS QUICKLY AS HE could will his mouth to move and took to the paths immediately afterward. The donkey had done well the day before, and he drew less attention in the rough trails this way. The all-terrain vehicles were closely monitored, and fuel was already hard enough to come by, so donkey was the only viable option.

It was a petulant thing, as was to be expected, but it was willing enough to keep moving and didn't wince at Archer's weight. The slow sway rocked Archer into a meditative state. He welcomed the wave of non-thinking. It had all been too much these last two days.

The same conversation played out in his head again and again.

"I am loyal. My loyalty is no question. But you have stretched me almost to my breaking point, Maeva." The vision of her green eyes floated before him; his heart fluttered at the imaginary sight. "But can I do this? I could never betray you, but now betrayal is pitted against betrayal and I don't know if I can stay strong in the moment when I must."

The trail ticked past him, the green lushness of the region made him fall further into nostalgia.

Ariane's eyes. The brown with only flecks of green. Her wisdom and innocence in those early days. Her clear intent and dedication. The future he saw in her eyes. In all their eyes. Their eyes weren't just beautiful like the Queen's; their eyes were powerful.

Yes, they would surpass Maeva. They would, and who knew what the world would become then.

The task started becoming clearer to him. What would the world become with three Queens all with righteous claims to Lower Earth's throne? All with the same fervor to lead, the same ardor to create change, the same power to control.

"I see now, Maeva."

With three such as they were, how could there ever be only one Queen?

"We all kill off the parts of ourselves that threaten our survival."

He knew it too well. The draw, the pull to be something greater. He had destroyed that desire in himself long ago. He had seen the danger, the risk, in letting that yearning thrive. It was best to remain the Queen's loyal aide.

Despite his nature. Despite his longing. Despite his need to dominate her.

All of that he'd long since laid to rest.

He took a deep breath.

Slowly the countryside turned drier, yellower, and his longing descended into deep, silent sorrow. Breaking grass reeds under the donkey's hooves grated on his ears. The wind had a hot sharpness to it. He had to pass to the other side of the Central Mass to reach the agreed location, but there was nothing there. Trees became cacti which became nothingness on dry rock and sand. Such little life. When the new generation had come, they'd been overwhelmed by the Central Mass, he remembered from his lessons, and it wasn't hard to see why. From this angle of the earth, it seemed to go on forever. With the right orientation, it was only a day and a half's journey across the eastern edge, but the first arrivers after the Final War couldn't have known that. Looking at the horizon, he could understand their fear. There was simply nothing there.

His eye caught a scorpion rushing under a rock, and he was pulled back into his body. Casting his eyes across the sand line, more scorpions came into view. And more.

There were thousands of them.

He closed his eyes and put his trust in the donkey. He willed the animal to know where not to step, or this really would be the end of the end. Each sway felt like an eternity as the creature lifted and replaced hoof after hoof. Archer saw the scorpions pull back underneath their protective stones every time they approached. It seemed they wouldn't attack unless they perceived threat. It was just as well, since Archer could think of no way to reassure the tiny deadly beasts.

They continued forward. Archer tightened his thighs on the donkey as he wiped the sweat that had dripped into his eyes.

I can do this. I must, and I will. They love me. They will believe me. And it won't be lies that fall from my lips, it is just what must be told for the world to find peace again. Peace across Lower Earth, that's what they always wanted.

He quit his meditative state and turned his mind to the practicalities. He reached deep in his pocket for the note without realizing how moving his hands would make it so difficult to stay upright on the beast.

He opened the note again, feeling spurred on by the Queen's words.

"She is waiting for you."

He fixed his eyes straight ahead and had no fear. He wasn't far from the next checkpoint. His faith lay in Queen and donkey to see him through another day, each hour growing closer to his mission.

The animal took one step and another until, at last, the checkpoint came into sight. The smoke from the fire rose high in the dusk sky.

34

—————

I was born for this.

Aria moved, soft of foot in snake steps that didn't move the earth as she touched it. She was on top of the ground, almost floating. Brambles and thorny vines caught her arms, but she healed them instantaneously as she moved deeper into the forest. All the years in East Gana had been leading to this.

Archer had explained it all in whispers in the middle of the night. The infiltrator had been sheltering in the Great Rainforest. The infiltrator would kill. The infiltrator had powers they didn't yet understand. The infiltrator had to be stopped. Only Aria could do it.

She had to stop her.

Archer would be there, behind her, just beyond sight. But she had to commit the act. This is what she had been trained for. They didn't know how the infiltrator would react.

Aria had felt Archer's fear as he explained it all. His fear was very real.

A fire crackled ahead, the sound of it so peaceful and natural, in what was to be the least peaceful and natural moment she had ever lived.

Aria pushed the thought aside. She had to be alert in the moment; she had no idea how the infiltrator would react.

Focus.

Aria pulled her awareness inward, trusting the sensations that boiled from within.

Breath moving eastward. She faces away from my approach. No scent. Upper Earth has found new methods of camouflage. Run scenario. Is there more than one? No. One heartbeat, barely discernible. Condition of heart: unknown. Imperceptibility due to health status or another camouflage tactic. Yet to be determined.

The fire came into sight, and Aria felt the doubleness of the other's heartbeat as it fell into perfect rhythm with her own.

Aria paused. The heartbeat was indeed so perfectly like her own.

Focus, you do not know what she's capable of. That is just a beating heart, like any other heart. She is the one who puts it all at risk. Upper Earth cannot take us over. I cannot let it happen. Her life ends and my reign begins tonight. By my hand.

The figure had no sensation of her approach. Draped in cloth, she was huddled by the fire, the smoke rising high into the moonlit sky.

She is both in hiding and marking her position at the same time.

The figure appeared to have no fear of being found, though her face was covered by a hooded cape.

The heartbeat intensified in volume, resounding like bells.

Or was it her own heart?

The sound filled her ears, like being in the tower of a church. She could hardly keep her eyes focused, the noise blasted in her brain.

She approached, at first slow, then faster, and then faster.

She steadied the knife and planned the trajectory to attack from behind, to drive it deep, no error in the target. The figure would never know she was there.

She pulled all her will from deep below, all her drive and all she ever had intended to be. She committed herself to the act and leaped forward, knife high.

But the figure turned.

She couldn't have known –

Aria had no time to finish the thought. Gravity was bringing her down as adrenaline rushed and the hood of the infiltrator shifted only slightly, only a sliver, but behind it, Aria saw her own eye staring back at her. She came down, knife in hand and landed it, deep. Time slowed and she watched the knife pierce the infiltrator, she felt it, almost as though it was in herself, rushing of pain and flying neurons with molecules rushed to the place as she landed strangely on her side, partly suspended above the ground.

She looked down at her body. A spear stood tall from her chest, just below her ribs and she had to close her eyes.

The infiltrator had pulled forth a spear, and Aria had not even seen it before it slid through her gut.

How did she move so fast? I landed the knife. I know I did. But how did she pull out the spear so quickly? How did I not perceive it was there?

She could not take the thought any further. All she felt was warmth. She marveled at her own physiological reaction.

I have no training for this.

She knew she was in pain, the madness of rushing from brain to site, and back again, messages flurrying in speeds she couldn't follow, the pain was only a fragment of the moment. She was consumed. And paralyzed.

Poison.

Every bit of every cell, every pathway, every idea, and memory had only one focus -

Do not give in!

Her consciousness pulled back deeper and her brain went into unnatural slumber. She pulled back as though in a tunnel that was sucking her like a magnet, the strongest magnet in the universe and deep she went, the force taking her down and backward, but she had no fear, no reluctance.

Only warmth.

She was enveloped by warmth, a burning hot but inviting warmth in the deep.

She turned her head, whispering the name she could rely on. He had to be near.

"Archer-"

Her eyes wouldn't focus, all was confused. Poisoned. Was this Upper Earth's doing? A poison-tipped spear? It was medieval but effective. Her eyes closed. She didn't feel the presence of the other anymore, the scout - the woman – the infiltrator.

Dead, she must be dead.

She had landed the dagger in the woman's chest just in time, it must have pierced the heart. The lump of body lay just beyond what she could see through hazed eyes. Now she had to get the spear out before too much blood was lost. She couldn't heal herself. Everything was spinning.

And she couldn't move.

"Archer, where are you?"

Time passed.

She couldn't heal.

Too much time, Archer should have been there.

He promised.

He should have been there.

"I'm here." At last, Archer stood over her. He was in silhouette from the fire, the flames rising behind him. She couldn't make out his face. He did not come any closer to her.

"Archer, is she dead?"

He stepped away, out of sight. Aria tried to send the blood rushing to her wounds, but she was so tired. Archer came back into view, though he stood several feet from her.

"She is dead."

"How can you be sure?"

"I am sure."

She hesitated. The scene was all wrong, but her mind wouldn't clear long enough to give her the answer. It had mostly gone to plan, but the scout's movement. Her face. It didn't make sense. The scout had been swift, silent, and focused.

Aria had to get the spear out and overcome the deep fatigue that was consuming her. She couldn't find the strength to heal. She needed Archer.

He was still there; his body cast shadows from the fire. And still, he did not kneel to tend to her wounds. He kept his distance, but the blood on his hands –

It was all wrong.

"Archer, you have my blood on your hands."

"No."

"I know my blood. I can smell it from here."

Her head rang, deep voices clamoring inside her, but the picture wouldn't come clear and she couldn't will herself to move.

"I promise you, Ariane, my little Aria, it is not your blood."

It is my blood. There is no sense; I can make no sense.

She heard his footsteps approach, the sound scraping at her brain as she struggled for consciousness. His breath brushed her cheek, heavy breath. A droplet fell on her brow as she felt his hand clutch the spear in her chest. She felt the slide of it being removed and finally she could exhale, weakly willing the blood to travel to the place, for the cells to split and renew. Nothing would move as fast as it ought to. Her eyes were closing against her will, her peripheral vision closing in.

He whispered in her ear, "I'm sorry."

She barely heard the words, but she felt the violence as a knife came down into her chest.

And again.

And again.

She could not lift herself. She could not think. She watched from the inside as cell after cell died and shriveled, slowing to a complete stop as her heart wept blood. Her body and mind faded until she had only a passing thought of death.

She let a long, last breath escape her lips as everything inside and out went dark.

35

Let it be quick.

He prayed that she understood why. Why he had no choice. Why he had to do this.

He couldn't bear to watch it even as he brought his hand down into her again. He closed his eyes. He forced himself to hold his breath as he drove it in further, her body unresponsive to either death or life.

He silenced his agony, his heart tearing apart as he pushed the knife even deeper into her.

Go quick, my Aria. Go quick.

She did not move.

He brought her into his arms and twisted the knife in her chest. He felt everything in her let go, little by little. Her legs, her neck, her back. The blood loss, the poison, it would be enough.

His eyes tightly shut, he curled her body into him, cradling her and remembering when she smelled like a baby. He couldn't reconcile the woman in his arms with the infant he'd once held.

He let the tears grow under his lashes and stream down his

chin. He tried to exhale the memories, spit them out but they caught in his throat. He was choking on memories and his lungs burned with them.

Dirty hands, mingled with their bloods, their singular blood. His betrayal made him black inside. His mind was black, his bones were black, his heart was black, his soul went black.

He stopped crying.

Eyes more tightly shut than before, he lowered her to the ground. He feared what would happen if he dared to look upon her. His body was almost too heavy to lift itself.

Right foot.

Left foot.

He stood with eyes still clamped shut. He took a step backward, and then another. Finally, he turned, opened his eyes, and walked away from the fire, the cold night, and his orchestrated scene of death.

He walked in a trance to a creek. He washed his hands and face, but nothing felt clean.

A wash of red went past his eyes, and he shook his head to pull himself into the moment.

Red like blood. Am I seeing blood before my eyes now?

Again the image flew by, and this time he was sure it was human.

Only they can move like that, only my Arianes.

And the Queen.

He stood straighter, listening, but hearing and seeing nothing.

I am going mad. The two are gone. My head is making memories alive from their dead bodies. And the memories are surfacing in the color red.

The figure appeared, far away. She moved toward him, but he couldn't make out the detail. Her movement, slow as the earth and then faster than he could see. It had to be one of them, or both of them together. Both at once, finally reunited in a single body.

He was caught in deer-like fear. Frozen.

I am watching them dead, now a single dead angel walking towards me.

She moved towards him steady and fast, yards away, he thought, but no, she was just there, now to the right, now to the left.

And then she was just in front of him, eye to eye.

But deformed.

For only a flash he saw the face he knew so well, but in a horrid twist of animal and child and woman with eyes abhorrent, red bursting from her head. He gasped in fear as her hands flew at his face and all went black.

36

The Queen stirred, then jolted awake. Upright, alert.

Something is wrong.

She closed her eyes to focus on the sounds of the fortress, the wind echoing through the corridors, nearly silent but audible in the distance. She perceived footsteps in the east wing, on the upper floor. Walking toward her. Then walking away.

The night guard; no reason for this alarm.

She didn't know what woke her, but whatever it was had hit her hard.

Has Archer done it?

She pushed the thought out of her head. He was not to tell her the exact day, this way she remained innocent to its knowledge. It could have happened days earlier or not for days to come.

Closing her eyes, Maeva heard the sounds of the people in her head. She heard their breathing, thousands of lungs lifting in slumbered breath, and an exhale, unencumbered and free. These sounds used to haunt her, for she felt she was never alone. No peace or privacy. Over time she had learned to shut out some of the murmurs.

But some sounds, especially the sounds of massacre from generations past, would boil up from within. It took all her focus not to be consumed when those sounds came. They were low and heavy. Her inheritance from her mother. And her mother's mother. And her mother before that.

And what about the two? Are they gone?

Perhaps. Perhaps, at last, it is done.

She let out a long exhale, one that seemed to have been waiting for years to release. Her body was not as swift to regenerate as it had once been, though in itself that was no cause for alarm. It was to be expected, even given her advanced capability of cellular divide. She would not be infinite; she had never expected to be. Still, she despised the sleep. She was over sixty years old, but her skin was as fresh as one in her thirties.

Her internal condition was a different matter, though she had been well designed indeed.

The freshness in the air swept along the Queen's bare arms. She lifted the heavy velvet cape that had long been the trademark of Lower Earth's queens. The summer heat lingered in her breath.

This night is too dark. The sounds are too loud and the night too dark. Where is the moon?

She roamed the halls, carefully avoiding the night guard, not wanting words to pierce her thinking. Sounds and memories rustled and she listened. She had to trust the voices now more than ever. She would be lost without them.

The announcement of the new royal - her successor - she would have to do it soon, now that the two were gone.

All things must ride gently and cautiously.

She stood still in the hall, allowing herself to go deeper within, to hear the voices that rumbled there. There was a message for her, she knew it, even if she couldn't yet decipher it. And all the better it happened in the dead of the night when she was alone. Not in front of others, not like the episode at court.

Perhaps I should have done this sooner. Perhaps this culling is long overdue. But how could I have known all the consequences?

A sound reached her ears from somewhere beyond the fortress walls. Maeva walked to the windows that faced the city. Central Tower rose in front of her.

Two lights on, floors seventeen and nineteen. Roman still at work. Good.

She was comforted knowing he led all research now, with his impeccable record of reporting. She calmed her breathing.

Her heartbeat accelerated, a change nearly in imperceptible.

Something isn't right. What then? It can't be the culling. It can't have gone wrong. Anything but that.

Archer wouldn't dare disobey her. Certainly, he would try to do right by the two; he would try to give them the peaceful and honorable death he felt they deserved. He wouldn't want someone else to do it and risk it being blunt and undignified.

But the feeling wouldn't leave her.

I should have known the calm would be short-lived.

Roman's body came into her view from the Tower, standing on the nineteenth floor, in front of the full-length window. Maeva focused in on his hair, his jaw, his gaze. He was far, but not too far for her. She could see the look across his face. His mouth was turned in angles, the skin pulled forward as he brought up his hands and buried his face in them.

From behind Roman, Archer came into view, his face twisting.

Archer.

From the nineteenth floor, Archer cried out, inaudible to all in the city except Maeva's ears.

His torment pierced the night and struck her ears with such violence that she recoiled before breaking into a run toward Central Tower.

37

"You're a complete mess, Archer. You're going to ruin everything, heavens help us, you might have already." Roman punched his cabinet. "What were you thinking, just leaving them there that way?"

"I don't know." The fever was getting worse and Archer thought he might throw up. A sob from deep inside him escaped his lips.

"You won't be able to keep this a secret." His words were spitting and sharp, but Archer could only nod. Roman stepped closer to him. "There is too much relying on this. If they live —"

"They don't. They can't. You weren't there!" Archer snapped, feeling guilt and righteousness and anger all at once.

"Do you think she knows? She must know."

"She knows. She might not know she knows, but she knows."

"You're a traitor, Archer."

"Archer, a traitor?" The Queen arrived silently as she always did, startling both of them and jolting them out of the argument.

"My Queen," Archer moved toward her.

"Now, now, Archer, you've had quite the accusation thrown at you. Be out with it, fast."

"I've done as you commanded," he spat out.

The Queen stared him down, a movement ticking within her eyes. He felt the guilt oozing out his pores.

She knows.

"Where are the bodies then?"

"I killed them, Maeva."

"You were to mark the bodies. Where are they, Archer?"

There was no hiding it anymore. "I don't know."

The Queen's nails slashed at the left side of his face. He reeled against the office wall, never having seen the hand raise from her side. She betrayed no evidence of the attack. She grew taller over him. Towering with fury.

He put his hands out to her "Maeva, listen, I have done everything you asked - " he couldn't bring himself to continue.

The Queen lowered her chin, burning her eyes at him. "I will go too far if I stay here another moment." She turned and ran from the room, away from the Tower, running faster than Archer's eyes could follow.

"Maeva, please!" He cried, desperate, coarse tears pushing out, a break in his voice. "Please!"

But she was gone.

38

Soft man! Spoiled man! Dead, dead man!

Everything had changed; the voices deep within had known before she did.

Imagine that I believed in him! The man with the code of Kings! Ha! I should have known. Weak, soft man.

Her instructions to him had been clear. She had faced threats from Man, from Upper Earth, from the failure of science and from her own birth's chaos.

She had conquered over the thousands of others, winning her mother's acceptance, winning the love of the people.

She had looked into the next generation and made the decision. The culling.

There could only be one - she'd had to make a choice. She had assigned the near-divine act of saving Lower Earth from eventual civil war to the only man she trusted.

The one. Only him. She had only trusted him. She trusted him because they trusted him, he could get close to them without suspecting. That's what she'd thought.

And now it was all crashing down around her. All because she wouldn't do it herself.

Oh, but I was a fool, wasn't I? I could have known. If I had listened to those who came before. I could have guessed he would betray me. Lucius was right. More right than he knew.

She ran to the fortress hill's edge, desperate to be out of sight before it exploded in her. A scream boiled from her gut, up her lungs, through her throat, and burst with such ferocity that birds sleeping across the city block flew from her in fear. As she moved deeper into the forest, her fingernails dug trenches in her hands, her fist so tight that blood drew and trickled down, melting into the burgundy of her velvet nightdress.

She quieted her heart.

Quiet now.

She felt the air slide into her nose. Her nostrils relax. Air cooling her brain. A rush of calmness. Sanity returning.

They must be dead. Certainly, they are dead.

She watched from the inside as she healed the lesions on her hands, willing the wounds to close, splitting new cells until her cheek had only a gentle glow of new flesh. A moment's pause and she was back in control. She began the walk back to her quarters in the fortress as the old queens spoke from deep within her.

"They are alive."

They must be dead. He did that much.

"But dead women don't vanish into thin air."

They're still human. Eaten by animals. They're gone.

Looking out from her bedroom window she saw a blur in the distance under the moonlight of the clear sky. She knew who it was.

Her last hope.

Her last Ariane.

She waited for the message. The confirmation. Thank goodness she sent for confirmation. She just needed to know that the bodies were there, or even just that there was no sign of them whatsoever. A sign that what had been too many was now only one.

One Queen.

One Successor.

One Future for Lower Earth.

Silent steps approached that no human ears could hear except those of a Queen. She raised her nose in the air but had no sign of scent of the one approaching.

No scent, no sound - the code has been perfectly executed in her. Just let her speak the words that they are gone.

Her voice spoke with barely more than a whisper as she passed the door. Almost as quickly as it came, it was gone. Only the words were left hanging in the air.

"I still feel them."

Questions rose and the Queen raced through her mind. Memories flew in and out as if single panels on a screen moving faster than light and she searched. She searched through years, through generations, for an answer.

She still feels them.

But their status is unknown.

They might be dead. She might be feeling them from the dead just as I feel those within me who are long dead.

That would be logical.

"Be pragmatic, Maeva." the voices chided.

"The two might be planning to come for you now. This might be the end of it all."

The old voices spoke, and she let them in. She dove even deeper into them, giving them space to maneuver, a stage on which to announce. This was dangerous, she knew that well enough. But she couldn't avoid them this time. The voices may have had their own motives, but she was never meant to play at Queen for a dying world. There was more she had to know before making her next move.

Inhaling deeply, she moved her consciousness into the dark

place inside her. She felt like she was suffocating but she had to ask the questions from those who came before. She pulled at her clothes, needing space, needing air. The sensation of the night breeze soothed her. She let herself go, into the deeper cells, into the old ones. She plunged in without hesitation. She dove.

Mother! Mother of mother! What do you say to this? Please! Please tell me what I must do!

She sought, begging in her deepest place, tearing into her code. She listened as the generations boiled up, dead but not silent. She listened to all that her mother and her mother's mother and her mother's mother's mother taught her.

It came back in a blast of explosion, and then, like a bomb's mushroom, it pulled back into silent clarity.

The Queen stood tall, assured, young and old at once. She set her eyes somewhere far ahead and nodded.

New plan.

39

Rose ran her fingers through the dark hair of the second sister-self sleeping on the edge of the water. She missed them already even though she hadn't yet left. She burned the memory in so that she could recall it at will. She wanted to remember the fullness of feeling she had when she held them close.

The other one was settled. She, too, a beauty. A beauty saved. A future saved.

It won't be long now. They will awake. Someone will come looking for them and they must fend for themselves.

She had to run.

Two sleeping sister-selves; a lifetime of anguish was beginning to come to good.

Sweet communion.

She felt their souls pushing at her heart and she wanted so badly to stay. To let them see her face. To show them her love, her loyalty to them.

Instead, she ran.

Unseen and unheard, she rode wind-like and arrived at his

doorway, the stench of morning and sweaty sleep emerging from it, but she didn't mind. She hardly even noticed.

40

———

Lucius heard her but pretended he didn't. That way he could feign surprise at her appearance in the door. That always made her smile. He loved to see her smile. It was like all the ugliness of life flew from her face and her eyes sparkled. They radiated when she smiled. No one could smile as she did.

You fat idiot, selfish too. After all she's done and you want to see her smile.

But he did.

He waited, feeling her eyes on him, but hummed to himself in the mirror as he slowly washed his face. He was desperate to know the outcome but pushed his anxiety aside. He wobbled on his semi-paralyzed legs but was determined to stay upright before spending the rest of the day in the rolling coffin.

Ugh, this body, Lucius cursed as he lifted the flaps of fat. He sprayed too-strong cologne and brushed his hair back in a comb-over for the single spot that was thinning, not that anyone would ever see the back of his head through the chair. But still.

Pride, my manly pride.

There she was, waiting, patient and silent, a faraway look and rosy cheeks to match her flaming red hair.

"Well now, look who has returned from the ends of the earth."

But there was no smile. Her bottom lip quivered and a tear fell down her misshaped face.

"How was your trip?" He tried to keep it light, but his voice lowered unintentionally.

She looked at the floor. Her chin nodded up, then down. Up, then down. She looked at him.

Lucius waddled closer and firmly grasped her shoulder. Trying to control his heart rate, he barely managed to speak.

"Were you able to get there safely?"

She nodded.

His heartbeat quickened. At least she hadn't been cut off before she began.

He had to know but was afraid to ask. Almost in a whisper, he breathed it out.

"Were you seen?"

She raised her eyes with a look Lucius understood to mean that she probably had been.

"That's okay, you've done your part. That was all you could do. You risked a lot, you see that, little fairy? You did more than your share."

She shook her head fiercely. "No."

"Yes, you did."

"NO!"

Lucius was surprised as the fierceness of her response. He didn't know she was capable of speaking loudly. He'd thought her hushed voice was another consequence of the DNA mosaicism.

She whispered, "It was my duty."

"Oh little fairy, come now." He pulled her into an embrace and felt her body relax and heave. She must have traveled fast.

He heard the blood rushing through her. It hadn't been easy, he now understood. She had been scared, so very, very scared.

"So you were frightened, little fairy?"

She pulled back enough that he could see the tears again welling in her eyes. "No, not afraid."

He pulled her in even tighter.

"Okay, it's okay now."

This de facto daughter. Most days it didn't feel worth the agony of seeing himself in the mirror, but he had so many reasons not to give up yet.

And she was by far the most compelling.

He took her face in his giant hands. Her deformity was a blessing to him, a sign of survival and grace. He knew that she was the superior race. More human than any of them. He knew it. After all, he designed her code for it.

"You did well, little fairy."

"Yes, Papa."

"I love it when you call me Papa." He kissed her rippled forehead and let her go as he stumbled to his chair. "Now make me some coffee."

41

The Queen had questions, so many questions. But they would all have to wait. Archer's state was precarious at best, and she preferred his ill silence to the ill blabbering she'd listened to all morning. She'd returned to the fortress, intending to return in the afternoon. Then she would demand he return to his senses.

You can never believe what comes out of a sick man's mouth. There will be ample opportunity to gather the detail later.

But she wasn't sure she wanted the detail. It had been done, clearly had been done. A single look at Archer's face and there was no question. She'd meticulously arranged it. The fears of Upper Earth were valid, Archer would be a normal vehicle for the conversations, both had been primed for the story. For the attack. For each other. There was no reason to believe anything in the plan had changed. He said it himself.

He had killed them.

And yet, the words of the Future Queen rolled back and forth through her mind. Could they live? Could it be possible that they all still lived?

What kind of misguided conscience comes to torment me now? It is done.

Irene slammed the bedroom door behind her. "Queen, we have two decisions that must be referred to your level. You cannot keep rejecting the arrivals."

Irene's voice grated on her.

"This business will not disappear in the distance. The priestesses know something has gone awry. The whole of Gana is talking – "

"Enough! Not today, Irene. You're infuriating! One day I ask for peace. One day."

Irene lowered her chin. "Fine. I will be back later. We must spread a message."

She needed silence and yet no matter where she turned, someone was blabbering in her face.

"Your bath is now ready," the waiting-woman said.

"Obviously, since it's in front of me and I watched you do it. Get out."

Maeva laid in the tub until the water went cold. Clearing everything from her mind.

But she knew the voices would be back.

Footsteps approached. Maeva groaned.

"I can't even see you yet, Irene, and already your presence is unwelcome."

"Maeva, the High Councilor representing West Strangelands awaits your company."

"Send her away, I'm about to take a bath."

"You invited her." Irene lowered her voice. "This was part of the plan, do you remember? You have to plant the seed of – "

"I invited her and now I'm sending her away. Is that clear?"

Irene approached the tub, her eyes flaming. Her voice came out as a hiss. "You are better than this, Maeva. This weakness you're wearing does not hang nicely on you. I don't have to say it. You know it already. There are things we are born to do. Perhaps it's destroying you inside, but that is no matter for anyone else."

"You lecture me?" She did not have the strength for a confrontation now. If only Irene would go away.

"I remind you."

"I have not forgotten."

"Then act the Queen. *Act* it, if you cannot *be* the Queen we need right now."

"Then here is my next Queenly command: Get out."

Irene bowed deep and low and turned to exit.

"You mock me?" Maeva felt the voices screeching inside at the insult. The affront.

Irene didn't turn around.

"I wouldn't dare, my Queen." She left.

The voices were mumbling, agitating, creating something inside her. A protest. None spoke a word loud enough for her to understand, but they weren't quiet enough to ignore. They rang inside her, making her veins quiver, and still not one would speak up enough for her to listen. She lowered herself into the tepid water, hoping to drown them away.

42

He felt the pillow wet under his head. The fever hadn't broken in days. Wilma wanted to call the doctor, but he wouldn't hear of it.

"I'm not sick." His insistence was more like the lazy swatting of a fly. The gashes on his face and neck felt infected, but that was the least of his concerns.

Wilma looked at him sideways. He'd lost track of how many times she'd said he was dying.

"Two weeks maximum, that's all you have left at this rate," she muttered under her breath, but loud enough for him to hear. Then she shook her head and went back to her apartment, knitting in hand.

He turned over in bed, fitfully moving in and out of sleep.

That face, her face, always in double, was in front of his eyes, regardless of whether they were open or closed.

"I'm going mad," he said to the ceiling fan.

Whomp whomp whomp, it agreed.

A guilty conscience kills cleaner than poison, the voice of his Willing Mother echoed in his head, recalling every childhood misdemeanor, white lies, and darker lies. But nothing, nothing compared to what he had done now.

Archer, Archer, the voice of his mother chastised in his ear. *You've been bad, so very bad, Archer.*

He shook his head to send the vision of her away, but she was a stalwart. She wouldn't budge from his inner ear, this dead mother's voice from generations ago mingled with the memory of her soiled apron from his childhood.

Slap slap, she wiped her hands on the apron sides, hand-print of coarse flour caked on her hairline. Slap slap, she smacked him on the ear, the sound pounding into his memory. "Horrid *boy,* you, *boy* who killed us all off when the world almost ended! It was *you!*"

He was sickened and sick, in his head and heart, but he had no words to get it out. Festering, the guilt weighed heavy in his stomach. He felt the burden with each beat of his heart.

In a blink, he was taken back. Ariane, crouching by the water's edge, communion with the creatures that lived within. Ariane, running across the barren field in West Strangelands. That peculiar way she moved, deer-like and free, but fast like a shooting star, her brown hair leaving visual memory in his eyes even after she was gone. Ariane. Always Ariane. Deep brown eyes with shards of green, like broken glass that cut into his heart. That smile which spoke of obligation and love. He was nestled between father and uncle, and sometimes something else he didn't let his mind consciously explore.

A passion for her. A driving need to hold her. Desire.

He had burned for her. Ariane, joy-filled. Ariane, feeling so deeply. Even now he remained lost between the two of them. How he loved them both.

The memory was burned into him, from the time he arrived in Gana, that time he took Ariane's hand, his little Aria. Seven years old but with the gaze of a woman. She'd led him like he was the child to the creek's edge.

"Archer, do you see the fish?"

There had been no fish to see.

"Archer, do you not hear them coming?"

There was nothing to hear, he was sure of it, a silly child, she was just a silly child. He'd always believed they were children like all children.

But the fish came, and how they came, the rushing monsters roaring toward them.

How the fish came.

There had been nothing to hear, no sign of them coming. And she smiled, satisfied and defiant. And so much more powerful than he.

He feared her. Oh, how he feared her.

He awoke with a start.

"Daytime, Archer." A gentle voice sang. "Daytime, dear Archer."

Now I truly am going mad, Archer said in his head. *The Queen at the foot of my bed, singing me awake? What dream is this?*

He dismissed the vision but stayed in his waking dream.

"Please now, Archer," she took a deep breath, her breasts rising in the square-necked velvet, and he was again struck by how beautiful she was in his dreams.

Blinking he waited for the apparition to fade away into his mother's voice and the daytime to turn to night again, but she didn't budge. Instead, she moved closer to him. She looked so real.

"What you did was good, Archer. It was right. It was what had to be done." Her face was even closer, she floated before him. His heartbeat started to pound.

He reached out, gentle giant fingers moving towards the apparition's face. He feared he would reach right through her.

What do I do then? How many bodies must I pierce? How much blood?

But the apparition took his hand, boiling hot in her cool smooth fingers, and brought it to her heart.

"Archer, you're a good man, I have a kind of love for you, the most you could ever expect of me. For all you have done, you have my loyalty and admiration. Do you feel this?"

Her heartbeat was suddenly drumming against his fingers, his knuckles resting fist-like on her bare skin. She opened his hand and held it against her heart.

Caress her! he told his hallucinating self, but he was too afraid. The flesh of her breast, so smooth and cold, clean and fresh. His eyes widened.

She gently laid his hand down on the bed again, where it came from, and stood up solid, towering over him. Cool Queen over gentle giant. Her cheeks tightened and her voice lowered as she looked him hard in the eye.

"Now get up."

43

———————

Look at this man. A complete wreck. How is it that this breed, this strain, this man ruled the world?

"I said, get up, Archer." The marks on his face and neck glared, evidence of his weakness.

She understood on a psychological level why he had turned into this mess. Unwashed, unshaven, distracted, open-mouthed madman.

And these are the genes of the men who tried to oppress us? I can hardly believe it.

And yet, looking down on Archer, seeing him in this state, Maeva felt something for him still.

Affection.

He is fragile. This man is fragile, despite his code, she thought. But responsibility is what responsibility is.

He had no understanding of her responsibility. He was incapable of it. All he'd had to do was follow her instructions.

"Archer, tell me, is it truly done?"

"I loved them."

The heat rose from deep within her, so many voices bursting with her own.

"Is it done?"

"I loved them. I loved you," his mouth hardly moved as he repeated the words again and again.

Loved?

Those eyes, pleading with her.

She hardened herself.

"How could you make me do that, Maeva? How could you?"

Her walls crumbled. He was so small. And somehow she didn't have the answer anymore.

"No more, Archer."

She left.

He promised. He must have done it. He promised.

He had promised, and more so, he promised he would never regret it.

Promises.

Men and their promises, the words of her mother, and her mother's mother, and her mother before that, snuck into the edge of hearing.

44

———————

The constant thump of her heart blasted between her ears. The scar under Aria's shirt throbbed. She hadn't had a chance to check its condition. But it could wait.

The hunter was still close.

Every breath was exaggerated; she tried to mute the sound of her breathing, but it rushed through her brain. Aria focused her attention on any movement across the forest that was out of place. She scanned for miles.

A twig snapped. A slight brush of leaves.

She leaped off again, running, running, running. She covered miles in minutes, even in her compromised state.

Assess condition: Injury well treated. Timeline and caregiver unknown.

She moved slower than the gentle shift of evening air. Listening. The sounds moving closer. Then away. And away. And away.

Continue northward, into Lakes Region. Thick brush and waves to mask identification.

She inhaled down to the base of her lungs, finally slowing as she approached the water's edge. Her reflection came and went with each small wave. She saw enough of her face in the water, enough to raise an alarm quietly in the back of her head.

Deep unconscious. Flesh healing time passed. Open wound. Slight irritation due to inflammation. Cells reuniting across boundaries, crudely cut.

The freezing cold water calmed and soothed. She cleaned off the wound with handfuls of it. The flesh in her cheek remained jagged, but the wound was not entirely new. She ran through her mind the process of healing – her current stage, how long ago it must have happened. The formulas rose and fell in sputters as her head still hadn't fully cleared the cobwebs of deep slumber.

When she had first opened her eyes, she'd heard her pursuer immediately. Instinct had taken over, and she hadn't stopped running since, not even long enough to consider who may have made her unconscious.

The chill will set in. This place is too exposed. Must locate shelter. Better awareness of the environs immediately required.

She perceived no danger. The only scent she found was her own. Another deep breath in and she willed her cells to find each other again, to grow, to multiply, to find each other and repeat. There was a sting in the cheek wound. But it was only flesh.

Water fell down her torso as she lifted the clingy fabric of her shirt. She saw the scar, touched it lightly, the hardness of it extending deep, reaching her kidney. The wound was well-dressed, well cared for, and had been for days. Perhaps a week. Perhaps even two.

And then the questions came flooding in.

She couldn't heal herself without some level of consciousness. How did she not know? She had no memory of the wound, no memory of the healing, no memory of new blood rushing to recreate. A fogginess, drug-like, settled across her eyes as she tried to remember the period before waking.

A sensation came over her, though it wasn't quite fear. Confusion at the unknown.

The word fear had long been shunned in her training.

Questions rolled in as she processed time passed, angle of the waves rolling over her feet, the position of the rising moon, and how many days had passed since she last ate. Her brain recreated itself in the moment, testing pathway after neural pathway, moving through consciousness to deep memory, and there she recalled a feeling of touch.

The hands of a stranger. Eyes closed, she had seen no one but knew someone was there. Flashes of red had moved past her eyelids, red and warm, but she had no answer to the question of who or what it had been.

Who was it? Find the answer. Find it, find it, find it.

Her brain rolled through options and answers and weighed the possibilities in fractions of a second while it processed the time passed.

Movement.

Movement behind her and she swung, landing on the ground, facing it in the stance of spider ready to jump. Her chest grazed the stones below her with every muscle active. Alert.

She perceived no threat at the figure - human, woman - though she didn't understand how it had managed to approach her. She had scanned the vicinity for any sign of life. The woman slowly turned, slow like the earth on the axis of the sun, and all time seemed to hold. Aria watched her spin with the rhythm of the wind, too familiar, like her own body moved, slower than time, undetectable in its movement.

The figure stood.

Their eyes locked.

Time stopped.

45

Hot and cold. Hot and cold. The flutter of butterfly wings, feathered wings, wings of water, gentle and smooth. Hot and cold. Ariane smelled the dusk. Dew of evening tide beginning its rush across the brush and trees. It stayed only a moment, fleeting, kissing the leaf edge before drifting into the air. Cool night air that touched but didn't rest. It was still summer. She began to process.

Summer. Evening. Dew. Lakes.

No longer in West Strangelands.

There had been an enemy.

Water kissed her torso. Arms were twisted without pain, but also without comfort and so she pulled herself upward. Righted the angles of her arms. Her brain adjusted to gravity, time, season. Spinning inside the days, weeks. She was not where she was, but where she had been wouldn't come to her; it was just out of reach as cells collided and re-joined, building pathways, building memory, and then it all came to a stop.

Period of unconscious is unknown. Time to process must be swift; unsure of immediate danger. Where is the enemy?

She did not sense anything nearby, only her own scent of

sweat and slumber mingled with the water. She heard no one, only the sound of a lone gull overhead. And so she waited. Eyes closed. Allowing her brain to focus on recreating past days. She was well. Inside, her organs flexed, testing their condition, pressing into tissue, sending signals.

The only discomfort is from disuse. They have been in slumber. Unnatural and necessary slumber.

Someone had put her there, into that slumber, and then moved her here, near Rainfields, horrid Rainfields of her childhood nightmares. She had been deep in unconscious, for there was no memory to rebuild.

Now the pathways re-joined, rediscovered each other, connecting and recreating skin and muscle and memory. Trying to make the days lost visible again. In stillness she rebuilt tissue, triceps, abdominals, knowing her current danger.

Body remains frailer than may be required.

She rebuilt the cells, first to exist, second to strengthen, third to remember the training. Training infused into muscle fiber and she inhaled. Still, no memory to be found of how she came to be where she was.

Scent. It struck from afar, out of place.

It was her own scent, but it was distanced from her at the same time.

Impossible. Or did I do that? Have I traveled to this place so recklessly that I left my scent behind?

Questions ran through pathways seeking answers, but none came. She had been in West Strangelands. She had been told of an infiltrator. She had been out there somewhere. Her scent still lingered.

Where? Close to here, but not where I now stand. I can't be in two places at once.

Unless…

The pathways broke, a brief second of pause and she lifted her head higher like a hare in a field of hounds. Without daring a muscle, she swept scent first and failed. Ears aware: water lapped to touch the rocks, birdsong. The earth rolled silent and she turned with it, turning to face away from the water, slow as dead time but alive in every pore. Only one grain of sand shifted in her spin, the sounds of it echoing in her excited, alert state. She was softer than gravity. Turning, she arrived unto herself.

She was staring herself in the eye.

46

———————

Neither of them dared to breathe, their eyes locked as the rest of the world, the lapping water, setting sun, sand under their feet, all faded into the background of this moment.

I am out of my body.

The shape in front of her, so perfectly herself, was more perfect than her own reflection.

Aria's mind paused, emptying itself in waiting. She was standing across from her body and couldn't explain it, couldn't even form a question for it. The rising red sun made it surreal. So she waited.

"A perfect reflection," said the other-self.

"Yes."

They stood in this way, both contemplating the unconscious and measuring the possibility of an out of body experience.

"You have a deep wound," said the other.

"I have," she said.

"Mine has healed better than yours," said the other, and then it became clear: they were not the same.

Each an individual woman, but sharing a single scent,

sharing a movement as slow as the earth and as fast as the stars.

They adapted their stance, each seeing it happen in the other. The indication of it was subtle; a slight change in the angle of their shoulders was perhaps the only sign, but they both recognized the distrust at once. They blinked their eyes; their shoulders relaxed again. They shared this moment across their gaze, telling and listening in silent communion.

I can hear her heartbeat.

They quietly listened to the double beat become one as they unintentionally fell into rhythm with each other. And then there were words.

Who are you to me?

It was clear and unmistakable - the words having been shared between them, across the silence. Questions slowly start to rise as pathways in their brains snapped into action, a willed movement of knowledge and memory crashing into each other deep in the rear lobe.

Have I known you before?
Where do you end and I begin?
What are we?

Stepping closer to each other, they each watched the healing, drying, and regrowth of the other's body.

And they felt it inside themselves.

Minutes passed in this state of active healing, skin growing over wound, vein rediscovering vein as new blood rushes, replenishing, cells dividing without immediate consequence of death.

"I know you."

"Yes."

Sister? The silent question between them.

No, the common answer.

"The same."

Questions decades-old reformed in their minds. Answers to

some left stronger silence to others. Neither woman spoke for the many moments it took to compute any memory of the other, of having seen more than one of themselves. They sought within for an answer before attempting to communicate it aloud between them. Words, they both knew, couldn't explain.

"I operate at more than seventy-seven percent."

"As do I."

And with that much was answered.

They were of the same moment, born at the same time to the same mother and of the same design. That was the only remaining answer with any scientific sense. The "how" of their existence was no longer a question, but the meaning of it would demand a new level of reflection. Both fought it; both felt the other fighting it. As it bubbled up from deep within, they pushed it back, assuring themselves the urgency of the moment called for more practical questions to be asked. Feelings could be explored later, if necessary.

"I am the Future Queen."

"I am the Future Queen."

They paused, again in silent computation of risks to realities, often arriving at a blank.

"I am Ariane."

"I was Ariane since before I was born."

"As was I."

Each leaned the slightest of degrees back, chins lifted. Their dark brown hair glistened in the rising red sun, casting fire colors across the whites of their eyes.

Both were now dry but for their clothing. They each intently watched the other continue to heal, feeling inside themselves the subtle changes that came so obviously from the other's body.

Something in the sensation of the other across space was as familiar as Aria's own body.

The gash on her face was closed on the surface; safe now from the risk of infection, but the scar tissue in her gut would take longer to break down.

Aria was more acutely aware now of the implications, as she inwardly explored the surface of the scar, the uppermost edge grazing her lowest rib, extending to her oblique, down and across the start of her kidney.

She explored the moisture of the scar tissue, the only indication of how long she had been unconscious. Five days, at natural healing speed, for without memory of the moment, she could not have accelerated it beyond the normal rate. It should have only taken a couple of hours.

"Five days. I've been out five days," and the other, Aria, nodded, running the calculations.

"Deep unconscious?"

"Must have been. I have no memory of the period. I did not accelerate the healing."

"Nor did I. But you were left to die with such a wound."

"No, the wound was dressed."

The other raised her eyebrows. Someone knew what had happened.

"I've tried seeking the memory, I hit a black wall."

"As do I."

She should have been able to replenish the cells in acceleration, even in regular unconsciousness. Someone had interceded, put up a black wall of forgetfulness, a treatment strong and unnatural, its effects ongoing. Someone had disconnected Aria from herself, for there was nothing there to retrieve.

"I've been made to forget."

"As have I."

They let their voices drop to silence; both held each other's eyes as they sought answers to the questions. Both sought a way to imagine this moment as temporary, fleeting, a brief crash of worlds that would soon dissipate back to reality.

Is she a living reflection?

Is she a shadow? Is she my shadow?

Could something be ruptured? Could she be false?

Continually the questions rose and fell again. A shared future was no part of their training.

They both heard the sound.

Without word or thought, they were both down, ground level, active, and still.

Movement, 100 degrees southwest. Human.

Both were aware of their common reaction, but they filed the observation away.

Survival was their priority.

And someone was trying to kill them.

Their ears sought evidence.

Breaking branches less than a mile away.

No discernible scent beyond our own.

Both found it difficult to interpret beyond their own mutual scent, but both were sure there was something in the distance.

The other hissed, her anger apparent. "Why are we being hunted?"

"I do not know."

"How can I believe you?" she spat out.

"You have no other choice." Aria did not look at her.

Ariane's eyes opened wider; she heard the truth in the other.

Danger had a sound, and they heard it blasting against their skulls. She was not alone in this danger. They were both being hunted.

"We have to move."

They ran.

Side by side, their legs lifted like deer strides over and above the brush and fallen logs. Pushing past branches, hardly touching the forest floor of damp leaves that would have made anyone else slide uncontrollably to the ground. They ran, crossing miles in moments arriving on the north crags, pulling themselves with ease into the high pines that masked their footsteps and heartbeats. One above the other on the trunk, their fingertips braced their weight effortlessly in the tree.

Ariane, below, said, "My vantage point west, clear for four point two miles. Some forest animals, known, normal."

"My vantage point east three point seven miles, unknown scent, moving further eastward. Otherwise clear."

Aria, above, climbed down hand-over-foot to eye level with the other and they shared the same thought.

Find safety.

Cutting across treetops, moving with the wing brush of birds, they were near-silent as they leaped their way, unsure still of their pursuer's abilities. Until that day, both had been sure of her individual superiority.

Now, they were not sure of anything.

In animal-like single-mindedness, they focused in deep concentration for the singular goal.

Shelter.

They found a mid-forest cavern, uncharted and natural. They covered it with leaves and branches, and animal dung to throw off their scent. Like fish into coral, they shimmied their knees and hips, elbows, and neck to find themselves twisted, but able to make eye contact.

Here they waited for hours. Silent, still, and thinking faster than they had ever thought in their lives.

They processed memories, seeking any evidence.

There was a series of recollections, lived experiences from infancy, the physical changes that came from some external force. Little had been difficult for them in the exercise of making meaning, a testament to the advancement of Central Tower's quest in genetic design. But when they had raised these questions with their carers, language having been in place from eight months of age, they had never been given a sufficient answer.

Their collective experience and unique experience blended into one now.

Hip to hip and head to head, memories passed between them like crayons as they began to draw joint histories. Locked eye to eye, they exchanged their childhood through single phrases.

"Phase one."

"Language and feeling. Phase two."

"Unique thought against collective thought. Phase three."

"Physical endurance and regeneration. Phase four."

"Meaning remaking. Phase five."

"Human connection. Phase six."

"Danger."

"Current age: eighteen years."

"Eighteen years, three months, four days."

"Yes."

The secrecy, the betrayal, of two Arianes in the world - it did not fit with what they'd been taught.

Their brains wove through years of experience, seeking a chasm, a moment when they knew each other to be real, something more than a fantasy, this other-self.

"You held my hand."

Neither knew which of them had said it aloud.

They snapped back to a place from long ago. The memory overtook them.

Before language and coherence, before meaning and relationship had sense.

Wrapped in the dark warmth, we were inseparable, unborn infants rolled into each other to feel the other's heart.

More dependent on our shared beat than on the fluid fed from the body above.

We moved world-ward.
We could not see.
But I felt you.
We held hands.
Held hands as we floated ahead.
Life and light.
But what we were to each other was unknown.
You could have been my own consciousness.
You could have been my beating heart.

There, in their burrowed safety hole, they found each other's body and rolled themselves in. Grasping, clinging, seeking that beat.

Together but longing.

A longing they had felt for so long that they believed it part of their existence.

A longing so fulfilled that at last the sounds of their brains dulled in quiet comfort.

They did not breathe.

Legs over waists, arms around necks and ribs, and faces pressed skull to cheek to chin. They laid in silence, neural firing slowed to glacial melts, neither was ready to consider any more than this moment and their shared reality. A single lifeline made twice over. Perfection, twice, in their haunted world. They understood now why they had never felt completely alone. They clung to each other willing again for life to begin. An urge so early, so strong, it overcame them, and they lay like this long after the night sky tore the wild day away. Each felt the movements deep inside the other. Even the voices they each had inside, the old voices of generations past, always disruptive, calmed in shock.

Aria, scar deep inside her, felt it throbbing. "Training is insufficient for this circumstance."

"Indeed." Ariane took a deep breath.

They shared this breath; the gentle breeze of the other caressed her face and it was too familiar, as though it was her own.

"I think I felt you, it must have been you."

"I, too, had those moments."

They actively sought those memories from when they had felt a wave of something, a vibration of electricity. Those moments when they turned expecting to see someone, but no one was there. The changes inside themselves that they had not commanded.

The other looked at her, head shaking slowly. "To even be given the same name. It's almost perverse."

"I had always believed the name Aria was out of affection, but now - now I know what stands behind the name."

"Aria." Ariane moved the word, this name, around her mouth. "No one ever called Ariane anything other than Ariane."

Ariane. Aria. This and the scar were the only discernible differences between them.

"Where were you, *Aria*?"

"East Gana."

"Aria of East Gana. How comfortable you must have been. How privileged in your seaside paradise."

Aria tried to read the spite in Ariane's tone but she did not have enough information to make meaning of it. "Where were you?

"Me? I was in West Strangelands."

Aria tilted her head. West Strangelands was as far as the terrain habitably extended. Called Strangelands for the darkness that set in from the high caves, glacier topped, where twilight lasted for hours and very little had ever been able to grow since the Mist settled. And too close to Rainfields. It was far, literally and figuratively, from her life in Gana.

"How are your wounds?"

"Healing," Ariane's shoulders relaxed. "They had been numerous but only a slight graze of the heart. The lungs had the greatest injury. You?"

Aria lifted her shirt and turned, evidence of the deep wound. "The primary remains thick with scar tissue. Several of the others were deep enough to kill. I should have died. I, too, was saved."

"But by who? This is mad. That you are here before my eyes is mad. Am I mad? Are we mad?"

"No." Aria lifted her chin. "We are a genetic experiment."

Ariane shook her head. "Lucius must be involved."

"He must be."

"And what now of us?"

In this new reality, they were not one Future Queen Ariane: inheritor of the throne, Future of the Nation, raising the land to renewal from the generations of despair since earth crumbled and boiled under man's feet.

The future of Lower Earth, the birth of generations in waiting, sat on the shoulders of the royalty. The royalty had been the driving force of society, seeing the people of Lower Earth regrow, replenish, become stronger and more resistant. Here the Future Queen was the symbol of all that was to come, of all that could be achieved, of the direction of humanity, where every child's face reflected aspects of the Future Queen's own image.

The generations who fought against all the elements to survive, who had relied on the natural royalty to maintain the world in peace, to find ways to rebirth society, they would look to Ariane for resolution.

Ariane, the Future.

Ariane, their Hopes Embodied.

Ariane, their Leader.

They were now two. Two genetically identical selves.

In a world where there was only one Queen.

47

Leaves stirred as footsteps gently swept the forest bed.

It was a movement as slow as the turning earth, invisible in the black of night. Using sensations and sounds that reached deep into the woods, she sought the two, hunting, knowing their scent, not knowing if they still lived. She swept across the distance seeking out signs of the code she knew so well. Hunting the sequence written through her own blood. She could not tell if they were alive or dead and the forest gave no sign. Scent and sight failed to uncover an answer.

The huntress turned homeward to report.

The Queen would be waiting for her.

48

They did not rest. They waited. All motion was on pause, but at the ready. They did not know their hunter and couldn't anticipate the next step.

"We can assume they believe us dead."

"That is the greater likelihood."

"A silent unknown death."

"That is most likely."

"What would have been your next step had I not been here?"

Aria ran the scenario in her mind. "The city. I would go to Geb."

"As would I. In hiding."

"Yes."

"Do you know Geb?"

"I was never permitted."

"Nor was I."

They processed the consequences, the unknowns, and the taste of shame at their ignorance. They sensed the determination in each other.

"Geb will be the seat of change."

"Yes. The priestesses of Gana have no more desire for independence. Not since the death of Habana."

Ariane's eyes were set in the distance. "They cannot possibly know we are two."

"The Queen would not have taken such a step as to divide us if our double birth was known."

"The Queen knows all, I am sure of it."

"The Queen," Aria stopped. "You are close to her?"

Ariane responded without hesitation, "No."

"Nor am I."

"I was close to no one."

"No one?

"It was my preparation. Solitude. My relationship to the land first. Second, to the people as a force for progress. The relationships would be built once I was seated as Queen. No one was to know me until then. For only the purest of relationships. The Queen rarely came. The only one who ever came was-"

"Archer?"

"Yes. Archer."

They sat in silence.

"Archer is across all my memories."

"And mine."

"I outgrew him."

"A long time ago."

"But there was an affinity."

"I felt it too. Can you name it?"

Aria paused. She could not. Several times she had considered it, this strange relationship with a man who came by choice and without reason. A pull between them. The voices had always stirred at his arrival but made no sound. He came regularly and without cause.

"He tried to be a father."

"He did."

"So Archer knows about us."

"And Irene?"

"The Commandante? Difficult to say. She avoids the priestesses."

"But she is a born Ganese."

"She is, but she left their ways behind long ago."

"So you know her well."

"No one knows her well. Habana knew her. Though I was always close to her genetic copy."

Ariane paused. "The Commandante has genetic copy? But the priestesses do not allow it."

"They didn't allow it for a very long time. But Irene made a strong case with Habana. Improved reproduction processes. More advanced techniques used in Geb applied to the Ganese and so on. So far there is only one, and it is of Irene, though in heart they seem quite different." Aria's eyes relaxed, "Leadon. Her name is Leadon. And she is nothing like the Commandante."

"They started with the Commandante?"

"It was the most logical."

"You had no threat from her, Irene's kin?"

"From Leadon? No, not at all. They aren't even kin. Irene gave her code, but nothing more. She doesn't even acknowledge Leadon. The Commandante's ways come from training. From experience. Not from blood. Leadon and I have been close since early childhood. We met not long after I was born and had much in common, being outsiders in Gana."

"We were born."

She paused. "Yes."

"I only had the Rainfields." Ariane looked away.

Aria felt a coolness down her spine. The sounds of Rainfields had rumbled in her for as long as her memory went.

"Rainfields," Aria whispered, memories of nightmares rushing through, "Do they still call you?"

"I hear them, but they do not call me as they call the Queen."

"They call the Queen?"

"I know it too well that they do. She is weaker than me. Than us."

Without speaking, Aria heard the heart quicken in the self across from her. She knew. She too felt it but could suppress the call, push it down with the other voices who threatened control, but who couldn't take her over.

"We are a stronger design than her."

Ariane looked at Aria, "Yes. But there are mysteries in her that I cannot explain."

Aria saw a flash of Ariane's memory. Small visions she knew weren't her own. But she didn't know how to explore them.

Head touching Queen's. Screaming. Beating. Stone walls. Fierce woman. Concrete floor.

"We leave at sundown." Ariane broke Aria's concentration. "Are you healed?"

"Sufficiently."

They held their eyes on each other and together turned to look off towards Geb in the distance. They calculated the voyage and threats, obstacles, and directions.

And they did it with duplicity of thought.

THEY WERE ON THE MOVE. ARIA'S BREATHING WAS SHORTER than it should have been. Her ability to control her functioning was more limited than usual. They passed through miles of forest and hills. Their arms touched as they sat in the brush.

She had taken no time to consider what it meant, this other person, this other self, now beside her in the fading light of day, as real as she was.

She tried to remember the events that took place during

her unconscious period. Every moment came back to her as a quiet hum and nothing more. She could only see it as an underexposed photo. There were vague outlines and she could hear some sounds, but the lull of unconsciousness drove everything else into silence.

Remember. Recall. Where was I before the beach? What chaos, what demon, or friend put me in that place? Put us *in that place?*

Each attempt to scan through muscle memory fell flat. Neural pathways reached their end. It was the darkness of a pillow covering her face. Even when the memory became clearer, it was all red, like a blanket over her eyes. And there she reached the limit of her access. No more memories to be found.

She grunted in frustration and threw a rock at a tree, denting the trunk. The other understood why.

"My memory is covered in red."

"And mine. I get closer, and then it slides farther away."

They moved in silence but for an occasional exhale at the minor effort to scale trees. They slithered between rock forms, small pauses for fresh water when they came upon it. Their bodies joined in mutual fabric, cut only by space.

They read each other's move. And they knew it.

Looking to each other, they recognized the shared awareness.

Familiar.

Dusk turned into night, and they moved ahead without pause, until they found themselves on city limits, a question rising in both their heads.

Decision required, they shared the thought.

Ariane spoke through the dark. "Enemies still unknown."

"Likely recognition on arrival in Geb."

"Agreed."

They looked at each other.

Not yet. She said without saying a word.

The other agreed with a nod.

They lowered themselves as rain began to fall.

Aria watched as the other prepared a small space, pushing brush and bush aside for them to hide. She crawled closer, keeping her low position but needing to look at this other again. Closer. The other looked up and they held each other with their eyes.

Remember.

Aria reached out. Her two hands cupped the face of the other-self in her palms. The rain poured down the other's face, through Aria's fingers, onto the other's neck. Ariane lifted her hands, hands as though breaking through a mirror, and placed them on Aria's cheeks. Her skin responded to the coolness of the water, heating in natural reaction, and the mist burned off. It rose into the air.

Aria watched as the face of the other became veiled in the mist. She removed the hands from her face, holding them in her own.

It was like touching her own skin, feeling it as only can be felt when you touch yourself from inside.

They remained kneeling across from each other as the sun set into darkness. The gulls overhead changed course to avoid their tower of steam.

They leaned forward, touching foreheads and the sound erupted between them, pushing breath at the end of their lungs. They sought out the memory, shared memory, turning with breakneck speed to the inside, firing and flaming their way head-first, hurtling into something. Remembering collectively what they could not remember alone.

They grasped each other as the red rose up in color and form.

Red, of soft touch in red, she was red.

She.

She who came when the red of their blood soaked the

ground. She breathed life back in. Somewhere, unseen, the coma thus given, thus gifted upon them.

Who is she?

I don't know.

They sought and searched within themselves and each other, embracing head to head, clawing at each other's memory, tight grip, to find it, run, run, run. Can't stop until it is there, pushing harder, heat boiling in their brains as they look for it, labyrinth of sound and smell buried, they ran the course within their memories, caught in dead ends, a something, a sound, a belief, a truth that -

She is like us.

But there can only be one.

And yet they were three. This duplicity of face and their red sister self, similar but a world different. The one who saved them at the edge of life.

They could not let go, could not let the power of their shared experience be lost.

Seek it!

Find it!

Go farther into it, what comes before?

Who is there?

Ariane's body jerked against her sister-self, the effort greater than shifting boulders. They were in deeper than they had ever demanded of themselves. They trembled against each other, flesh slapping with the movement inside, and they were upon it, so close.

Go, my sister self, stay within, stay with me. Do not shy away.

I am with you, I am here, and I feel you from the inside.

I feel your scar.

I feel your rushing blood.

What do you see behind the red?

What do you see?

They saw frames of memory, moving pictures of complete

lives led, and the fear of all that came before and what would come and the moment they hid inside themselves. They saw the moment they hid from their own death, saw it coming, and hid away with only a sliver of hope to one day emerge from it.

There, in that place, it crashed upon them both.

It was him.

They thought it to each other. Pulling slowly apart, they breathed the same word, the same enemy, the same betrayer at once.

"Archer."

49

———————

The sun was setting on the horizon. Side by side, they entered the city, down the hill in snake slides. Chests flat, they rose at the undocumented and forgotten gate of Old Geb City. The Geb of the first peoples' day. The stone gate stood against the wind, a searing wind that emerged from the peaks of the Leeside mountain range. The gates were mossed over, a wet surface drawing up from the watershed below. The moisture beaded on the surface, sliding under Ariane's touch. Aria and Ariane looked at each other, the slightest of nods between them before one headed north and the other south.

Northbound, Ariane passed the ruins of the originator's time, long before the Mist. The city of ghosts' way, the superstitious people called it. She stepped through the foundations of a structure, gentle of foot, not letting her weight penetrate the mud. But still walking as the common people walked. Drawing no attention should she be seen out of the corner of someone's eye. This was a time to blend.

Southbound, Aria met the river intake, its wide creek and smoothed stone, the crystals of water shone in the moonlight. All her senses heightened, she sought signs from every direction. She perceived no sound now but her other self; they still had not breached the modern city limits.

She slowed her heartbeat, the sound of it irritating, distracting her from focus. Slowing her breath, she caught the slightest of sounds off in the distance. A stone moved.

Northbound, Ariane heard the stone shift. Someone was walking in their direction, walking towards the old city gate. There would be no reason for this, not at this hour. Miles apart, they each found their cover. One in the river bank, the other in the broken foundations of an old structure.

Humming.

It wasn't recognizable as a tune. Neither could be sure what it was, the voice low and full, a woman. But the song was off-kilter. It rang flat and sideways. Safely distanced from it, the two struggled to keep a hold on the sound. It was disjointed; the sound bubbled through the humming woman's throat.

Northbound, Ariane caught the smallest of sights of the moving figure. Her breath stuck in her chest. The woman's size was unmistakable, the manlike face and square jaw too memorable. The sweat on the giant woman's brow, the sneer, the delight, and stench of blood and duty mingled in the night air. Ariane knew exactly who it was. That face had been burned into Ariane's brain. She had come to West Strangelands more than once. Always to take someone away, someone who would never be seen again.

Marian. The Queen's Guard. She who disguised herself as a Sister in the Strangelands and had committed such horrors there… Ariane knew exactly who she was, though she had changed so much.

She is a distortion of her former self.

Ariane watched the murderer, an explosion of who she had been, all perspectives and all angles stretched. The face half-alive, half-dead, seeming to rot under the moonlight. Ariane was clenched between fear and disgust.

The woman-beast turned its head, snapped it like a whip, and caught Ariane's eye.

Ariane jumped back and away, silent at windspeed, flying sideways into an old tree trunk half sawed down.

She saw me. I saw her.

The eyes had blasted through Ariane, wide eyes, massive eyes that looked fist-like, inhuman, overgrown for their sockets.

Are we being followed?

Ariane tore herself out of the sight of the memory to scan her surroundings in manic review.

Scent.

Sight.

Sensation of ground movement.

Sound, silent. Where are her footsteps? Let her walk away. Where is the sound of her steps?

Not daring a breath, Ariane waited. A short moment later, the humming recommenced, and the footsteps carried on in the direction they had been heading from the start.

Ariane held the air on her tongue, feeling the stakes growing higher before her.

There is no predictable conclusion to our arrival in Geb.

Lying flat against the river loch, Aria in the south sought to understand the sensations running through her body. She'd heard the head snap, knew it was looking away from her, but felt the gaze land on herself. Not herself.

On her other-self.

She burned under it, panicking, feeling infant-like in cold sweats. It wasn't her experience, she wasn't the one being sought, but she felt it deep into herself until the air turned to wood and she was against it. The other one was against it. She was against river rock and tree trunk, in two places at once. She fought her logic to accept it.

She couldn't see the scene, too far, too blurred. Her mind stayed at a distance while inside she was flying, blood rushing to the heart pumping faster and harder against her will. The other's fear vividly inside her.

The humming continued, grating, low discord, and Aria felt the other relax. Resting her head against the side of the loch, she wondered how life would continue with half of herself always somewhere else, with someone else.

Is this how it is to be, forever?

The question rose and had no answer. Firing calculations predicted scenarios without certainty. There was no answer to a question never before asked.

In unison, they restarted their movement from their separate locations, heading east. First low, then growing taller, they simultaneously recognized the need to act "normal". To walk as the common people walked. Draw no attention. Blend.

Listen to the city, they shared their thought.

The collective breath of Geb surfaced and settled with the sounds of lives closing down for the night. Closing doors, closing cupboards, closing shutters, closing eyes. First children, fluttering eyelashes, and slowly the rest of the city's inhabitants.

Ariane listened to sighs and whines, complaints of this and that, meaningless words, light sorrows, and gentle pains. A cry from over there, a momentary wail, the commonness, so common. Ariane marveled at the simplicity of it.

They took cautious steps, a regular pace, regular gait, shoulders held suspended between alert and feigned disinterest.

Sobbing.

Someone sobbing without voice but with such raw emotion that they felt the weight of it. The sound carrying across the city to them. The voice behind the cries was familiar, known to them. A voice of their childhood. A voice that had once soothed them.

And then deceived them.

Archer.

Emptying their lungs of air, they controlled the rising heat on their necks. They observed their anger, and then set it aside.

No rashness, no revenge.

Not now, not yet.

Let him heave it all up, his guts and his heart.

Let him taste his treachery, eat the bile of it.

Now is not the time to confront him.

That time will come.

Walking the southern perimeter, Aria saw the skyline. The rocky cliffs of the west that blended into the fortress. She sat on the hill to absorb it before her, determining the safest route to avoid risk. At least as much as could be foreseen.

Central Tower drove up in the middle of it all, a shocking phallus from the angle where she sat.

Incredible that it was allowed to remain standing. But then, it had been built by men in the height of their power, just before they were to lose it all. It fit well with man's history that this symbol was their hospice and comfort.

Turning her eyes to the fortress, she assessed it for movement. From her position, she could only distinguish the heavy curtains masking lamplight.

The fortress. It was supposed to be her seat, her great reward for killing the infiltrator. That had been the story, the lies, they'd been told.

Nothing is as it was supposed to be.

NORTHBOUND, ARIANE ROUNDED THE OLD POWER STATION. THE electrical combines whirred, deafening those who lived in its wake, the very few who lived in the Power Hub. Ariane adjusted her hearing to listen through it. The last stop before Cork Town commune, the limbo between modern life and life on the outskirts. Outskirts of the city - outskirts of society - the border between them was marked by the power station.

Ariane looked down the unpaved path that was the only entry to the windy alleys of Cork Town, unafraid of being spotted. No one would recognize her in these parts; everyone here had their own story to tell. She carried on forward, pulled deeper into the city. The buildings began to rise around her. Low at first, then swiftly lifting higher into the sky, old blocks blended with new blocks, the concrete's grey darkened in night's shadow. The moon was barely visible; the light it cast was weak.

A woman passed her, oblivious, uninterested. Ariane noted the shape of her hips, which were perfectly like her own. This woman stepped with habitual rise to rise, just as she did. There were no accidents in their design, Ariane was sure.

They have pulled from our DNA for the Willing Woman program.

Another woman crossed, an older woman with her jaw set.

Set like Ariane's was set. So clearly her own.

Focus. Or we will be too distracted in our own image to hear danger when it comes.

ARIA IN THE SOUTH HEARD THE WORDS OF HER OTHER SELF, recommitted to her path, and walked dead into the center of town.

She caught a scent but couldn't place it.

She sought throughout her own memory and the planted memories of the old voices in her. She ran the scent through, but there was no clear match. Too weak a reference, but she understood clearly.

This scent does not belong.

.   .   .

ARIANE IN THE NORTH HEARD THE THOUGHT AND RESISTED THE urge to run inwards to the city. She kept her gait steady, her vision clear.

And then the scent hit her too.

Rounding an apartment block it struck her, pungent, unrecognizable. Slowly, even slower, she sought it out.

Hound to fox.

ARIA IN THE SOUTH RAN THE ALLEYS, NEAR INVISIBLE, HER speed unnoticed in the break between buildings. She took the risk; the scent demanded it. And then she was there.

A wood stove burned in the ground floor apartment of a Cork Town street. Here was the origin of this scent. Aria saw a woman kneeling in front of it. The woman's back was rounded over, looking at something in her lap. Her shoulders lifted, her head rose. Aria saw her profile. She was almost right, but yet not quite. The curve of her nose, the angle of her brow. Aria inhaled sharply as Ariane arrived beside her. They gazed a moment longer before sharing the thought.

She is not one of us.

The woman stood and turned, as Aria and Ariane pulled themselves out of sight against the concrete window block. Backs to the wall, hidden in shadow. They heard the woman's steps, heavier than any in Lower Earth when her heel struck the ground. It was the smallest of details. The woman may have passed unnoticed in the street, but for Aria and Ariane, it was all too obvious.

A scout is living amongst us.

They looked at each other in the fading dusk light and ran through the hosts of possibilities, the predictions, the ratio of likely to impossible.

Nothing was impossible anymore.

Their logic had been faulty from the start, but the neural

pathways autocorrected and laid avenues before them hereto dismissed on the wind.

Time passed this way, hooked eye to eye while the worlds of danger and possibility spoke through them until they were interrupted with a raindrop. It landed on Ariane's cheek, and the other saw it. All thought paused and they shared a nod to find shelter.

An abandoned sewer duct gave them privacy and peace. The small pipe warded off curious onlookers. They pulled their bodies in tight to each other, sliding first pointed feet, interwoven knees, hip to hip, and bust to bust with arms stretched overhead. They slithered inwards to the pipe and to each other.

Mouth to ear they heard each other's near-stopped breath. Ariane with head on top rested her cheek on the other. And while it seemed they could get no closer than they were, they came to hold each other in embrace, the resting muscles now pulling in tighter, their cheeks pressed. The Ariane of Strange-lands felt the warm breath from the Aria of Gana above her. It met her own exhale on its procession; the air rolled seamlessly from one face to the next, across the landscape of themselves. The two breaths moved as one into the black metal of the pipe below.

They moved on before dawn, having shared the night in turns of rest, changing heart rate their sign to take guard. They glided outwards from their resting place, gentle writhing to free themselves from the pipe's constraint. The outline of Central Tower consumed their view and together they began winding their way towards it.

Ariane slid into the crack of a slightly open window where a child slept. She re-emerged with fresh clothes, close enough in size for an appearance of decency. They slipped on the leather soles as they walked.

The sun threatened to rise as they calculated entry points to the Tower.

Front, impossible. Rear, challenging but possible. Windows and half balconies of fire ladders, preferred.

Everything appeared shut tight against the night's rain.

If we are fast.

If we are agile.

If we can maneuver quickly enough.

They took the first ladder in a jump, the second in a step, and then tried the next window on the rung. Locked shut. Thrusting upwards they pressed against each entry for some give. And they found one.

It lifted easily below her fingers, and the other nodded approval. They were hidden enough by the metal fire escape that their entry would be unnoticed.

50

———

R oman's mind raced at the Queen's words. He couldn't believe what he was hearing.

The backroom men were right. She's going to cancel the Male Program.

He tried to control his thoughts and just listen without weighing all the consequences at once.

The Queen took a deep breath and continued. "Our resources are limited. Time is running out. We've been at this for a very, very long time, but the urgency of this cannot be overtaken by a pipe dream. Roman, we need to move on. We need to prepare this world for the inevitable. War will be on our doorstep within this generation."

"My Queen, I - "

She lifted her hand, but her eyes stayed trained on him in that disquieting way she so often did. He felt like he was being eaten alive, being absorbed into her.

Roman looked to Archer, who stood in the corner, staring, unmoving. He'd been a wreck ever since he'd reemerged in the Tower two days earlier. His skin had yellowed.

"I am sure you have much to say," she waved her hand.

"But first, listen. I am no fool, I know you have access to the records. But beyond all that, you must understand that when I was born, I was among thousands who wanted my place." She took a deep, almost labored breath. "What set me apart was not simply superiority. No, no. I was born with an instinct that goes back to our first generation. Perhaps the greatest gift the Mist gave us, passed down the royal lines." She came close to him. She took his hand and placed his thumb on her cheek, his fingers wrapping along the side of her neck. He kept his grip loose, but she squeezed his hand, encouraging him to grasp her throat tight.

"Feel this. When I call on them, feel what happens, and don't try to explain it."

She closed her eyes. He was wary but knew better than to speak. He couldn't imagine what was going to happen. So he waited.

Her eyes tensed, her brow pulled in, and then he felt it, the rushing, the blood that moved like a waterfall, blood flying through and across her body. He felt it, a mad river rush, chaos over rapids and crashing, her blood crashing into itself. His hand pulled tighter into her, like a magnet pull, he worried he was strangling her, but he couldn't stop it. He finally forced his hand to pull away.

Is she human? Even our designs can't produce that.

"This is how I know, Roman."

He was frozen on the spot. The backroom men were both right and wrong. She was something apart from the rest - he'd felt it in her.

He'd felt it with his own hands.

"Do you need me to explain it any more to you?"

Still, there must be a chance, however small.

"What happens to the Male Program?"

"It's on pause. It's not over. Nothing is ever really over. But we have to focus now. The time has come, Roman. Today. We need to look across the entire country and put ourselves one generation from now. Come with me." She took his hand and led him to the window. Below the people were starting to come together, a gentle movement of masses and the occasional laugh or call that rose above the din. He searched for the right words, the right argument, but the rush of her blood had washed his head clear. He was walking in a dream.

"You see? They know nothing of what is to come. But we do. Roman, I don't want to order you. I want you to see what I see, and tell me what must be done." She guided his head delicately to the window, fingertips under his chin. "What do you see?"

He hesitated. "Ignorance."

"Yes."

"Peacefulness."

"Yes."

"Laughter."

"Yes."

He looked at the Queen. "Life."

"Yes," she smiled, so beautiful, so soft. "Life worth preserving."

He nodded.

But it was not only life he saw.

He saw death. Death of every man who ever could have been. That was what she was telling him. There would be no pause on the Program. They would all be long dead before any chance of a living boy would be viable. He felt it.

And there was nothing he could do.

"You want a campaign?"

"Yes, Roman, a campaign. One that will ensure we have enough to fight when the day comes. An evolution of the Willing Women to something more, something greater. A program for the next generation of Lower Earth."

"How many?"

"That's your job, Roman. You're not just a scientist anymore."

Roman cocked his head.

A political role? Perhaps this isn't the end.

He looked at Archer, who hadn't shown the slightest reaction. Hadn't made a sound. His forehead had a light layer of sweat as he looked off somewhere in the distance with his lips slightly parted.

Roman felt the Queen looking at him sideways, curious, waiting. Her brow melted with bemusement.

"You will be making history, Roman. You - and the next Queen."

Next Queen? Already?

He could only nod.

Scouts among them. War. A new Queen. A massive program of increasing population. He saw there was only one path available to him. Everything else closed, every other fantasy, every other hope.

This is what she is telling me. There is only one answer I can give.

"I must get to work."

"I'll expect you to report daily."

"Yes, my Queen."

"You call me Maeva now. Everything has changed."

"Yes, Maeva."

And she left. As quick as she came, she was gone. Archer, who hadn't moved since the Queen led him in, continued to stare at the space where she'd stood. Roman glanced at the latest male sequence on his desk and prayed this day didn't mark the death of his dream.

HOW PAINFUL, THIS EXPLAINING AT EVERY TURN.

Maeva rushed back to the fortress. Having Roman on her

side was the most important first development, especially given Archer's fragility. When his hand was wrapped around her neck, she could see it in his eyes, she knew she had him. She'd squeezed his hand tighter, curious at his reaction.

The flow of the blood struck him hard.

His touch felt good. It was so rare she felt touch like this. Meaningful touch. She relished it, the heat, the variety of each finger, each finger's pressure, separate, quivering. She'd closed her eyes for just a moment to take it in. His touch blended with her rushing blood. The voices screeched from within, excited. They always loved it when she felt threatened. An ecstasy resonated somewhere deep inside her, somewhere forgotten, in someone else's life.

She let him release her.

It will all move ahead now. Roman will see to it. And he certainly won't stray with Archer looking over his shoulder.

Archer, notwithstanding his current state.

AN ANNOUNCEMENT RANG OUT, NOT WITH MARY'S VOICE, BUT A man's. Adam and Sara jolted upright at the sound.

"Colleagues. This is Roman of the first line, nineteenth floor. On this Tuesday of fourteen generations since the Mist."

Across the building, movement ground to halt. Roman's voice echoed through hallways, labs, clinics, and offices. Faces found each other with confusion, curiosity, fear. This was unprecedented.

"What is he doing?" Sara asked.

"I have no idea." Adam had heard no word of any new programs, nor setbacks. His stomach knotted.

"Today at what will be a special Tuesday Briefing you will learn some troubling news. I won't go into the details here," he paused. "That is for the Queen to tell. However, there will be a role for us, a new role and duties that we must take up for the good of our country, for our future. Our work is not simply to further society. Our work is to preserve society, protect our way of life, and lead us all into a future where we can be certain of survival."

"What on earth has happened," Adam muttered.

"Make your way to the main square for the briefing at the required time. You will be told more in due course at our assembly tomorrow."

"I'm going up there."

"I'm coming with you."

Roman's door was open and they saw Isaac's back, sitting across from Roman's desk, his posture unreadable from behind.

Roman stood, not saying a word. They all waited.

Sara broke the silence. "Well?"

Isaac swiveled in the chair. "There's no use. He's not telling."

Adam and Sara turned to Roman, who shrugged. "It's not for me to tell."

Sara lifted her hands, incredulous. "And that's it?"

A voice spoke up from the back of the room, "That's it. Don't you get it? This is all coming from a place much higher up than any of us."

They all turned to find Archer learning in the corner, near the window that faced the rear of Central Tower. None of them had seen him there when they walked in. Archer looked yellow, his eyes dark and his shoulders pulled forward. His voice was weak and rough.

Adam knew what this meant. The Queen's hand made this happen, whatever *this* was. He walked toward Roman, noting that Roman's nostrils were flared, despite his attempt to stand tall and strong.

He's in a delicate state.

"Okay, okay, Roman, we get it. We would have liked to get

the news early, that's all," he smiled, trying to be charming, trying to be nonchalant, "You know where to find us when the time comes."

"Yes. In the meantime, you all have important work you should be doing."

But no one could move just yet. Roman had always been set apart, but a torrent had grown between them and him, a boundary they couldn't cross. Adam read the room and saw this was not a battle they should take on. Not now.

"You heard the man," Adam again put the on the smile, "Let's get out of here and let the boss think."

Isaac lifted himself out of the chair and moved toward the door. "Yep, lots of important work. And I'm guessing more important work is coming our way after today's special briefing."

Roman didn't try to hide his relief. He offered a quick, not-quite-genuine smile. "Later," was all he could get out.

The door shut behind Adam, Sara, and Isaac as they moved toward the elevator.

"And now?" Adam said, hushed.

Isaac jumped in, "We don't have long."

"We really don't."

"I'll make arrangements for early disclosure of 4957. We'll have to induce," Sara took a deep breath.

"Today?"

"Today."

They all agreed in silence.

With no more words, they walked in a trance to their desks, looking out the window into the square as the first wave of the crowd was met by the second and third, none of them expecting anything different from this Tuesday briefing. None of them with any hint to what was going to happen in the Tower. Adam saw Sara bite her lower lip.

"It is now or never," she said, expressionless. "I was always pretty sure that we were as good as dead."

ARCHER TURNED TO A SMALL CHAIR IN THE CORNER OF Roman's office once the others had left and let his weight fall into it. He felt Roman's eyes on him. He knew he looked ill, but he didn't care. It had taken everything he had in him just to get out of the apartment. For the rest, he just didn't care. Another set of judging eyes made no difference now.

"Are you just going to sit there?"

"For now." Archer couldn't meet his eyes. His stomach turned.

"You do as you will. I have a lot to prepare before the briefing." Roman paused. A wave of something gentler came across his face. He waited, said nothing, and then left.

Archer let out his breath, at last, the drama of the morning catching up. It was like only half his brain was working. But even so, the weight of everything settled on his chest as questions flooded in.

The same questions. Always the same questions.

Why? Is there any answer to how a man can be so manipulated? Is there no right or wrong in this earth, just two shades of wrong for a simple moment of right? It was so fleeting, had felt right, but it's left behind so much wrong.

Was there really ever any choice in it anyhow? Any of it?

Something moved.

The space below the wooden cabinet moved. Archer was sure he saw it.

My eyes play tricks on me. Again. I cannot trust myself anymore.

He shook his head.

Not enough sleep. Or water. I must be dehydrated.

It moved again. Then the curtain top was waving though

there was no breeze in the room.

"I'm hallucinating," he said out loud. "I need water." Archer looked around the office but there was no sink, no spout, nothing. Just the silent office writhing around him.

He rubbed his eyes.

When he removed his hands, she was in front of him. Eye to eye their noses almost touched. He turned away from the mirage.

But she was there too. They were both there, the dead and beautiful Arianes he had held in his arms as they bled.

She's looking into me, into my heart, my weak heart, oh heavens, such a weak heart. I must tell her, even if she is only a ghost. I have to explain why I did what I did.

He opened his mouth but no sound would come out. It was stuck in his gut, retching on the inside. They circled him, close, speeding up, he saw nothing but whirls of color. They were too close and too fast. He felt her brush against his arm, the back of his leg with another one of hers, she was there, they were there, and there were surrounding him. He felt as though he were dead alongside them. They danced this sick silent dead dance. He felt their blood again oozing down his arm, shifting the hairs, resting thick, old burgundy wine on his skin.

Gliding across the floor in a dead girl waltz, he looked out the windows to the west where groups of people started to gather, preparing for the special briefing though it was still hours away. He couldn't bear to see the crowds as he halluci-nated above them. He felt the heat of their dead bodies against him, but couldn't seem to snap himself out of it.

Look at them down there. They know nothing, these people. Nothing of regret, the taunting of the past. Nothing about the workings of our world. Nothing.

He could almost feel their breath on him, but he knew ghosts didn't breathe. He turned, aiming himself away from the square, anywhere else that he could be alone with his hauntings. Away from the rising tides of voices gathering for the announcement.

He moved across the office, falling into their bodies, his memory of their bodies. Rebounding, back erect, their rubber dead bodies soft as he fell against them. He tried to set his eyes, to focus a little more, but his head was spinning faster than time. He opened his mouth again, but still no sound came. The ghosts remained silent as they whirred around him.

They are too close. I can't see them. Let me just rest my eyes on them one more time. Maybe they will understand if they can see it in my eyes.

He saw an ear, a lip, a cheek. Felt her breath, sweet and cool air on his neck, and then the other one breathed against his cheek. He took in the sensation but their breathing suffocated him, and he stumbled against the window on the other side. They had danced the length of the office. At least below this side of the Tower, there was no one, no voices, no little heads busily rushing about. Below was quiet, abandoned.

Just a little air, more air, I can't breathe in this madness.

They pressed up against him as he half opened the window, his body feeling their bodies. His body betrayed him, their bodies pushed against him. He didn't understand the rush happening within him; this unused place that was so long dead suddenly coming alive, pushing against them. He felt his head would explode, he was going to be sick. Sick with shame. Their bodies and his body and their burning heat against him. He saw nothing but her eye, one eye, and then four eyes across his face, their heads touching side by side. He couldn't bear it another second, their beautiful brown eyes with broken glass green cutting into him.

Not another second. Don't look at me. Don't make me feel. Not for another second.

He turned, climbed the window, and fell with relief to his death. His body broke into a mound between the dumpsters below.

51

Lucy had slept well, despite her belly always seeming to be in the way.

She was still relatively small, certainly smaller than many of the women she had seen carrying around the city. Even so, she felt the little being's movements every moment of the day. Even its heartbeat seemed to echo in her head.

As she lay down to sleep, she tossed and turned, talking to the little one, humming and getting lost in thought until a rumble reminded her that they were two in the bed.

"Now, now, little one, what are you doing in there, tickling me from the inside?" she giggled, high pitched and worry-free. It had been, even by Lower Earth standards, an incredibly easy pregnancy. Nearly from the moment it was inside her, Lucy had felt a kind of peace. It wasn't just emotional, it was physiological, and her body responded with jubilance. Her skin was clearer, her back was stronger, her legs carried her tall. The horror stories she'd heard of raging hormones and swollen feet, sleepless nights, and cramping had bypassed her completely. It was only the fact of having a tummy larger than she was used to that prevented her from sleeping like, well, a baby.

She was fascinated. It was nothing like she expected, somehow. Despite all the news, the stories people told, and the leaflets she read in school - somehow when she was lying in bed and heard the sound of that life inside, she felt like she was a part of something bigger. It was only four months of pregnancy to endure and then she'd have played her part in society. So what if she hadn't passed her exams? Seventeen was a viable age to be a Willing Mother.

"Can you see that sky, little one?"

The sun rose deep red. Lucy let her eyes rest on it until it burned too much to keep looking.

"It is beautiful." She blinked but the burn of the sun stayed in her vision. Laying on the little sofa, she let herself drift off to a dreamless nap.

The doorbell rang.

Lucy started. She didn't know what time it was.

She was greeted by a woman with dark hair and dark green eyes, who smiled hesitantly. The woman looked nervous.

"Hi, Are you Lucy, Lucy of the Crynal rating?"

"Crynal, yes." No one else had used that term except Doctor Easom.

The woman smiled, visibly more at ease.

"I'm Sara of the seventh line. From the Tower. I'm going to need you to get dressed as we have discovered some complications with your pregnancy."

"You come here... you make house calls for testing?"

Lucy was confused, but perhaps this was all part of the process. It was true that she had never asked how they would be in communication with her. The calendar on the fridge had made no mention of these tests.

"Not tests, Lucy. It's time. You need to give birth today."

Sara's brain madly sought the right words.

Find the right thing to say, come on. Make the girl, this exceptionally young girl, feel at ease.

Lucy had to be completely confident in Sara's hands. If she suspected anything was unusual, she might go to the clinic and inquire, or worse. Sara gave a gentle smile with as much authenticity as she could pull together.

"I know this is surprising." She let her face grow solemn. "But we fear for your health and the health of the child. You could be in imminent danger."

Lies, they needed to collect pre-birth samples and then induce. Sara hoped she lied as well to teenagers as she did to adults. "Can you be ready in ten minutes? I can wait."

"Yes. Yes, sure."

In a bit of a daze, Lucy turned and exited the room. Sara let herself into the neatly-arranged though small apartment and closed the door behind her. The seconds felt like hours. Finally, Lucy emerged and slid her feet into sandals, opening the door and leading the way out, trance-like.

"Thank you, Lucy, I understand this was unforeseen."

"The clinic is that way," Lucy pointed in the opposite direction from where Sara was leading her.

"This needs to be done elsewhere, Lucy." Sara took in a deep breath. "The clinic is not prepared for the special needs of this delivery. Did Doctor Easom explain to you that you have the Crynal phenotype?"

"Of course, that's my ID."

"Yes, but did she explain that as a result you carry additional risk?"

Lucy visibly tried to remember. After a moment she lifted her head. "Doctor Easom never said risk. Never. Special, that was the word she used. And select."

"All that is true, Lucy." They continued walking.

"And - " Lucy stopped.

Sara's breathing was shallow. They were on a tight timeline. She needed the girl to walk.

"And what, Lucy?"

"She said I was never supposed to do this. As in, any of this." Lucy stepped ahead with more conviction than she'd had before. "Let's go."

Sara tried not to smile with relief.

"You can trust me, Lucy. This is what's best for you and for the baby. Because you have selected this route, there are additional consequences. But be assured, this is for all of Lower Earth. You chose this, you recall?"

"Yes."

"It's going to be okay. That's why I'm here. We're going to the seventh floor of Central Tower."

"Okay, right." It looked as though Lucy might say something more, but she didn't. Sara heard her muttering quietly to herself but could only pick out a couple of words.

"Naïve. I knew it."

They walked swiftly through the streets of Geb. Mary's face was alit on the screens for the entire mile-and-a-half long journey.

"And so this campaign will begin within forty-eight hours." Mary's voice was more shrill than usual. "The Queen will tell you all. Come to the square for the emergency Tuesday Briefing in just over one hour," the screen blared. "We will be more numerous, we must! At last, we have the rallying cry to increase our world, to reclaim all that was ours before the Mist! We are all a part of this, the changing human landscape. Be on time, do not delay," Mary tilted her head forward toward the camera, "Your attendance is essential."

Lucy looked over at Sara.

"Don't worry, we have an exception. We're almost there."

Thousands of people were on the move, heading towards the main square. Everyone was pressed shoulder to shoulder;

the streets weren't wide enough to take the human traffic. Sounds blared out the screens in a cacophony that at once put the crowd on edge and also somehow kept them contained. Mothers held their children's hands high so that they didn't get separated in the orderly but uncontrolled channel.

Lucy took Sara's arm. Sara searched across the faces for someone familiar, anyone who might see them and report, but the mass of people became denser the closer they got to the Tower. All dark-haired women of average to tall height. No one stood out. The Direction had become the norm - Sara could see it across the moving mass of women.

She let them be pulled along by the crowd, everyone was heading towards the Main City Square. They could duck out just before and enter Central Tower mostly unnoticed.

Sara had never seen the streets like this before.

THEY WOVE THEIR WAY THROUGH DIFFERENT LANES OF DESKS, mostly empty as the historic Tuesday Briefing had most staff already out of the Tower and milling in the streets. Sara tried to look natural. They were largely ignored by anyone they passed.

If anyone asks questions, she is simply Lucy of 4968, a test case that required mild modifications, a normal review at this stage.

Anyone who looked at the file would see the same, and they would be dismissed. Normal behavior.

And all lies.

Sara calmed her breathing. She had to be absolutely sure of herself now, to put this child-with-child at ease. It was true, Lucy is the best hope they had, but Sara had never liked it when they took girls this young into the program.

She isn't a Willing Woman. Lucy with the Crynal phenotype is barely more than a girl. Easom would have seen that, seen the ID, and chosen to forget her age. Too valuable, too special. Too opportunistic, that Lydia Easom.

Sara shrugged it off. She and the others had to deal with the reality at hand, not the one they wished they had. If they didn't induce in the right conditions then there was the chance it wouldn't make it. If they waited, it might be too late. They'd be discovered.

They arrived at the laboratory, sterile and well-placed behind all the other labs. This was the least used, the least accessed. Sara could see Lucy was once again doubtful. But this windowless defunct room at the end of an unused hall alone made it the perfect place.

Adam and Isaac had set it up in relative privacy, just "doing Sara a favor" when asked what they were doing.

"Hi Lucy," Isaac squeezed out of clenched lips as they entered. The light layer of sweat on his brow was disconcerting. He'd been edging towards a heart attack for years. Or maybe worse – physical degradation.

God, don't let him keel over now. Sara touched the lava amulet, an involuntary reaction conditioned from childhood.

Lucy took a very slow step forward, seemingly surprised to see men. She looked back at Sara.

Adam stepped forward. "Lucy, my name is Adam Lane. You're going to put on this gown in the adjacent anteroom while we finish setting up the equipment here." He handed her the folded gown and waited for her to respond.

She did as told, silent, and cooperative. She walked to the anteroom and closed the door. Isaac looked at Sara, Sara looked at Adam. Adam watched the door as it clicked shut. They stood unmoving, listening to the shuffling behind the door, none of them ready to act. They looked at each other with a mix of fear and dread.

And then conviction.

It started with Adam who stood just a little taller, and that was the only signal they all needed. They looked at one another, rooted solidly to the ground and ready. This was the first critical moment.

The anteroom door creaked open. Adam, Sara, and Isaac turned to face Lucy, their shoulders collectively set and their eyes clear.

"I'm ready." Lucy kept her chin low. She looked even younger in the medical gown. She kept her hand resting on the lava stone around her neck.

Adam lowered his voice, casting a smile to the girl that was just right for the moment.

"Okay, great. Come lie down here. This will hurt, but it is necessary. You're going to have to endure this, Lucy. And then soon you'll be ready to give birth. Are you ready?" He looked her in the eye, head tilted, an air of confidence and under-standing.

The room stood still, and time seemed to have stopped; not one of the foursome dared to take a breath.

"Yes," Lucy whispered, and they broke her skin with the needles.

52

The two looked away from the window. Away from Archer's body. His mad scrambling towards certain death nineteen floors below had never been their intent.

They rested against each other, backs to the window, arms touching. Quieting the squall in their minds. Ariane rested her head on the other one's shoulder for just a moment's pause.

Archer's mad utterances as he had stumbled toward the window confirmed it for them. It was what they had believed to be true, for Archer took orders from only one master.

The chaos of the moment passed and they shifted back into shared strategy across their thoughts:

The Queen must be held to account.

We must find what we came for.

We will confront her with evidence.

Aria walked to the window facing the main square. The people below come into view, the fortress in the distance a black swatch against the grey sky. The Tower would soon be empty, the announcement having raised alarm across every floor. As soon as the Queen began to speak, they would have free reign. It was the richest possible opportunity to find any answers the Tower might hold.

A voice rang out on the loudspeaker.

This was their chance. They moved with the speed of a fox being hunted. Doors and corridors led them from answerless files to blank stares of half-aware guards. Anyone who mattered was at the briefing. The Tower was all but a tomb, even though just minutes before the bustle in its hallways had been constant.

Constructed as a series of circuits, the Tower was a maze. Ariane opened one door to find herself facing two more that led in opposite directions. They understood the math behind it and agreed their course wordlessly. The sensation within them, the communication, had become self-evident. The silent agreements came naturally. They glided, hips nearly touching, as they moved in perfect rhythm. They searched behind each corridor, lab, and office, into the vacated spaces.

They went through pages upon pages as the voices outside gained in volume.

These files are meaningless.

Variations on code for stronger gut flora, resilience to malaria, development of brain cell regeneration. But none of that mattered to them now.

They were looking for secrets.

Likely the files on royal gene development are not stored here.

Likely in the fortress.

Or with Lucius directly.

They turned a circuit and at once were hit by multiple voices, strained and nervous, off in the distance but in the Tower. They could hardly make sense of it. The voices came from a different floor, but the two easily followed the source of the sound. They moved quickly, but slow enough to take the safest route around the last few prying eyes.

Mary's eyes came alive outside on the screen, the light glaring into the Tower.

"To the square, all of Geb, the time has come for the Queen's briefing. This is a time for bravery and celebration of how far we have come. There is much to say. Find your way now before the Queen takes her place. Come, listen to today's announcement, for, People of Geb, all People of Lower Earth, today is a day that will be remembered! Make your way to the square!"

The two approached the door from which the strained voices emerged. The room was next to a stairwell that gave access to a sewer pipe; a most unlikely spot for a meeting. They listened.

"You need to relax. This won't be easy, but it won't be as bad as you think, either." A woman.

"Have you done it?" A young woman whispered.

"No, but I've witnessed it. And it's been designed, you've been designed. You specifically, Lucy, you have been equipped to do this better than anyone. Do you hear me? Look at me, keep your eyes open and your muscles pushing."

"Which muscles?"

"You'll know. Can you feel it?"

A scream from the young woman escaped the doorway.

"Shhhh. Sara, keep her quiet!" A man.

"It'll blend in with everyone going to the square, this is the perfect moment." Another man.

"Can't you give me something to make it easier?"

"Too risky."

"He means that a natural birth will be best for you and the - child."

"Oh - this is not what I expected."

"No one expects it, sweetie. You're doing just fine."

"Just keep your voice down, damn it."

"Give the kid a break."

"You give me a break, Adam. We've all got our necks on the line here."

"Why is this happening to me here? Why can't I be in the clinic?"

"Lucy, we explained, you are the beginning of something entirely new. This is so far an untold story."

"That doesn't even make sense!"

Something hit the door, like a body being flung. Aria and Ariane looked at each other, jumping to a new vantage point, just out of sight, in case the door opened.

And it did.

"That's it, I'm out of here."

"I'm sorry, I didn't know my leg would kick out like that."

"Lucy, you're fine. He should have stood further back."

A fat man waddled past, wiping his forehead, not noticing at all the two identical bodies clasping at the ceiling above him in the adjacent hall. He just walked by.

They craned their necks and saw a wreck of a room, sheets hanging on the walls in a pseudo hospital cube, a table in the middle with a young woman spread eagle, a baby's head just beginning to crest from her body.

"Shut the damn door, Adam!" The woman's voice hissed.

A man's hand reached out from the unseen, slamming it shut.

The sounds of birth continued. Aria and Ariane looked towards each other and moved back to the floor. They walked away in slow, measured steps, the scene of chaos behind the door no wiser to their presence.

They reached the center of the floor, the open landing that looked down and up the entire building, as the Queen's voice echoed on the speaker.

"My people, my children, my friends."

Ariane looked at Aria, searching her eyes, before jumping over the rail, falling the seven floors to the lobby.

"We have reached a new era in Lower Earth's history. And you will be a part of it."

Aria leaned over the rail to find her other self below, looking up to her. They nodded and agreed. Time to separate. They would find each other again when it was necessary. Ariane moved across the floor as if floating, an ear to the speaker, an ear to the door beyond the hall, and the life-giving underway behind it.

"You know of the campaign. You know of the threats we face. But soon, my friends, I will have news to share that will set our world alight with joy!"

The crowd erupted, but Aria's ears were consumed by the gasp of first breath coming from behind that door. The cheers outside continued but Aria shared the thought with her other-self.

The child - the sound - it is not human.

'Hush, hush, child, please," Aria heard the voice of the woman consoling Lower Earth's youngest inhabitant. "Now Lucy, I have to go. And I have to take the child with me."

"But just a moment, please, let me hold my - "

"You have done something wonderful, but Lucy, you cannot see it. I can't allow you - "

The voice of the young mother lowered to a rasp. "What is that?"

"Lucy, you have to understand - "

She hissed even quieter, "What *is* that?"

The man's voice spoke, "Lucy, you have done something wonderful. You have given life to someone who will change the course of history. You have - "

"Get it away from me," Lucy's voice was barely audible to Aria. Barely more than a breath. "Get it away."

The child was silent, not so much as a whimper since its first moment on earth. Aria wished she could look beyond the door, but this was not the day, neither for her to see it, nor for her to be seen.

She ran the stairs to the roof of Central Tower with even more questions than when she came.

On the opposite side of the Tower from the crowds, Aria watched as a cat found Archer's body, and curled to sleep in the broken twist of his dead right arm.

53

―――――

From the Queen's perching place on the balcony, a sound reached her ears that was barely more than a gasp. She waited, holding the quieting crowd in suspense as she tried to listen to whispered words down a passageway at the back of Central Tower.

54
____

The child lay silent but for the occasional breath in the box where Sara had placed it next to Lucy. Lucy continued to refuse to look. Adam had been present in multiple test births and he had never been shocked by the sight, but he couldn't see the little body from where he stood.

They watched as Lucy redressed. She then walked out the door without looking back.

Pulling back the light muslin, Adam gasped. He then understood Lucy's reaction.

"What is it? I don't recognize it from the code."

"It's beautiful, Adam. It's what we have."

There was no reference for this. Normal head and ears with some oversizing; facial shape that was just about right - something wrong with the eyes - but as soon as the torso came into view, the contortions were painful to look at, though the child seemed to be perfectly comfortable.

"We don't have long," Sara spoke through clenched teeth.

"Let's do what we must." Adam took a deep breath and forced his eyes to take it in.

This is what you created, Adam. Now look on the creature as you should.

Adam smiled and removed all covers. The child was quiet and patient. Curious.

They took the post-birth samples as quickly as possible, gathering them into a protected sack. True refrigeration would have to wait, they had to get out. Still, the child didn't make a sound, despite the syringes and grafts.

It was as if it understood.

There was no sampling protocol to cover their current subject, but they were nonetheless adept. Swabs of mouth, ears, and anus. Protected, tagged, sorted. Stem cells collected during birth, set aside, stored, tagged. The blood samples were the most extensive, as they did not know what to expect. They planned for all possibilities, drawing tissue from organs and muscles. Protected, tagged, sorted, stored. With each minute Adam's brow became damper and damper, his heartbeat accelerating. He felt like he was running a sprint but at the finish line was a gladiator pit. He again looked on the child's body.

"Move," Sara pushed him out of the way as he stood frozen. "We can do all the thinking we want later. Now we act. Lucius is waiting for us."

"Yes, later," but he didn't budge.

"Now!" Sara hissed. "You take the child, Adam. You take it in the sack. This is it." Sara's strapped everything to her body. All the samples, protected, tagged, and sorted, were stored against her abdomen, armpits, and ankles.

One last look at each other, and without further word Sara burst out the stairway door. Adam could hear her running down the first few floors of the east wing, while he remained.

Outside, the Queen's briefing was wrapping up in the traditional way, thought its message had been anything but traditional.

"The screens tell you all. They remain your friends. I too

am your friend, your Queen. As ever, you know that I belong
to you, even more than you to me. Be kind and be strong!"

This is it.

Looking at the quiet baby in his arms, who asked for
nothing and had a look of gentle query on its face, Adam
stepped out into the corridor, full of purpose, but breathing
shallower than he wanted.

Just walk, Adam. Left, right, left, right. A normal day.

He held the bag open, not wanting to close in the
newborn just yet. The baby looked into his eyes with a
tender smile, or at least an expression of comfort. Adam had
to take the internal stairwell. It was steep and deep into the
heart of the building, but he couldn't see any other way to be
sure none of the returning employees would catch sight of
them.

Outside, cheers rose from the square. Even in the heart of
the tower, Adam could hear them. He lowered himself down
the escape ladder. Step by step, with each rung he inhaled,
though he felt like he was never breathing out. He became
light-headed.

"Damn," his foot slipped just a little on the edge of the
rung.

Now is not the time to pass out.

With the baby strapped to his chest in the large duffel bag,
he descended lower and lower. The weight of the child and his
responsibility pulled him down, yanking at his lungs. He tried
to focus his mind.

Just one step. Take only one step at a time.

The cool damp air of the basement swirled around him,
and still, the newborn was silent. Adam looked at it with
wonder. It looked right back, with equal wonder. Adam smiled.
The baby stared and began to stir, the fabric of the sack
cutting into its arms and sides, cutting off circulation.

"Shhh, shhh, now." Adam realized he was completely

unequipped to coo a child. This had never been part of their plan.

Moving towards the fire door, Adam shifted the baby's body, adjusting it so the bag looked like any other bag someone would take to work. He moved the child to his side, farther from his core, trying to look natural.

A sound emerged from the sack. It was quiet, barely audible, but it was out of place. It was the only sound to emerge from the child since it first came into the world.

"Now, now, this isn't the time for that." Adam played with its little arms and tried to smile reassuringly. Stuffing the sheet around its body, he protected it as much as possible, knowing that as soon as he walked out the door, he had to pretend his bag was nothing more than a change of clothes. It would be a delicate balance to keep the child quiet as it bounced against his hip on the street. Adam wasn't sure what to expect, but he put the thought aside, zipped the bag, stood tall, and walked out into the late morning sun.

Each step was a strain, but he tried to move with the appearance of confidence. The streets were near empty along the west end of the Tower, and he felt a sense of relief for it. He heard his breathing echoing in his head; his little precious package at his side remained unmoving but for the occasional shift or roll.

Now what?

Suddenly their planning seemed to fly from his mind. Everything felt different and new. Walking on, going through the same city streets he'd walked his whole life, he saw each corner with new eyes.

The turn onto the main strip was the hardest. His mind played tricks on him. People emerged from the square in vivid conversation. He thought each set of eyes was out to get him, or his bag. How could he possibly keep this living, breathing secret in front of them?

He froze in a moment of absolute paranoia, then jolted himself out of it.

You're a statistician, he told himself, *ignore your feet and run the probabilities.*

His steps fell into a rhythm; the panic subsided. His mind raced up and down the potentialities. No one was paying any attention to him. They were all engrossed in the aftermath of the Queen's announcement, anticipating what might come. He listened to their conversations as he passed.

"You really think we're heading to war?"

"Such incredible discoveries!"

"We're going to be fine."

"Perhaps she's finally gotten Gana under control. You know they are mad out there."

A young woman brushed past him, gently knocking the bag.

"Oh, sorry," she said and carried on, but the baby began to shift and, in a low rumble, emit a sound that didn't belong on the street.

Adam swiftly stepped into a recessed doorway and unzipped the bag.

"Shhhh, quiet now, this is it, we're almost there," facing the door, he prayed they all just keep walking by. He put his hand inside the bag to gently stroke the child's body, but he felt the disturbance, the strange twisting, and jerked his hand away. The child noticed and began again breathing quickly, warning of more sound to come.

"Shhhhh, no, no, shhhh." Adam urgently tried to comfort it. He stroked it, putting aside his judgment; after all, he had been its savior. It should have been terminated long before this. But here they were. Looking at the generosity in its eyes, Adam knew he was right to believe. This would be the child that would change their course of history.

Little by little the child settled.

Slowly Adam stepped out from the door frame, glancing left and right, and walked to the next alleyway, trying to keep the bag immobile. He had to get off the streets where people were bustling about. The risks were too great.

He turned the corner into the alley and allowed his eyes to shut for just a moment. The fear was overcoming his ability to see.

And then he heard her.

55

———

The Queen's ears perked again at the sound.

A baby's cry should not catch her attention. No, this was something different. Something unidentifiable. It was audible only to her even across the din of the thousands greeting and laughing. The sound was clear as a bell, undeniable, and she couldn't ignore it.

She cocked her head. The sound was somehow both familiar and new.

Thousands of babies were across the city. They all cried. But they sounded the same as each other with only minor variations.

This sound - this had a depth to it. It wasn't loud, wasn't far, and wasn't the cry of just any child.

She took a moment to take in the surroundings, allowing the remaining crowd to watch her think.

The Tower is quiet; most of the staff are here. Where's Adam?

The fortress had the normal rumblings, people moving at a quicker pace than usual. Steps heavy with the food platters, swift movements that were excited and cheerful.

What then is this threat?

"Is something wrong?" Irene asked as the Queen turns around. "Your look as if-"

"I don't know." The Queen turned back to look at the crowd lingering and chatting, none of them aware of what was happening among them.

Irene approached, climbing the platform alongside the Queen's seat. "What is it?"

"A sound."

"A sound?"

"It doesn't belong."

Irene cocked her head, "A scout?"

"No."

"I'll prepare the Guard."

"No, not yet. First, I will go."

Below the people continued milling and greeting each other in a state of general excitement. A group of women demonstrated a little dance routine, a spontaneous performance that brought a crowd around them. They sang and taught the simple movements to their onlookers, kicking and waving their hands. Others caught on and even more joined. From above it was like watching a flower gathering petals as the women moved towards different centers of activity. The Queen saw nothing of note in them, nor to the east, nor to the south.

Where did it come from?

Maeva scanned across, seeking anything out of place.

"Could it be a child from outside the city?" Irene offered. "And therefore a sound that is unusual to your ears? Perhaps from Gana, as you know we have different ways of raising children-"

"No. I can tell a baby's cry. This isn't a baby. Or it isn't - " she couldn't find a word to describe it.

And then she heard it the sound again.

It's not human.

She was out of her seat, across the square and walking past Central Tower in the moment of a breath, almost invisible to everyone but Irene, who had witnessed her ways many times before.

The Queen moved almost leisurely past Central Tower, listening through the floors. There were only sounds she recognized. Tapping, and clinking, turning of pages, doors. Nothing out of place, not now.

She could smell it, a mingle of fluids and skin, almost familiar, and yet with a tone so distinct she finally recognized it. She recognized it because it was in her own skin. Familiar and foreign, for only a few beyond the Royal line had it.

But this scent was contorted, debauched, something terribly wrong, out of place.

She quickened her steps. First, she saw the sack.

Then she saw the man.

He turned with the being, whatever it was, into the alley four hundred feet ahead. Maeva moved and was immediately there.

Turning the corner, the betrayal came more clearly into view.

Adam's back was to her; he didn't see, hear, or sense her. She watched as he opened the bag and paused before caressing the anomaly.

"Why, hello," she said, sounding and feeling curious, but the voices began to grow from deep within her.

He turned and met her eye to eye.

His act will not go unpunished!

The voices rose from within and Maeva let them guide her hand to Adam's throat.

56

———

Lucius waited for what felt like years for any report. Holed up in his Cork Town flat, he didn't move more than a few inches once the designated hour arrived. He tried to pause all thoughts, all expectations. So many times he'd learned that things never went to plan. And so he waited, hovering somewhere over real life but with the occasional jab of pain, fear, or thrill. Adam and the others would get there when they got there, and no sooner.

In that suspended state, he found a quiet peace with the past.

Memories floated by his eyes, he exhaled them away like wisps of dust caught in a sunlight ray. Off it would go - and he knew that all those moments that came before had always been leading to this. He felt himself becoming new. A freshness inside him that he had almost forgotten; he hadn't felt it since that moment at Rainfields when his *piece de resistance* had been ready. When the incubation program had been at its height. All the belief and faith he'd poured into that program, the opportunity to find the genetic mix that would finally overcome the Mist.

But that was before he knew the Old Queen had twisted his dream into her own reality. His faith had burned to the ground that day in Rainfields.

Rainfields.

His spine stiffened.

The smell of the burning came alive in his nose again. It had been fierce, that burning. He felt himself being taken out of the now, taken back to that time.

RAINFIELDS.

Watching sun turn to cold, burning cold and the fire. In his former body. His real body.

In her madness, she hadn't seen him approach from the east while the sun set in the west. She was a frenzy of black skirts and black hair.

Maeva.

She had raced past from left to right, far wing to near wing, pulling it down, ripping apart the station, cursing the land and the sky and her mother. He could not hold his eyes on her. The speed and imprint of color as she moved hurt him to watch. He stayed back, knowing any movement risked catching her attention.

So much he hadn't known, and couldn't have known. The limits of his own arrogance. The limits of his physical body, which was then still tall, broad, muscular, refined. Whole. Functional.

He could not have known his landscape for the Male Program would become the Old Queen's sick riddle on her own genetic offspring.

Maeva. Still so young, barely eighteen. The queens who'd come before had all begun their reigns much, much later. Lucius wondered at the consequences of an adolescent queen and felt he was watching some of them before his eyes. The young Queen tore away at what had been his near-triumph, his almost-greatest success. All the incubators smashed; the files ripped. She set them on fire.

He felt her pain with her. He witnessed it, and he experienced it, somewhere deeper than he knew feelings could be felt.

The young Queen rested but a moment on her haunches. She was consumed, livid, the scent of wrath seeping out her skin. And yet – Lucius saw it – she was fragile.

It's my fault, I made her fragile, the voices - it is my fault, I pushed the design too far.

Overcome with shame, Lucius had to hold her, to comfort the girl. She was the closest thing he had to kin.

The pull of her emotion, raw and magnetic, drew him in. Her eyes were seeing beyond, into the distance, to the cliffs. He watched her step in a trance, deathly slow, like the earth had stopped and all was frozen but the sound of her dress brushing past her calf as she pushed on through time and space.

Her lungs expanded with each breath and he could hear it in his ears like he heard his own breath.

Is it her breath or mine?

He was suddenly aware that she was walking to her death.

Just like the old Queen. His instinct rang out the alarm. He didn't know whether to run to her or to run away.

If she jumped, he could not bear to witness it.

This is it, he thought, *this is how it feels to love a child.*

Closing his eyes, he listened for the voice of human instinct.

He followed her. Stepping with as much silence as his body would allow, taut and tight, he controlled each muscle's move. He could not emulate her walk, though he tried. She barely left any sign of having touched the ground, slow with the spin of the earth and light flutter of breath, her feet brushed by. And he followed. The sound of the crashing waves grew, becoming like thunder as they approached. Was it coming for them or were they going to it? He couldn't tell as his eyes tunneled in on her. He didn't dare look away.

She stepped.

He stepped.

She sighed half a breath. He held his closer in.

He heard her name coming from the cliffs.

This is madness, he thought, *I'm being sucked into her madness.*

Louder her name rose into the sky, and she looked for it, frightened. Her eyes, such deep green, he was swimming in her eyes, feeling her fear, following too far behind to save her if she really walked to the edge.

She won't walk to the edge. She won't.

He stopped.

She was walking to the edge.

Panic alit and suddenly he was back in his body, hard and fast slamming into it.

"Maeva!" he cried out, screaming against the waves and wind and that voice that drew her forward. That Old Queen's voice calling her forward. He screamed against it, screamed at her.

"You are mine, Maeva! You never belonged to her!"

All the air was sucked out of the earth. He was sure of it.

Nothing moved.

"Mine, Maeva. My child. Not hers. You are only her blood. I am your creator. Don't go, don't go to the edge."

He froze.

No sound, no breath, no time.

The waves seemed held in place, frozen white bulbs waiting for the clock to start again.

She turned to see him, staring into his soul with blazing eyes.

And she ran.

Inland.

He saw only the imprint of her body where it had been. She was gone. He felt the absence of her as she ran past, the panic that had remained in place after she'd gone. The memory of panic. Only after several minutes did he find the strength to move.

She was saved.

"Saved."

The memory lifted and he was left back where he started.

Did she even know it was me? Had she seen me in that flash?

He stared down at himself. So much had changed since that day. But he was still the man he had been, though stuffed inside all this mess of body. He was the man who had saved the Queen, saved his design, saved her from that unknown silent enemy who called her name on the waves.

The current moment washed over him. He was still waiting alone in Cork Town, waiting for someone, anyone, to arrive at the door.

"Heavens, what is happening out there?" he asked himself aloud.

When his fairy appeared back at the door, he felt no comfort. It was the look on her face.

"Ah, yes, there you are. I was just thinking it was time for news."

She didn't speak.

"Come now. I'm ready. I can handle it."

"No." Her deformed face twisted.

"Yes, dear." His heart was pounding. "Come now. What is it?"

A tear rolled down her cheek. She choked on her throat, seemingly unable to make a sound.

"No words."

Lucius stood. He took a deep breath and waddled over to her. He didn't want to ask. But he had to know.

"Just tell me what you saw."

"He won't be coming. Adam won't be coming." she inhaled the word, "Ever."

Lucius nodded, short and fast nods. His head nodded without stopping.

The mass of red hair waited, her chest rising and falling in swallowed sobs.

"Yes, yes - " he kept nodding, "One could expect that." Nodding. "He was only human."

His silent sobbing began, and she ran into him, holding as much of him in her arms as she could.

He sobbed for his only son, for the world's only son. The one who could have changed it all.

The whirr of the fan drowned out the quiet violence of angry tears.

He held his little girl close, her red hair full and falling over him, comforting. He knew she was hurting inside for him. But this was his loss. He felt it in the center of his gut, the center of his soul.

He didn't hear Sara come in.

Didn't hear her opening her cloak.

Didn't hear the vials clink as she unstrapped them from her body and placed them on his little metal table.

57

Aria turned to Ariane.

"Do you feel this?"

"Yes. They hide in plain sight."

The two were only just beginning to understand the real situation facing Lower Earth. The foreigner they had spotted on entry to the city was not at all the only one.

There are scouts everywhere. They shared the thought, still stepping softly around corners and keeping their heads low. A woman caught their sights.

The first sign was a burst of hair. Hair that waved just so, wind-like in its movement. It was out of nature for the peoples of Lower Earth. They knew it immediately and watched the villain from afar. She turned and looked in the direction of Aria and Ariane, but didn't seem to know she had been identified.

"Perhaps they aren't as perceptive as we believed," Ariane whispered.

"How long do you think she's been here?"

"She seems at ease with the people, speaking and moving like them. It has been some time."

Aria nodded, processing.

Situation more advanced than believed. Scenarios are multiple without more input. Impossible to calculate the consequences until more is known.

"Do you think the Queen knows?"

They ran the probabilities through their minds, but the pathways came empty. Too many variables, too little information. The Queen's behavior too erratic to know.

The woman lifted her eyes at that moment, catching them staring. She shifted her weight, turning slowly, unremitting, and holding their glance. She continued to do the wash but did not let her eyes lower. She held the two in her sights, her hands slowly running up and down the washboard, moving with grace and simplicity. A smile started to curl on her lips.

The two perceived her evil intentions.

"We must move."

"She will expose us."

"She's already decided she will."

"I sensed it too."

"Run."

A voice rose behind them, not unfriendly but filled with the menace Aria knew would follow.

"We must be more careful," Aria lowered her voice to a whisper. "We don't know what they know."

"Any one of them could be after us."

They looked at each other and shared their uncertainty.

"Nothing is as the Queen described."

"We have no time to reflect on it."

"Listen!" Ariane pulled Aria toward her by the arm, her fingers pushing imprints into her skin. "I hear others." The stood, listening, becoming aware of how acute their situation was. "We cannot continue running recklessly around the city."

"They will catch us out immediately."

"We need a plan."

They pulled their faces further back under their hoods.

Stepping as the ordinary people did, one foot at a time, they made their way into the shadow of a new city apartment block, into the back range. The only sound was the sewage pipes blasting into the grate behind. They would be left alone here to think.

Aria recalled the moments her body changed in the night, the muscle that shred and rebuilt without her will. Finally, she understood. As they stood in the shadows, their muscles flexed in response to each other.

The reflection has my face and my body.

They cut the cells and shared them between us.

We live the same physiology. We can read the situation better together.

We are far more powerful together.

They sat side by side in identical folds of legs and arms on knees, back to the wall as putrid thrusts of sewage filled the air in smell and sound. They held each other with their eyes, searching in behind them. Knowing the answers were inside. She only had to find them. She inside she.

They leaned forward, bowing their eyes, letting them close as they felt the heat from the other approach. Waves of heat, so palpable and so real. So close and familiar, their first memories flooded in shared moments of joy and fear.

Their heads touched and burned fires between them. They exhaled the heat with a barely audible cry.

Together they were so much more.

Their molecules moved faster, harder, than they ever had.

Together, their firing synapses made apparent what was only a hint when they were each their separate self: their lives depended on the next twenty-four hours and on how they handled the city of betrayers, for the betrayers were everywhere and would seek them out.

Their lives depended on the Queen.

The organized chaos of weighted options flew between them faster than light.

To see the Queen immediately: not sufficiently informed. Run: but stay within the city. Be amongst them: but only with great care. Together: no. Separate: no. Other options: in hiding, suspicious; in daylight: apart; appearance: too close, too clear. Someone will know.

Someone knows already.

The scout with the washing.

She plays the long game.

She has been here for years.

Perhaps her whole life.

She will betray us.

She will betray us all.

And they had their first answer.

They ran through the city, returning to the washing place, just in time to see her packing it into the bin, strolling as in any other day to the line.

She is the enemy.

The washing woman's head snapped to them, eyes set as the leopard on prey.

The two took their posture; this was the defining moment.

Does she hear us think?

The woman smiled, rotting teeth behind the soft, rosy lips, they couldn't tell if she heard or was just responding to their stare.

They were upon her without pause − hands on neck and twisting - and then they were gone.

The body laid limp in the streets, snapped neck so gentle that no one would know the cause of death until they cut her up, if they cut her at all. She'll be called out as a flawed design, just another death from a period of flawed designs. They would only discover the cause if someone dared to dig deeper, beyond the customary way.

They ran to the deepest southern tip of the city, on the edge of the jungled mass.

They breathed heavy air into heavy lungs as they fell against the palms and slid down to sit. Knees folded, heads on crossed arms. The rough dead palm leaves beneath them cut into their cloaks, leaving impressions on their skin. Without thinking, they smoothed the spots from the inside. Moving heat and blood, just to find a moment's comfort.

"We have killed an ant on the crest of an anthill."

Ariane nodded. "She died very easily."

"They are not hard to kill."

"But perhaps hard to identify in the crowd."

"They have blended well."

Ariane nodded.

They sat in deceiving stillness. Waves of information crashed through neural pathways to old sounds and smells as their heads in present time pulled together like magnets, closer to each other, unable to avoid it.

They were held hostage by the force of a lifetime of absence of the other.

Which next step?

So much more makes sense and yet rational thought has lost its luster.

The movement of space and time in their memory blended with the present moment and they came up empty, mutual emptiness in seeking answers for their next move.

Their heads touched and the flame reignited between them, so hot it burned, seeming to meld them, welding them together.

This is what we trained for, she said without speaking and the other felt it.

It was not to have all the answers, but to face the unknown and lead in the right direction.

That is what we were trained to do.

This is what we were born to do.

Underneath them their feet lifted, pulling them erect as

machines. Looking into the city, it was no longer the capital of their youth, the empire of their dreams.

The city was their enemy.

They postured against it, backs inclined toward the wind, and they ran in different directions. Separate and solitary, they met the city head-on.

58

"We have found three so far, and we can expect more," Irene burst through the heavy door as though it were made of tea leaves, the force of her people apparent in her eyes. They were on fire.

Maeva closed her eyes and tried to focus. She heard the flurries of people moving about the fortress but she couldn't emerge from her quarters. Her mind was consumed in visions of the new Willing Woman campaign.

She was certain it would be insufficient. They had to move faster and at a greater volume. Incubation was the only way. But the idea of restarting the Rainfields program, whether or not it was in Rainfields, horrified her. After all she'd done to put the nightmare of incubation behind her, her destruction of the laboratory, how could she even consider it an option? Wouldn't that be taking Lower Earth directly down the path she'd tried so hard to avoid?

Her eyes settled on Irene.

"Huh, what? Three what?"

Irene leaned forward, shaking her head.

"What is going on with you, Maeva? Haven't you heard it all this morning?"

"I sent the women away. I had to focus."

"Three dead bodies. That's what we've found so far. Cork Town. They didn't look out of place there. But certainly, there are more."

"Three dead bodies. Alright."

"We aren't sure of the method of kill yet. Given the lack of visible injury, I'm guessing poison or broken necks."

Maeva sat back in the chair, warm velvet feeling rough. Even her skin was on edge. Every cell in her body was on hyper-alert, feeling every wisp of fabric or air, her nose overwhelmed by every stench, and oh, how the city stank. Her nervous system screeched threats at her. An increase in murders in Cork Town was an alarming trend, but not the worst risk she'd ever faced, certainly not in times like these.

I cannot follow the logic of the problem. I'm getting too old for this.

The thought hit her in the face like a fist. Standing up to another round of threats would not be as it always had been. The time was fast approaching to announce the new queen.

Irene glared, her nostrils throbbing. Her warrior blood was running hot, Maeva saw it pumping just below the surface, red flows of it tumbling as a mad river.

Maeva took a deep breath.

"Bring it down, Irene. This is not new for us." If she could just calm Irene a bit, diffuse the situation, that would give her time to think.

Time. I've never needed time before.

Irene's neck seemed to pull her even taller. She took slow but deliberate steps towards the Queen. "Not new? I'm not sure we are speaking the same language here, my Queen. They are conspirators."

"And we'll treat these murderous traitors the way we have always treated traitors. To kill even one of our women in

Lower Earth is to betray us all! We will find them and lock them up or see them disappeared as the people so love to say, whatever we must, but do not create such panic to serve your own ambition."

Maeva cocked her head, watching Irene while trying to act as dismissive as she could find.

Color rose in Irene's cheeks and the left side of her mouth curled down.

"My ambition?" She took a few more steps, tentative now, seeming to hold herself back. "You are misinformed, my Queen. It is not the killers who are the traitors."

The Queen felt a tic, a reaction in her shoulder, involuntary and uninvited. The voices would come soon. She prepared an insulating cushion against it.

"The dead women are scouts. They are all scouts. They are Upper Earth's scouts and they are living amongst us," Irene spat out, "My Queen."

The voices exploded.

You're too late!

Too consumed with your own foolishness. You stupid woman, murderous blood sister!

Here's your punishment, they are amongst you now and where have you been?

What have you been doing, you silly Queen-Child?

Playing Mama to genetic freaks you allowed to live on, you wasteful, stupid fool!

"Hush, damn it!" The voices deafened her.

"I cannot, my Queen. Permit me to do as must be done. This is not an age for strategy and refinement. We are already at war."

War! What have you done!

Since the Mist, we have been protecting it all. And now you - you have turned it into chaos.

You will be the downfall of humanity.

We will all become subservient again. All will know what you have done, what you have failed to do.

"I said stop!"

"We haven't even begun, my Queen. We have much to do."

So much to do, Maeva, while you were pandering about, concerning yourself with the murder of your own children, look what a mess you've created now.

How have you forgotten it all, the generations we've spoken in you, for a moment such as this?

"Give me the word. My Queen, Maeva, this is the moment! Say it, say it now. Tell me I can do as must be done. And it will be done." Irene was growing before her, or perhaps she herself was shrinking. Suddenly she was barely more than an ant before this mythic woman, her beauty and force so fierce that Maeva stood speechless before her.

"Now, my Queen! Say yes, say it now!"

Now, Maeva, Fool of Queens! Say it!

This was it, her defining moment. It would be one of her last, she knew it to be so. The treachery and future blended into one vast barricade and she closed her eyes to it all.

Face what you have done.

She opened her eyes. Walked to the window. The people below were so small, like molecules bumping into each other before bouncing away again. A world only in itself of any importance. This contradiction of design and nature, man's advancement left in a woman's world. All for what?

The response came in a small sound, deep within.

We will have to find out what this world was made for. We cannot remain blind for much longer.

The voice was buried so far inside the cacophony; she could hardly make it out. But it rolled on repeat, a record trapped in time, waiting for this moment.

Keep it alive. Keep this world alive. It's the only thing worth living for. Keep it alive for the world as it could be. Keep it alive -

It lurched forward, louder from that deep place, the beginning of life.

The first innocence.

The first meaning.

The reason for all reason, and Maeva was filled with a godly benevolence from all the generations who ever gave life.

Her holy tribute, her only calling.

Her eyes cast out beyond the city, to the edges of the world and it all became clear. She was the life-giver and preserver of life. She was their servant in word and deed. The screeching voices went silent in the instant of the thought and for the first time, the color of light filled her eyes.

The time had come.

Everything stopped. The people, the air, the smells, and all time. She turned and took in the sight of the beautiful warrior who was waiting on her word. The word that would define their future, the word she alone could speak. The word that would rally them all and turn destiny to a new sun.

It is time.

She nodded her head low to earth and high to generations past, calling the world back to movement as Irene's dark eyes beseeched.

Maeva smiled at the tomorrow in her mind.

"Yes."

Irene's chin drew higher and she turned, bringing the whistle of the Guard to her lips.

"Irene!"

Irene stopped in the door, standing between the Queen and call of her birthright, whistle in hand, chest heaving with excited breath.

The Queen spoke with firm intent the words she had always known would one day be her legacy.

"It's time to bring forth Ariane."

Irene nodded slowly, her purpose painted her face in hues

of yellow before she burst with the clamor of war on her tongue.

59

———

Ariane felt it like a wave moving across the city, even before the Queen's Guard marched out. The air became thicker and anxiety was drawn on the faces of those who knew the rhythm of the city was changing. From her separate vantage point, she listened.

"What's happening?" Ariane heard a soup seller ask of a guard who paused to look down the crossing lane.

"Nothing."

"Obviously it's not nothing. I haven't seen the guard out like this since I was a girl."

The guard pretended not to hear.

"Is it a storm?" The soup seller ventured, desperately looking for answers. Ariane stayed in the shadow behind them, unable to read their faces but hearing it all in their voices.

"It's a kind of storm."

"Oh, well, then the screens should be announcing something, right?"

"I don't know what the screens should or should not do."

"Right, I see."

The guard maintained her place, looking off in some distance. The soup seller tried again.

"Could it be that -"

"I think that's enough questions for now."

"Yes, right." She dropped her head and seemed absorbed in stirring the pot.

Another guard joined, but the conversation was cryptic. Ariane strained to make sense of the words.

"She knows."

"All of it?"

"Commandante says so."

"Then it is so."

Does she know of us? Or only of our deeds?

Weighing the possibilities, Ariane listened for a sign from her other self, any news for perspective. She had not yet mastered this listening for herself at a distance, the concept somehow jarring that she should listen to her voice in another body and recognize it as such. Until now it had only ever been her own calculations by the millions to decipher - with this other it was suddenly exponential, all the possibilities. And yet in some moments, there was only one loud and clear response. She couldn't be sure if it was her own or gifted from the other to her consciousness.

Has it always been this way? How many of the voices within were actually this other one speaking directly to me?

She couldn't find an answer. She had spent so many years in lonely isolation, she still didn't trust the idea of sharing her thoughts, much less sharing body and mind. Everything she'd ever learned spoke of her independent superiority. Separate, alone, strength in solitude.

Will this other self be my undoing?

She listened to the other voices of her surroundings. From her crouching spot under the concrete slab of the rain grate, the pictures were coming together of a city in the stages before a siege. The people seemed to sense it. She could make out pieces of conversation from across the city.

"Movement in the alleys – Night Watch reinstated - heard hushed voices speaking of others - closing gates - children told to go inside - "

"Word of 'others' - what others? You know of others? Me neither, not possible - foolishness. Yes, guards. Troublesome, I'll give you that."

"Closed down - moved - told me to stop, but I do this every day in the same place so I can't see why."

"Obviously don't want to tell us."

"Don't want to worry us."

"Maybe, maybe not."

"Stop the conspiracy theory."

"Wasn't me who started it."

She could hear children crying across the city with soft voices of Willing Women rocking them, hushing them lovingly, the same anxiety in their voices as the others. A quiet song floated to her, an unseen woman to an unseen child. Ariane felt her muscles relax at the sound.

Be lifted, darling bright eyes
Be lifted away
Feel your heart lighter
Your spirit at play
Be lifted, wise child
Know night-time from fear
Know daytime from bright lights
Know that I am here

The refrain continued, a backdrop to the tight voices and questions of the city. Ariane envied the child in that moment, the sweetness and intimacy of a mother's voice in times of fear.

How many times had she wished for comfort? For her

mother's love? She had always known it was unattainable without knowing why.

Now she knew.

All the deception, the statements of Ariane being the 'one and only'. It was all a farce. The burden of knowing crushed her lungs.

Aria laced her way up the pipes and mechanics of Central Tower, up the maintenance staircases and fire escapes. Everyone on the street below was distracted by their own business though, from where she sat, the sound of boots on asphalt dwarfed the usual noise of the city. Keeping her body stiff against an exhaust pipe, Aria took in Geb from above. The scurries of some with unmoving others were an unorganized weaving as the Guard began moving through the streets in formation.

An unannounced parade? It seemed to be, but to what end? A display of strength?

The answer rose in her, loud and clear, setting off momentary panic.

They've found the bodies.

Aria calmed herself.

This is an expected response. The Queen would have understood the significance of the deaths. But does she know their origin?

Unlikely, but with some statistical significance.

What is happening in her head? What is the most likely? What is the least?

Whatever is the least likely is what we should anticipate.

She willed the thought to the other, not knowing if it was received, not knowing if this was even a way they could consciously communicate. There was nothing in her studies to indicate even where to begin.

Collective thought?

Shared thought cannot be the same.

"Do not be fooled by commonplace appearance," a voice lifted from street level. "You were trained for this moment. You were designed for it."

Aria shifted against the pipe to face east. The voice was not near, perhaps from the base of the fortress where a contingent was preparing. But she knew the voice. The Commandante had a way of speaking that she couldn't forget.

"Be bold and smart. Ask the right questions and otherwise say nothing at all. Do you understand?" A quick nod from the lines of cloaked women replied. "If you are not sure, bring them to the prison. If you are sure, then do as you must." Another nod. "The Queen is relying on you. Lower Earth is relying on you. I know you are capable. Report back at first shift's end after receiving from the initial round's review."

And the guards dispersed.

Irene stood strong as the women moved out like rays from her into each corner of the city. Her shoulders were broader than Aria remembered, her eyes deeper in their darkness. She appeared to be in her element. A woman set to lead. And her face was the spitting image of an older Leadon. Aria blinked to take the sight of her friend away; she had to see the Commandante before her, not her childhood friend.

As Irene's eyes began to scan across and up, Aria shifted again to the west. It was not the moment to be discovered, though Irene did not have anywhere near the capability to see her hiding spot.

Even so, it was not worth the risk.

She slipped back into the Tower block. The guards would soon be arriving there, and she intended to find the best location to observe their actions.

She found several floors abandoned, unsurprisingly since the loudspeaker had announced a meeting in the first-floor auditorium. Aria ensured that she stayed in the folds of curtains and shadows of cabinets as the final stragglers filed past her, rushing. There would be too many suspicious eyes in the auditorium. Best to wait it out and listen from afar.

She passed by the door to the fatal office, Roman's office, where Archer had jumped and they'd had their first insight to the events happening as a backdrop to their current situation. She felt a chill run from the nape of her neck and watched as tiny bumps arose on her skin. She made no attempt to stop it, though she could have.

Dread. I deserve this. I didn't know he would jump.

She passed that door by.

There are others, let this one stay closed.

Roman's most sensitive material won't be here.

The Central Tower assembly hadn't yet begun, though the staff had already filed into the auditorium. Aria had most of the Tower to herself. Two voices asking questions in quiet tones reached Aria's hearing as she touched the seventeenth floor's main office door handle.

"This cannot be because of us." The voice stood out because of its panic, the heartbeat of the speaker stopping Aria dead in her tracks. Someone was very afraid.

A traitor? A scout?

Surely whoever she was speaking to couldn't also be a scout; they would not be so reckless as to congregate together.

"Just wait. Be normal."

She recognized the voices. It was they who had birthed the infant. Two of them, the third was absent.

"This is anything but normal."

Aria forced open the locked handle of an abandoned office down the hall as the conversation came to an abrupt stop. The heartbeats continued in her ears. She waited for their next words.

"What do we do about Adam?"

"Shut up," the man hissed. "That has nothing to do with this. We won't know anything for days yet."

A sharp exhale came from the woman and the beating hearts continued.

Aria scanned the office, seeking broken patterns, anything out of place. Any hints.

The neat pile of folders on the desk.

The voices silenced as heels clicked on a wood platform in the Auditorium one floor below. A voice began on the microphone.

"You will have noticed the presence of the Guard." A voice of authority. A man's voice. The Primary Overseer, Roman.

Aria picked up the pile of folders. Varying colors, same ink across them all.

"This is not standard, as you know," the voice continued, "Nor is their mission."

One folder was worn on the corner. The others were pristine. Aria let the others drop back on the desk and opened the worn green folder.

The voice on the microphone carried on about creating new practice, seeking out from within, no cause for alarm unless you knew there was cause, but Aria only half listened. The code on the page had her transfixed.

It was the basic code of men.

In it she could see, clear as day, how it had all gone wrong. There was something unnatural planted in this sequence. A voice inside her screamed it out, a voice of an old generation and one of the first.

The voice explained why it had been done and what it had been intended to do.

Come.

Ariane heard it somewhere and couldn't identify the direction, but knew the sound and, above all, her own voice, from afar.

Her feet lifted her directly. She swept the city through alleys and shadows, heading to the place from where it came. Heading to Central Tower.

The flurries of people were speeding up. She turned her head left and right but no eyes fell on her. They were in their parallel world with the guards moving them indoors, removing them from the streets. Sellers and children and walkers-by; inside, the guards asked questions, unending questions. Ariane listened as she went.

"And you were born here, in the capital?"

"You are of which Willing Woman?"

"And you attended which academy?"

"When did you leave the Lakes Region?"

"And you harvested in the East Fields when?"

And, and, and - the questions were incessant to those being interrogated.

The guards are gentle enough of tone but unrelenting in manner. They are seeking, but it isn't me they seek.

It isn't us.

So the Queen knows the dead women were scouts.

Five dead so far, if they had, in fact, found all five, had somehow already been identified by the fortress. She weaved through the questions-asked, the eyes-demanding and the eyes-fearful, none of which had any interest in her.

Ariane turned a corner and caught the edge of a block, tearing the flesh off her shoulder because of her speed. She paused just long enough to close the wound. She watched the skin come back together, the blood, hot, underneath the surface, heal and bind, as it always did. When she lifted her eyes, there was a child before her, mouth, and eyes wide.

Ariane smiled quickly, but it faded. She did not know what to say.

Find your voice, Future Queen, this girl is one of your people.

"Are they looking for you?" the child whispered before Ariane could find the right words. The girl tilted her head toward the guards whose voices preceded them.

"They might be, child."

"Then you should run."

Ariane smiled and touched the girl's shoulder, before crossing the block in three steps to the east.

"Wow," she heard the girl whisper in her wake.

They found each other on the roof of the Tower. Aria to Ariane, they walked to the center, grasped each other by the back of the neck, and spoke with only the quietest air.

"The regulatory signals in the basic male code," Aria started, holding a printout of the DNA sequence between them.

Ariane looked at it, searching through training and data. "A single point mutation."

"The response is to die."

Ariane nodded, the meaning too clear. "It consumes itself."

"Hence the obesity."

"At just the right age."

"Yes."

"It's an old mistake in the code, or else an old objective."

"A bioinformatician likely from the early generations."

"On royal command, likely."

"After the Betrayer King, we can expect."

Ariane nodded.

There are many betrayers in our midst.

Perhaps the men are not the only ones designed to die out.

The data will support it when I take the fortress.

When we take the fortress.

When we take the fortress.

How will it be as 'we'?
Training insufficient.
We must remain we.
We must defy their history.
We are the ones to do it.
Yes, we are.

They nodded and turned their heads to the west, evening sun rising like a beacon to their destination. The fortress awaited them. They knew the Queen was within.

It is time, they each thought to the other.

60

———————

Even before they walked through the door, they felt what was on the other side of it. The air held a different quality. They both knew it immediately.

It reeked of danger.

She is there, no doubt that she is there.

"What are you waiting for," they heard from the other side. That familiar voice, ever unreadable.

Did she know we were coming?

Minds rushed to find answers in the Queen's tone.

"Don't keep me waiting."

It was decided.

Without hesitation, together they pushed the door and found the Queen seated, facing the window, her back to them. Her straight spine gave no answer to the questions flying about in the room like guillotine blades. "My dear Ariane," she stood and turned to face them. "And Ariane. Understand, I didn't intend to put you in this position. I was equally shocked that you were two. Indeed it had never been my intention." She looked at Aria, "Ariane." She looked to the other. "And Ariane.

What a debacle. What a mockery." She inhaled deeply. "I had to make the most of the situation. View it as an opportunity. Determine which course would best prepare a Queen. She looked at Ariane of the Strangelands, "Solitary and severe?" She turned to Aria, "Or connected isolation?" She turned away from them both. "But I needed some kind of insurance. You must understand at least that much. You were both too unpredictable at the time. I didn't know how deep the sequence ran between you. I had to take precautions."

Looking at each other, they affirmed their course. Ariane spoke, "You must have known we would figure it out."

"Figure what out?"

They looked at each other again, the Queen seemingly asking an authentic question. They moved their eyes to the Queen, knowing they had to keep their attention on her.

She is the outlier.

She is the danger.

Upper Earth remains a distant enemy - the Queen is flesh and blood.

Aria approached the Queen.

"You have changed the course of Lower Earth, Mother. We will be taking the decision away from you."

The Queen gave no response.

Ariane spoke, "We will be making the decisions from now on."

The Queen laughed.

She dares to laugh at us?

The two felt their hearts quickening. Their breathing deepened. They both recognized the anger boiling up inside themselves.

Like insulted warriors.

Like incensed royalty.

"Respond to us, *Mother*," Ariane spat out.

The Queen smiled.

Aria stepped beside Ariane, "Do you think this is a game?"

The Queen looked them over, her lips pursed, bemused.

"We have never asked for anything from you. Yet you sit like a statue, a mute, blind and-"

The Queen simply raised her hand, but the energy charged within it stopped the two silent. A mother's demand and a Queen's command. Something was seething from her, up her spine, out her arm into her fingers. They saw her lip curl.

The Queen spoke, barely above a whisper. "You are taking liberties."

Their hearts quickened again.

Ariane burst, "You have taken too many!"

The Queen laughed, deep and hearty, almost jovial, almost sinister.

"You are both girls. Still just girls. I had wanted so much more from you. So, so much more for you." She stood and turned as slow as the earth moved. "I always loved you, as much as could be expected from a Queen to her offspring. But listen now, this isn't personal. Look at you both," she sauntered to Aria, putting her fingertips under Aria's chin, lifting it, "So close to perfection and yet," she released Aria's chin and walked to her bureau. "You couldn't be what you needed to be. It is you who left me with no choice. I saw it ever since you were children."

The Queen sat on her chair, turning her eyes toward the files on her bureau.

"What is that supposed to mean? You intend to reign forever? Go against the royal policy? Abandon your own principles?"

"Is it greed, Mother? Or did our greatness put you to shame?"

"I feel no shame," her eyes lit. "There could only ever be one queen. I ordered you dead, and I felt no shame. My calling is greater than that. So was yours, such hopes were on you. Believe me, I was sad to see you had failed. Mortally failed."

The two instinctively moved into a crouch. The sense of danger they had felt was not, and maybe never had been, Upper Earth.

It is our own mother.

How we respond now will define the coming generations.

The Queen read their movement.

"Girls, there can only be one. They're always could only be one. Do you think this touching homecoming will last? You know as well as I do that your communion will be short-lived. Try to reign together and you will be the undoing of Lower Earth. End of everything the generations have worked for. Don't think our little family reunion will last beyond these walls. Your time here is nearly over." Her eyes glowed green in the sunlight streaming through the window.

It will not last longer than a minute.

For Lower Earth, Ariane, for Lower Earth!

They all together broke into a leap, hurtling themselves into the air. They met the Queen in the rafters, her velvet gown streaming to the floor below. They were three arms' lengths away from each other, squatted on the rafters, when time stopped. Mother looked at daughters, daughters looked at mother.

Between them, collectively, came a fleeting stroke of regret.

The Queen mouthed words. Silent words, inaudible to the two. It was as though the Queen was looking at and through them, speaking to an unseen presence. They strained to listen but could hear nothing.

The Queen inhaled, words still on her lips as she grasped either side of her draping velvet gown. With muddled words she tore it off her body, spinning, falling into the rafters and righting herself as Aria and Ariane watched, confused, unprepared for the sight of their nude, muttering mother.

She's gone mad.

The Queen righted herself on the floor. Long scars of decades of self-mutilation throbbed in pink against her olive skin. "Come, Aria, come."

Aria looked to her other self, her sister self, the human form of her own code. Ariane nodded.

Adjusting her stance, Aria jumped down to the floor. She approached her mother with careful, deliberate steps.

The Queen held her arms out.

"Aria, my daughter. Come."

Her naked body rippled with muscle despite her age, her abdominals expanding with her lungs, her tight breasts showing no evidence of the births she gave. Only the scars gave any sign of weakness.

A voice alit in Aria's gut. The voice of her childhood who had begged for her mother's embrace. Aria sought to read the Queen's heartbeat. It was slowed, calm, contained. A complete change from moments before.

She is torn between us.

"Please, my Aria, come."

Aria looked up to Ariane in the rafters, who was observing with hawk eyes. Ariane gave no sign of thought.

I will not betray you, Aria thought to Ariane, hoping she heard. Hoping she understood.

Aria let the Queen's hands grasp her shoulders, pull her in closer.

The Queen embraced Aria, her naked body clenching her with such fervor, such intensity. Such love. Aria closed her eyes for a moment and begged her mind to stay sharp and focused. She felt her vulnerability, the rawness of an emotion she had felt for as long as she could remember.

Connected isolation. It had been torture. Her desire for love, raised in her by the priestesses, and yet explicitly denied as part of her preparation.

"Close your eyes, Aria, picture the future. Tell me, what do you see?"

Aria closed her eyes and felt her other-self move away.

Is she gone? Because our Mother called upon me to come close?

"Tell me, Aria. Pay the other one no mind, not now. We are here and we are together. This is what counts. What do you see, my daughter."

Aria could tell that Ariane was gone. Something inside her that had been full was emptying. She tried to stay focused on the moment.

"I see Lower Earth." Aria squeezed her eyes tighter. "I see the men and I see the civil war. Violence. I see what we must do. I see Lower Earth's eventual prosperity, the strength of a common people rallying behind one cry for justice, equality, and commitment to our world."

Recognize her bias. Run the scenarios, she has other agendas. Give assurance.

"I see us ruling together, Mother. I see it all."

"Oh, Aria." The Queen pulled her even tighter. Aria felt lost in the sensation. "I know you felt this so deeply. I know this is what you always wanted from me. I never could give it. Aria, I tried." Her mother breathed the words, "But I couldn't love you knowing one day I'd have to kill you."

Run! Aria thought at her other self, only hoping the message reached her in time. *We are more deceived than we thought.*

Then her thoughts vacated.

Everything turned red.

The Queen released her from the embrace and Aria looked down at her chest.

A dagger point burst through her chest from behind.

The dagger twisted.

Shredding her.

Slashing into her heart.

Aria of East Gana froze in open-mouthed dying. She looked up to the rafters, but Ariane was nowhere she could.

"You see nothing, Aria. Your conspirator, betraying two-faced double self, has fled and left you to die. She won't be back. She was raised for solitude. It was an experiment that failed. She thinks only of herself. It's why she could never be Queen. Now turn. Look upon Lower Earth's future. Lay your eyes on your assailant and at last, you will understand."

Aria's brain demanded regeneration, but her heart pumped mad blood in all directions. It poured down her chest.

But she had to turn. She had to see. She rallied every cell of energy to remain standing as her feet slid, slipping on her blood as she turned.

Another version of herself stood before her. She had Aria's face, her shoulders, her stance. But the eyes were wrong. They gleamed green. Something in her was angular. Stark.

The self across from her stepped back, Aria's blood oozing down her hands and arms. She watched Aria with cold amusement, watched her dying.

The Queen whispered from behind. "Your mutual brilliance was a stroke too imprudent, reckless, too emotionally driven to be Queen. But never doubt that I loved you. Ariane shall reign, yes. Ariane shall reign, and you shall die for your country."

Aria's blood flowed in furious chaos, cells colliding and exploding, dying as the oxygen decayed, such crushing inside her. She couldn't move, it took all she had just to stand; she could only stare herself in the eye.

"Who are you?" Aria's eye twitched as she fought to focus. A small flash of recognition crossed the killer's face.

"I am Ariane." The other one paused, searching Aria's eyes. "You must know me, you must have felt me, just as I felt you." Aria's face was dying but she asked the question with her eyes. "Oh, so perhaps you didn't. And perhaps that's why I can do what you never could. We may have been three, could only ever be one Queen."

Blood-covered, this unknown Ariane leaned in to Aria's ear and spoke without hate and without love.

"Be proud, Ariane, you are dying for Lower Earth to live."

61

A cry pierced the air. A heartbroken sob from the flurry of red hair, and Rose ran, full of grief from behind the Cork Town pub.

She felt it. She knew.

Aria was dead.

62

—————

She looks so small.

Maeva stood over Aria's body.

Such love in her eyes. She had such love for me, of all people. Such love for me.

A swell began in the soles of her feet, moving up her like quicksand. It was heavy and dark, rolling up her body.

Her kneecaps, her thighs, her hips, the bottom of her ribs. The weight of quicksand pushed at her though there was nothing there.

I'm going to drown on the air.

Collapsing to the floor, she felt the thunder inside her. Deep and far, ages and generations of anger and despair, from that dark place within her, the voices burst out her mouth, almost inhuman, a sound from the beginning of time. The sound was a vacuum, silent it went out and then returned from where it came.

She gasped, hardly able to breathe. She lowered herself down to the floor, pulling her body in, grabbing at arms and neck in a grotesque embrace. She smelled death on her; but even then, it was like a flower, wilting petals in the sun.

Rocking, rocking. Mother whispered love at Aria's empty shell. She hummed a gentle tune, one that floated up from a voice inside. She'd never heard it, no one had ever sung to her this way, but it came to her from a place where once someone had loved another.

I found you where the river ends
Where the river bends back into itself
I saw it go on the way I came
Rushing back now, back to the lane
But in this place where it met itself
I saw my reflection looking back at myself
A reflection of me, how I used to be
But when I looked closer, I saw it was you
You smiled at me from the river bend
Where the river ends and takes me home
I saw your face in the river rush
I saw you blush, for you saw me
And so, my dear, I know you're near
I know you'll come where the river runs
I know I'll find you once again, where the river ends
Where the river bends.

SHE PULLED ARIA CLOSER INTO HER, BURYING HER FACE INTO her shoulders and neck.

"Ariane," she whispered to her, but her cold skin gave no reply.

She felt a cool hand run across her shoulder blade.

"That's enough now." The young Ariane spoke into the Queen's ear.

"Not now, not yet." She couldn't let her go.

"It is time. You must change your clothes and address the people."

Maeva felt weakness rolling over her. Just a few more moments. Just a few. "So soon?"

"They are waiting."

"They are waiting," Maeva repeated, and the sound of the words fell deeper inside, calming the quicksand, quieting the voices. "They are waiting."

"They will have heard the sounds of death. The people are afraid. They are coming to the square. They are waiting for you."

The bright, beautiful face, deep green eyes commanded her, even though there was no command in her words. The Queen heard it and straightened her spine.

"No, Ariane, they are waiting for *you*."

They both lowered their chins in a nod of understanding and respect. The Queen lifted herself taller, chest first, and walked in vacant meditation to the sink. Her reflection was no longer her own. She saw all who came before and all who would come after looking back at her. She washed her hands, her face. Pulled her hair back, tamed the errant strands.

This is as it must be, she knew. She took a new gown from the wardrobe, casting it over herself as she walked.

Perhaps it could have been different, had the world been different.
But it's not.

Maeva took one last glance at Aria's crumpled body on the floor.

In another world, she would have been Queen.

She raised her eyes and saw Ariane, this Ariane, whose shoulders were back and set with strength.

Yes, perhaps in another world, Aria would have been Queen. But this is the world in which we live. This is the Queen for the Lower Earth before us.

Maeva lowered her chin but kept her eyes on Ariane.

She turned toward the air of day, walking anew, feeling the

freshness of it on her cheek. She stepped out onto the balcony. The hum grew quiet in the crowd of thousands.

Suddenly there was no sound across the masses; nothing moved throughout the city.

Indeed, they are waiting.

The Queen inhaled.

Air of today and air of tomorrow.

She spoke.

"You have all come. Without knowing it, this is the day you have waited for. This is the moment you have wished for. For all the fear we live in today, here is something that is certain. This is the world we have created together, and this is the land where she will reign. Queen Ariane!"

She emerged into the sun, this Ariane of the people. She smiled into her mother's eyes as the cheers rose around them, the sound rolling into the hillsides, up the skies, surrounding her, all for this Ariane. The shouts were of celebration, confusion, delight, and shock. So much change in so little time, the Queen knew the people were reeling. The campaign to prepare for war. The Guard across the city. And now Ariane. Fear ran as an undercurrent to their present celebration, she heard it in their hearts, in the rushing blood.

Maeva offered her hand to the new Queen and led her forward to the balcony's rail.

The robes fell long at Ariane's sides, deep black and velvet, she glowed brighter than innocence, her olive skin in hues of the sun. Her cheek, her lips, her brow were more perfect than perfect. Her blood ran with the voices of the past. Maeva heard them as she held her hand. She had to pull away, for Ariane's voices were shouting at her now, burning the flesh of her palm.

Their eyes locked on each other. In this new Queen Ariane, Maeva read both assurance and threat.

The people are right to be afraid.

Turning her back to Maeva and her eyes to the people, Ariane bowed. The crowd cried louder, tears and wails, whistles shrieking as the people thrust their confidence and hopes and loyalty at her feet.

Maeva watched as Ariane took them in, looking the people in the eye, casting her benevolence down.

There was not one mouth that wasn't cheering, no hand not in applause, no eyes not alight with wonder at this perfect new Queen. Ariane drank them in, peace across her face as she read the crowd.

Then, off in the distance, Maeva saw Ariane's eyes halt, just for a moment, yet a moment too long. Maeva followed her gaze, but it was too late. She only felt the waves of the moment flying back, hitting her like shrapnel, giving rise to uncertainty somewhere deep inside her.

The voices rumbled.

Maeva squinted, but the streak of red hair ran the perimeter of the crowd before disappearing altogether into the distance.

63

Rose felt this false Ariane's eyes on her, and she did not shy away. She saw what was behind this new Queen's eyes. She saw it.

And she despised it.

The voices began to again rise up, the voices that she had silenced so long ago. She let them now speak into her blood, muting the sounds of celebration around her.

She is no queen. She is false. She is treacherous. She is vile. She is no Ariane.

The crowd all fell quiet in her ears. Her voices spoke in unison, the same words and same message, though they tussled over each other, a mass of sound speaking the same words. She heard them and she recognized them.

And she knew they were right.

I am the true Ariane.

She had christened herself "Rose" all those years before.

Now she let "Rose" die in the afternoon sun.

She would be who she was born to be.

She stared at this new Queen who stared back, willing her to hear the truth that the voices inside her proclaimed.

I am the true Ariane. And I am the rightful Queen.

Rose turned, at once slower than time and moving faster than light, feeling the eyes of former Queen and new Queen burning into the back of her head as she ran.

She did not care.

She removed her hood and stood tall, letting her twisted face feel the sunlight upon it. Letting the shame burn away. She stood taller than she'd ever been, tall as a Queen, and she ran, ran toward and away as the voices inside her shrieked with delight.

THE END

PREVIEW OF CULLING: LOWER EARTH RISING, BOOK 2

Chapter 1

Meet Leadon, Aria's childhood friend and a warrior priestess of special blood…

Leadon's throat was dry with ocean air. Empty boats bobbed on the ocean, gently rolling over the waves as the tide moved in. Fishing rowboats ducked alongside sky-high ocean vessels built in the generations before the Mist. Leadon watched them dancing on the water, but her mind was off in the heavens. Her heart ached for her absent friend.

Five years had passed since Aria had been declared Queen. For Lea, it was a lifetime ago.

She walked away from the ocean, toward the river that ran up alongside the main village.

Aria. Give up on the Aria of your memories, Lea. She is Queen Ariane now. And she has no time for the likes of a mere subject like you. Know your place.

Leadon sighed into the river, watching it rush on. She

kneeled for a moment, remembering how she'd watched Aria rearrange the stones so that the currents would invite the fish back.

Her boots nearly soaked through but she didn't see a single fish. She walked on, following the twists and turns of the riverbed. It wound along and up, rounding the hills before reaching its destination. Lea approached the end of the town limits, the low wood fence the sign that she ought to turn around. But she wasn't ready to go home yet.

Her fingers ran along the wood fence, little splinters catching in her skin, then falling aside. The fence was as old as the new world. More than four hundred years had passed since the settlers after the Final War had laid down borders in Lower Earth. The warrior priestesses had been on the land for generations before and had never needed borders to know where they lived. Then a wooden fence became all that created peace between them and the settlers' society. It had worked.

And then it didn't.

No fault of the fence, Leadon thought, *People were the problem.*

She wasn't sure who had been the first to negotiate with the new peoples. Nor why. These weren't the stories recounted over fires in midnight rituals. They could begrudge those forbearers all they wanted. Nothing had changed since the first warrior priestess had started making concessions. Maybe it was during the wheat shortage. Or the period of the locusts. All of Lower Earth had suffered then. Desperation was a powerful driver for change. For loosening limitations. For giving in.

Now the Ganese weren't allowed to leave the broader Gana limits. At all. East and West Gana, despite their cultural differences, were united under this decree. Only travel allowed that didn't require written authorization was to the capital city via the Geb Free Route. And the Ganese leaders had all but forbade the warrior priestesses to go, even though they were allowed.

The short wood fence turned to stronger timber as Leadon reached the border of Gana proper. It didn't look like much. A wooden gate, unlocked. Tall and crooked. Unprotected wood making a hatch that didn't keep anyone or anything out.

But it kept her in.

If only Leadon could get permission from the Keeper of the Chief. But Batrasa had held the role for several years, and Batrasa would never let Leadon go. Not even if she explained why. Batrasa had been skeptical of Leadon from the start; maybe even since before she was born.

So she didn't ask.

She put her hand on the wood of the gate that was latched in diamond shapes. She could see through to the plains. A couple of days' journey to Geb. How different the world was there. Twenty-two years she'd lived, confined in Gana's borders. Two days' journey was all it took to change worlds, though Leadon had no idea what that would look like. It only came to her in stories from the few who'd traveled to negotiate new terms for Gana with the capital. She dreamed of one day taking the Free Route to Geb, to follow the steps of her people when the settlers had first established the city.

"Leadon!"

"What? What?" Leadon felt like she'd been caught, though she wasn't doing anything wrong. Only in her imagination was she breaking the rule. She couldn't be persecuted for what happened in her imagination. Not yet anyway.

The woman cocked her head as she led a horse toward the stables on the edge of the village. "Why are you so startled? It's almost time for the quorum, we've got to prepare."

Leadon closed her eyes. She would one day find herself in real trouble if she missed the third-day prayers quorum.

"I'm coming. Of course, I'm coming. Just doing some morning exercise," she lied. "Cooling down from climbing." She mustered a smile, "Thanks, Miliah."

"Nothing to thank for," she patted the wide neck of the deep chestnut-colored horse. "We have a responsibility to each other."

"Indeed."

Miliah nodded and turned, the flaps of her leather tunic slapping her sides as she went, the Ganese steed walking proud at her side. Her breastplate was ceremonial; Lea couldn't see why she'd be wearing it for third-day prayers. This wasn't a special day.

Or is it? Where is my mind? No, today is not a skills parade, nor a sacrifice. But I'm missing something.

She left the gate out of Gana behind her and walked towards the village center. Even though they still called it a village, it had the population and activity of a city. More than a hundred thousand of them now, ever since the Willing Woman program had been more accepted among the priestesses. As she arrived, the city was already bustling. She had to find her quorum quickly.

"Lea, thank heavens! Get in here and prep the stew." Her quorum lead, Shyanne was running between a boiling pot and sizzling root vegetables on the fire.

Lea walked to the pot and gave it a stir. "Goat? Today? What is going on?"

"Where have you been, Leadon?" Shyanne came over and put her hands on Lea's cheeks. "Incredible how you live in your own head. The whole morning has been buzzing with it. Batrasa has called a full quorum."

"A full quorum? What? Why? We haven't had one since Habana died."

Shyanne lifted her hands, urging Lea to recognize some seemingly obvious fact.

Lea shook her head. "Batrasa - is Batrasa dying?"

"Why else would we have a full quorum? Stir the pot, for heaven's sake!"

Leadon stirred but her mind was absent. Batrasa, dying. If true, it could throw all of Gana into disorder for a period. No one expected it this soon. Habana's successor hadn't even been announced. Batrasa may have been the Keeper of the Chief, but she was no Chief. How could this happen? And who would step in next?

Anyook is too rash. She's probably the most likely selection, but we'll end up bandits and thugs if she has her way. Just because she exudes power doesn't mean that she has the makings of our leader. Priyantha? Possible, but she is too concerned about her inner circle. Mitam? Maybe, she's a bit young, just had her woman's day. But she's promising. If only she had more experience. If only Batrasa could hold on a few more years - announce Habana's successor and provide training. Look how her training of the Queen has worked; Aria will likely be the greatest Queen Lower Earth has ever seen. Much of that must be due to Batrasa. How I miss Aria. If only Aria would step in and help decide.

"You're letting it burn, Lea. I can smell it from here."

"Sorry," she picked up the pace of her wrist's twisting. It was a large pot. They'd be responsible for feeding three hundred mouths. Every feeder house would be.

Maybe I can get a few moments with Batrasa. Perhaps she would listen to me, given my background. I could convince her to ask Aria. I mean, Queen Ariane. If the Queen made the announcement, then everyone would have to follow. Habana had always been attentive to my ideas. I know that I was a genetic curiosity for her, but still, she seemed to appreciate my insights. Maybe Batrasa will do the same.

"Leadon! The stew, for heaven's sake!"

Leadon and Shyanne bumped through the growing crowd as they took the cart of stew into the center of the village. Most Ganese would be there, except for the very ill and those overseeing the borders. The lookouts were more ornamental now than anything else, their roles nearly defunct. But when Leadon looked up and saw them at their stations, she felt a puff in her chest. They stood as still as statues, a message facing the rest of the world, an enduring message. The border lookouts had been there since the outbreak of the Final War. And they'd be there until the next assault on their tribe, whatever that may look like.

But the lookouts couldn't do anything about the water sickness, the drought, or the crop viruses. Their skills fell far short of the threats in their modern world.

For all those microscopic invasions, Gana was reliant on Central Tower in the capital. The researchers of Central Tower were revered throughout Lower Earth. Without them, all society would have died off in the second generation after the Mist. The Mist had already killed most of the habitable land on the planet. How blessed they were that Lower Earth survived the worst of it. Their native home. One of the last strongholds on Earth.

Their enemies weren't biological weapons from a far off enemy or adversary, but rather the land on which they lived, which seemed to be in a constant state of flux. Invisible enemies in the shape of bacteria, parasites, viruses from the old world that had managed to travel on the Mist's back, surrounding the planet in places they never belonged. The Ganese had been gifted in finding ways to overcome them, but they had their limits. Some illnesses they just couldn't outsmart.

"Look out, coming through," Lea led the cart through the first few hundred who'd arrived. Some wore the garb of West Gana. Lea loved how the long, white tunics flowed from their shoulders to their waist to the ground, how it caught the wind and flew like clouds behind them. Under the translucent cloak were the standard leather tunics, bodices with iron rings for attaching weapons, and the fur hangings to cover their legs. But the white over-layer caught Lea's breath every time. The West Gana population was fewer now; most had been called back to East Gana for agriculture. But the old theology was alive in the West. Lea thought they were more connected to the earth than the Easterners who looked out at the ocean and dreamed of something more, something greater. The Easterners had kept up the ways of sailing like the old generations, the boats maintained, especially for the management of the Forgotten Islands Prison. Certainly, there was good in the ways of the East and the dreams of what was out over the water.

But Lea admired how the Western theology focused on the here and now. They were grounded and realistic. They favored plans over dreams.

The crowd grew; Lea couldn't see across the central meeting point, there were too many women in the way. Their skin rich and dark like their land, hair long and woven. Most had taken the time to prepare for the full quorum. Leadon felt a sting in her stomach and tried to flatten her hair. She too was a natural Ganese, even if she was different from all of them. Those who knew her genetic background gave her sideways looks, always second-guessed her motives. They treated her as though she was never supposed to have happened. As though Ganese should not play with genetic codes the way the settlers' descendants did. But Leadon had been given no choice in the matter. She'd just been born that way. A genetic design, an intentional copy. The only one in Gana. Warrior priestesses like Ahnira made their disdain known.

Lea saw Ahnira coming toward her, and she mustered her nerves. She inhaled deeply, trying to calm her breathing. Ahnira pulled her cart up alongside Lea, her lips taught.

"Aren't you supposed to be setting up on the fourteenth corner, Leadon?"

"That's where I'm headed."

"Get moving then."

Ahnira pulled her cart away without waiting for Leadon to give any kind of response. A call came across the shell horn.

One long, two short. They had only a few more minutes before Batrasa would appear.

"Go, go!" Shyanne pushed the cart forward.

"There's people there, stop pushing!"

"No time, Lea, no time."

Lea eased the cart into the fourteenth corner and joined the crowd in the center. The clinking of iron on tunics clanged as bodies turned to look for Batrasa, though she hadn't yet emerged from her hut. The sound of the iron was musical, and despite the charged ambiance, Leadon found herself grinning at the excitement of it all.

"What are you smiling about? Don't you know this is a full quorum?" a voice assaulted her, a shoulder bumping into her. The woman was tall, broad. Strong shoulders and glaring brown eyes. Judging eyes. Leadon refused to feel shame.

"A full quorum is not by its definition a sad occasion."

"You inherited something funny in that blood, replica."

"Replica?"

Shyanne's voice pulled Lea out of the conversation. "Leadon! Over here, I found our quorum house."

Lea watched the woman and the woman watched Lea for a few steps, and then she was in the crowd.

Replica? They call me that?

The noise of feet stepping and iron chinking and nervous conversations surrounded Lea as she tried to follow Shyanne's path. She picked up pieces of other peoples' exchanges as she went.

"Do you think she identified someone?"

"I thought this would be a council decision."

"Upper Earth attack maybe?"

"Not a chance, we have haven't seen sight or sound of them since the scout removal."

"But they could, theoretically."

"Who's accompanying Batrasa? Could this be her final rite?"

"No, she wouldn't leave it for the last second."

"Maybe she didn't know, maybe she-"

"Wanalia, over here! Our quorum's near the ninth corner!"

Lea and Shyanne reached the other women from their quorum just as the shell horn called out for silence. One long signal, no mistaking it.

"Where were you?" Niapal hissed.

"Where were *you*? I was setting up the cart. You were probably off at the boats again."

Niapal lowered her voice. "Of course I was at the boats. We had no warning."

Lea sighed. "I know. I was caught off guard too."

Niapal took Lea's arm. "We might need the boats more than ever. We could be at the beginning of very difficult times."

"We could be."

"Hush, you two," Shyanne gave them each a light slap on the back, "She's coming."

All sound flew away on the wind as the horn echoed out to the forest beyond the village. Slapping leather against bodices and legs were the only sound as the fur door covering of the hut pulled back. Batrasa stepped into the light.

"She has no accompaniment," Niapal whispered.

"Maybe that's promising," Lea replied.

"Hush."

Batrasa looked out over the thousands of gathered women, seemingly still in her thoughts, not looking at anyone in particular. She closed her eyes and inhaled, her ribs expanding under her ceremonial priestess robes. No sign of the warrior she'd always been. She'd abandoned the leather and iron for softer custom.

Lea could tell this full quorum would not be what any of them had thought.

Batrasa exhaled and finally set her eyes straight. She looked at the women, one by one, those in her immediate radius. The women parted, giving her a pathway through the crowd, but Batrasa lifted her hand.

She walked first to the left, following an imaginary labyrinth. She then turned right, into the crowd, women stepping aside as she came. Those she passed absorbed the sight of her, she who had led them for the past few years, since just before the coronation of Queen Ariane. Habana had been Chief for two generations, more than eighty years. She and Batrasa had quarreled, all of Gana knew it. Habana had wanted Batrasa to lead until her death, to take over the role as Chief. Batrasa insisted it had to be someone of the next generation. The fight had lasted days. Two elderly women with voices that echoed through the village. They let everyone hear their argument; they hadn't tried to hide it.

Batrasa began to speak, still from within the crowd. She was far from the podium in the center of the square. Her voice carried through the village square to waiting ears.

"Warriors. Priestesses. We of Gana are women of many faces."

She continued her spiral through the crowd, inlets opening before her.

"I have many secrets. They inform my ways. To you, I might look erratic. Obscure. Maybe even senile." She touched the face of a woman as she passed. "Glowell, how tall you've become." Batrasa stopped, taking in the woman's height, her breadth, her muscled arms, and chiseled face. "How you've changed." She carried on walking. "We are all changing. Lower Earth is changing. I will soon change. I will pass into the world beyond this one, where our ancestors will greet me. I can only hope they will be pleased with what I've done." She stopped and let out a sigh. "I did what I could. I failed many times, I know." She nodded her head to the beyond, her eyes set on the clouds above.

Lea couldn't unhook her eyes. They were held captive on the sliver of Batrasa she could see through the crowd. She felt the eyes of everyone cast in that direction, through Lea, through everyone. All eyes pointed at Batrasa, waiting.

"You've seen I am unaccompanied. I am not the Chief. I was only ever the Keeper. I have asked the souls of Habana and those before her for guidance. Habana, who went just before Lower Earth's transition in power. Her judgment was already foggy with oncoming death. You were there, you recall. Only a strong leader can admit when she doesn't have the answer. And so we find ourselves here today."

"Is she going to say who the successor is?" a voice behind Lea asked.

"Today is a day of reckoning. You all expected an announcement, I'm sure. But I will not give you such relief." Gasps emerged from the crowd. "There is a reckoning to be had. Humility. Shame." Batrasa stopped. "Women of Gana, you have become too proud."

"How can she say that?"

"Does she have any idea what we seek?"

"How can we be proud when we remain tethered under Geb?"

"Stop!" Batrasa raised her hand high. "Your very words are your condemnation! Think on this, women of Gana. Who among you is the least? Who among you have you most cast away? Who is she that will stand forth when you have fallen under righteous weakness?

Leadon felt her heart racing, as though Batrasa was speaking directly to her.

Batrasa arrived in the center of the village square, stepping onto the podium without use of the many hands which offered support.

"You might call me hard for these words, but truth is hard to hear." She looked out, no one dared to speak, lest they be labeled for the rest of their life. "I will announce nothing today but this: she who will lead you must be prepared to be hated by you. She who can withstand such hate and ostracism is she who will stand when you have fallen. It is she who will find you justice, liberation, fair negotiation, and honorable position."

Batrasa stepped down from the podium, her cadence like a conversation with their society. "Do not speak to me of this. Do not ask. Do not parade your feathers like a proud peacock." She wafted her hand as though swatting the thought away. "I must rest now. I will call upon those with whom I must speak, but make no assumptions. I hate your useless assumptions. Dangerous assumptions."

Batrasa reentered her hut. The electricity that had run through the crowd before her arrival dulled into a charged hum. Lea served the stew as the line of women passed with only nods of thanks as they went by. Lea looked over to Shyanne who kept her eyes on the serving spoon. Lea's mind ran a thousand miles a minute.

No announcement? Too much pride? If only Aria were here. She could talk some sense. She could influence Batrasa.

Lea sighed as the spoonful she served splashed out of the bowl.

"Watch what you're doing," the woman snapped in a low voice. " You'd better not have tainted the food. I've always wondered if you're a spy for the Sisters."

"Tainted the food? Why would I even do that? Your tongue is sharp but your wit is dull."

"Lea!" Shyanne hissed.

She spooned a second helping as the woman glared at her.

"Move along," Lea said. The woman turned, shaking her head as she went.

"Mind yourself, Lea." Shyanne kept serving but spoke to her. "You walk such a thin line."

"And why is that, Shy? It's not because of me, it's because of what I represent. And how is any of that my fault?"

"Don't speak of it. That only makes it worse."

"I've been silent for twenty-two years. Don't you think the time has come for us to speak of such things?"

"Hush. Damn it, Lea. Clear up here. I'll go back and start in the kitchen."

Lea let the air huff out her nose. Speaking to Shyanne wouldn't change anything. But she was tired, so tired, of having to stay silent.

The note slid across the dirt floor of their quorum house. The curtain flapped in the doorway as the messenger passed by. Niapal and Lin were closest and jumped upon it.

Lin was always fastest and she snatched up the paper as Leadon put the last of the kitchen implements away.

"Leadon," she whispered. "It has your name on it."

"Me?"

Lin nodded and passed the paper. Leadon looked at it for a moment before reaching out. She'd never received a message before. She was second cook in a feeding house and tried to keep out of the way. There had never been a reason for anyone to send her a message, and she'd always been glad for it.

She touched the paper and her stomach sank.

Is it Aria? Has something happened? Or could it be Irene? She hasn't been back in so long.

Irene. The Queen's Commandante. Dedicated servant to settler Queens. Irene was well into her fifty-fifth year but remained as true as ever to her warrior roots. She took no prisoners. She led the Queen's Guard and enforced the disappearances. She was revered and feared across Lower Earth, the only Ganese of high position in the Fortress.

And despite more than thirty years between them, Irene was Leadon's genetic twin.

GET CULLING ON AMAZON

ABOUT EDEN

I started writing the Lower Earth Rising series at a time when I was pretty sure the world was moving towards a nuclear war. The news spoke of certain presidents of certain countries who weren't getting along.

I was panicking. What could I do to stop a coming nuclear war?

The answer, obviously, was "very little". But I needed some way to deal with the intense nervous energy it was giving me.

I started writing...and then I didn't stop.

I imagined what the world might be like after such a war, and the land of Lower Earth took shape in my imagination.

Now, here I am, launching this series out into the world. Being a new author is tough - many other authors who have seen success have been at it for a long time.

I would be really grateful if you could leave an honest review on Amazon, as that will help me to continue honing my craft as a writer, as well as shape future Lower Earth stories.

The world can be a scary place; I write to escape it.

~Eden

Acknowledgements

I won't be able to thank all the people who have supported me in this acknowledgements page, the list is just too long. The good news is that I intend to keep on writing until I've had a chance to thank absolutely everyone.

Mom. Always in my corner.

Dad. I see you up there.

Rory. From sandstorms to boardrooms. Amazing.

Barbara. Thank goodness you said I had a novel in me.

Christine. My #1 Beta Reader.

Alana. My #1 Fan.

Albert. My #1 Offshore Fan.

Freefallers, nothing like this kind of group, especially under lockdown.

Ally, you see? You can do anything.

Laura and Anna and Hélène and Gillian and Shannon and Rainer and Elaine and Micah… you all doubted me a lot less than I doubted me. That's love.

And thank you to the members of the Selfsame Readers Club for all the encouragement you've given to this burgeoning author. I hope my stories will keep you coming back for more…